WRECK ME

A.R. ROSE

Edited By: Virgina Carey

Proofread By: Nicole Bucciarelli, Kaitlin Keys, & Amanda Bentley

Ridgewood Series
Between the Flames
Wicked Games We Play
Marked By Cain

Standalones
Wreck Me
Only One Night

Twisted Heroes
A Captain So Callous and Cruel
Siren

With a Kiss
Sins of Sorrow
The Sinners
Sins of Bliss

"You may not control all the events that happen to you, but you can decide not to be reduced by them."

MAYA ANGELOU

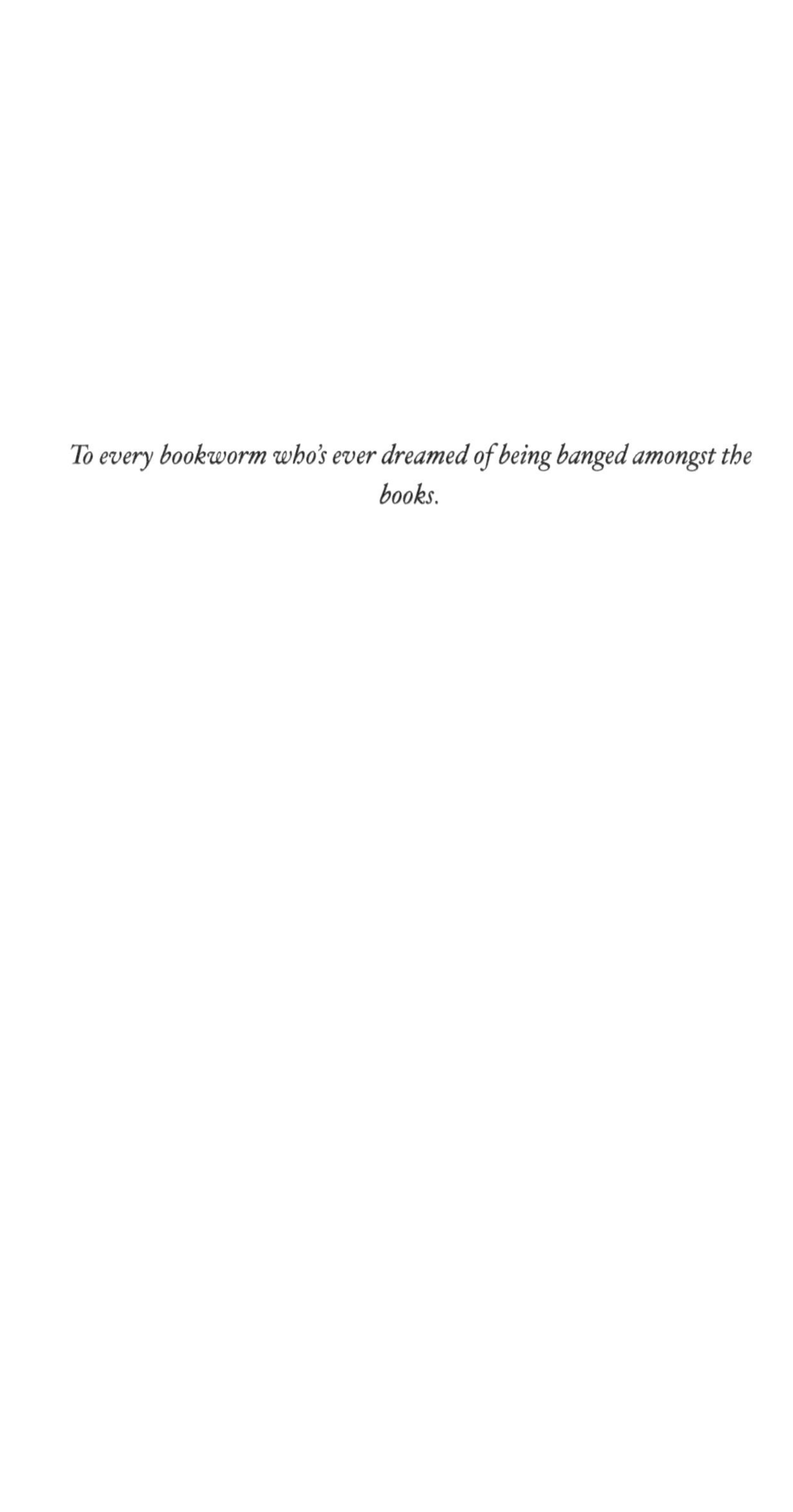

To every bookworm who's ever dreamed of being banged amongst the books.

A NOTE FROM A.R. ROSE

Wreck Me is a contemporary romance novel created for adults. This story depicts adult scenes and situations.

Reader discretion is advised. Wreck Me contains content that may be triggering for some.

Your mental health matters. For a full list of content warnings please visit www.authorarrose.com/content-warnings.

For those of you ready to begin, I hope you enjoy ❤

CHAPTER ONE

ISLA

"I'm so sorry, Miss, but I can't let you check out a library book when you have a dollar twenty-three balance due on your account. The system won't allow me to override it."

"I... but, I somehow left my wallet at home..." I frantically murmured to the older gentleman behind the checkout counter as I sifted through my Louis Vuitton bag. A fierce heat coated my cheeks as the embarrassment set in and sweat pooled at my hairline. The eyes of several other library patrons watching—*judging*—my every move grew heavy on my back. I bit my tongue to keep the tears that flooded my eyes from spilling over.

If my father could see me now, he'd be staring at me with a smug grin on his face, readying himself to gloat to whoever would listen, saying I'd come crawling back to my trust fund any day now. Since the moment I had left the house with my luggage in tow and hopped into my Mercedes S Class—which, unfortunately, he had paid for—I had been the object of his ridicule.

Actually, let's back up.

Since before I was born, I had been the object of his ridicule. His lack of confidence in me was not something he was interested in hiding.

It had been a long couple of years at college, and despite being excruciatingly tired of ramen noodles made on a stove that only worked half the time, I had refused to ask for any more help than the agreed-upon amount my mother sent me monthly. We bickered for weeks about how much I should receive and, ultimately; I had won. I would receive monthly deposits to keep my modest one-bedroom apartment's rent paid and the utilities on. My parents also covered my car insurance and cell phone bills, so my primary responsibilities were food, gas, and anything extra I wanted to buy.

Fourteen hundred dollars.

Some months I had extra to spend, and other months, such as this, my empty wallet was "accidentally" left at home in fear I would spend my last few dollars on something stupid.

Poor little broke rich girl.

God, I still sounded like a snob.

The clearing of a throat snapped me back to reality. "I understand, Miss, I do, but perhaps you can come back later when—"

"Excuse me, sir? I can cover the balance for her." A man who looked just slightly older than me stepped forward from his place in line with a five-dollar bill in his outstretched hand.

Words escaped me as I stared at this stranger who had just become my library knight in shining armor.

Short chestnut locks fell in front of his deep brown eyes while the rest hung haphazardly, looking like it desperately needed to be brushed. His light gray t-shirt clung to the muscles that were so clearly hidden beneath, looked worn and had pinholes scattered near the collar and hemline. My eyes traveled further to take in the rest of his appearance, and it conflicted me with what to think. He didn't look dirty, per se, but he looked unkempt. It was hard to tell if he was poor or if he just didn't care.

And I was judging. I was judging the man who had stepped up to pay my dollar twenty-three balance so I could check out a freaking library book.

Sometimes I really hated the way my parents conditioned me to think.

My mouth hung agape when he turned around and I finally got a good look at his face, not just his profile. His eyes were so dark, they were nearing black. I bit my lip to keep from salivating over his sharp features and the sexy slight bump in his nose as if he had gotten into one too many fistfights. He was everything I dared to dream about, and everything my father would hate. The sort of bad boy slash grungy 'I don't give a damn' vibe he emulated made my heart skip a beat.

Trying my best to hide my idiotic smile, I could barely register a coherent thought as he paid the balance. The *beep* of the machine processing my book's check out emitted into the air. My smile faded, bursting the lust-filled bubble I was caught in, as he thrust my now checked-out book into my hands and rushed past me to dart out the door.

"I—uh," I stuttered, my brain catching up to his hasty departure, before I flew toward the door after him. I had to at least thank him, right?

The cool, early-fall air assaulted my senses as I stepped out onto the library's stoop. My library knight had just barely made it to the street corner when I screamed out, "Wait! Stop! Please."

To my surprise, he heard me and stopped immediately, but didn't turn around. I moved as quickly as my Jimmy Choo's would get me to him and nearly collided into his back, my body gaining more momentum than I had expected. With his back still to me, I could see the movement of his chest rising and falling by the way his shoulders slightly rocked, as though he was angry and trying to rein in his temper. Still, he didn't turn around.

"I—uh," I stuttered again, finding it hard to formulate the words. "I wanted to say thank you. For paying my balance at the library. I left my wallet at home," I lied, but I didn't feel the need to explain the truth. "It must have fallen out of my purse when I sat it down on my entryway table. I should have double checked when I got home earlier, but I was so excited the text had come through from the library saying the book I put on hold was ready. So I just grabbed everything and ran out the door. I didn't realize my last book was overdue and I would have a balance on my—"

"Do you always ramble when you try to thank someone for a deed that doesn't deserve praise?" he questioned, his voice dry and petulant. Slowly, he turned his body so he could see me, pinning me in his gaze.

I stared at him with what I could only imagine was a shocked expression. People, especially men, weren't typically curt with me. My entire life, I'd been treated like a porcelain doll, spoken to like a child, as though I couldn't understand. Raised in a family where children were to be 'seen, not heard', and unfortunately it was something I had grown accustomed to.

The candidness was refreshing.

"Excuse me?" I questioned back, wondering if I had, in fact, heard him correctly.

This time, he turned to face me completely, and I sucked in a breath, overwhelmed by his very presence. "I paid your balance. It's not a big deal," he told me with a hint of irritation in his voice.

The entire world faded to black around me. The only thing I could see was him, and the only sound I could hear was the pounding of my heart. "It is a big deal," I whispered, unable to look away from him. His eyes dipped down to my lips before snapping back to mine.

I was dying to reach out and touch him—his face, his arm, whatever I could.

What was it about him that made me feel like this?

His eyebrow shot up, and he assessed me through narrowing eyes. "It's really not. Like I said, it was a dollar."

"Dollar twenty-three," I corrected, as he turned away again. Without thinking, I reached out, wanting to stop him from leaving. My fingertips brushed against his, and he instantly yanked his hand back like I had electrocuted him. He took a step away from me, his brows scrunched together in a glare. It still looked like he was about to flee, and the air constricted in my lungs. "I'm sorry. I don't know why I did that."

He grunted, not giving me any more of his time, before he turned on his heel and walked away.

"Wait!" I shouted desperately, following him. "Please, wait a second. What's your name?"

His head shook slightly, but he didn't stop again or give me the decency to turn around as he spoke. "You're better off not knowing, Starlight."

Starlight? What did that mean?

"What kind of answer is that? I want to know." My tone was demanding, prissy. It was the tone I often used when I wanted to get my way—an art I had perfected.

He ignored me and kept going.

"I'm Isla, Isla Donohue," I called after him, but his pace didn't waver as he kept walking down the busy sidewalk. I, however, stopped walking and watched him weave through the bodies, never once turning to look back at me. My shoulders sagged and the feeling of defeat washed over me.

I hated not knowing if I would ever see him again.

My library knight in shining armor.

Two paper bags stacked full of groceries threatened to fall from my arms as I struggled to unlock the front door of the piece of shit decrepit house I shared with my equally shitty old man.

Almost twenty-two years old and I was still living with my deadbeat dad, who still hadn't learned when to put down the bottle.

Shoving the door closed with the heel of my worn sneaker, it slammed and shook the entire frame of the small two-bedroom, one-bath roof over our head.

As usual, dad was passed out on his old as fuck, blueish-gray recliner wearing only boxers and a stained wife-beater that barely covered his giant beer belly. His mouth hung open as he snored, with a bottle of Jack about to fall out of his grasp.

"Fucking cliché," I murmured to myself as I readjusted the grocery bags and stomped into the kitchen. Setting them down on the kitchen counter, I started pulling the contents out of the bags to put them away.

I needed to get the hell out of this house, out of Ridgewood all together. This city had nothing to offer me—it never had. Nothing more than crushed dreams and a broken family. Can you even call it a family, though, when it's just you and your alcoholic Pops?

Back in high school, I had dreamt of going off to college, living in a dorm, and partying my way through the semesters, just like the rest of my friends. But lady luck had different plans when I received acceptance letters to every single school I applied to, just no scholarships. Guys like me couldn't afford college, let alone an Ivy, without a scholarship.

So, unlike my friends, I stayed behind, stuck in Ridgewood pushing through community college. Eventually, I transferred to Ridgewood University to finish the last portion of my bachelor's degree in science. I made it through the years by applying for every grant and private scholarship I could get my hands on and financing student loans for the rest. It wasn't ideal, but I needed to take things one step at a time. Step one was getting the degree. I needed that stupid piece of paper to get a move on with my life, and I wouldn't stop until I had it. My degree would get me one step closer to being a forensic analyst. Later I'd figure out how to pay for it.

My curiosity about science began when I was young and wanted to play mad scientist by mixing random things together. But after years of watching true crime shows after my dad had passed out, drunk off his ass, I developed a new curiosity about things like blood spatter and evidence—crime scenes in general.

After many discussions with my high school science teacher on the topics, he encouraged me to pursue a career as a forensic analyst or something similar. I had no idea what it was, but after spending some time researching, it seemed like a solid option. And working for the police department would just be icing on the cake, knowing I'd have a job that'd pay me decently and give me something I hadn't had in years: health insurance.

Yes, I had officially hit the point in my life where I was looking forward to having health insurance. My current job at the Pack N Mail gave me some money in my pocket and kept me fed, but the owner didn't offer health insurance for part-time employees, which I had to be, thanks to my grueling school schedule. I had been maxing out my units to try to finish sooner—shave off a semester or more—eager to find a department that'd hire me on and allow me to gain experience in the field.

The closer I got to finishing, the more I daydreamed about which police departments I would apply to. With every hopeful glance at the map, my eyes wandering over different cities and states, the pit in my stomach grew. I would never leave Ridgewood. How could I?

It was because of my dad's addiction to alcohol that I stayed. If I left Ridgewood, my old man would drink himself to death. He already basically did, killing off a bottle almost daily. Passing out, breaking shit. He was a messy drunk, and there were times I had to clean up his vomit and piss, too.

I hated it. But what kind of son would I be if I left town knowing it would ultimately mean my father would probably die?

I resented the life I lived and frequently wondered what type of life I might have if my mother had stayed.

The preemptive guilt of abandoning my dad had me in a

chokehold. I was stuck. He needed me around to babysit him. Do welfare checks and shit.

Life had me by the balls and was laughing in my face, shitting on me every chance it got. It was as though I had a neon sign on me flashing "BAD LUCK STRIKE HERE", because it was literally one thing after another.

That's how it'd been all week long. My car's dash had more lights on it than a Christmas tree, and a new light indicating another problem just popped up. My boss cut my hours this week because she had incorrectly scheduled another employee and had to make up their hours. And if that wasn't enough, I completely fucked off and forgot about a huge test I needed to study for in advanced chem and probably fucking failed it.

Just when I thought I was really down on my luck, sitting at the library working on my anatomy homework, I saw *her*, and I suddenly felt like the luckiest bastard alive.

Isla Donohue. *Isla*.

Even her name was as mystical as she was. I had never seen such a strikingly beautiful woman until I saw her in the library, gnawing on the end of her pen, deep in concentration. Her stack of textbooks told me she was in college, thank fuck, because it was practically love at first sight and if she had been underage, I would have died. From the looks of it, she was taking business classes, which baffled me since the clothing she wore screamed *money*. I would guess she didn't need to work a day in her life, but despite the shiny exterior, something told me she was more than what meets the eye.

For nearly two weeks, I felt like a stalker as I sat at a table directly on the other side of the shelves from where she sat, my position giving me the perfect vantage point to peer at her through the books.

Like. A. Fucking. Creeper.

Yet I couldn't stop myself from taking the same table every single day hoping when she came in, she'd find *her* table, too.

And she always did, like the good girl she was.

My intention was always to watch from afar and silently worship the ground she walked on, but when she forgot her wallet and couldn't check out her book, I could hear the wobble in her voice—practically see the quiver of her lip. She was embarrassed, and I wanted nothing more than to shield her from the embarrassment. Reflex kicked in and before I could stop myself, I had already made myself known.

The moment I opened my mouth was the moment I knew I had sucked myself into her orbit. Stepping out from a few people behind her in line, I offered to pay her balance, and I handed the guy a five. Once I could see the transaction was finished, I practically threw her book at her and bolted out the door as quickly as I could. The book I had wanted to check out was left abandoned on a shelf by the exit.

Maybe it'd be there waiting next time. Or maybe I'd forget the title and it wouldn't even matter anymore.

I *had* to run. She was too pretty, too perfect. Too out of my league.

The world crashed down around me when she caught up with me, calling out for me to stop. To talk to her.

And then she touched me... I almost fucking lost it right then and there. The raw fucking need I felt to pull her body flush with mine and kiss the shit out of her—like I said, I nearly lost it.

Even her name was beautiful—one that'd haunt me in my dreams.

Isla Donohue.

THE UNMISTAKABLE SOUND of glass shattering pulled me from my dream and I groaned, rubbing my fists into my eyes to wake up. The red glare from the alarm clock on my bedside table read it was nearing three in the morning, and I cursed my father for whatever drunken stupor he had found himself in this time.

Tossing the comforter off my naked body, I stepped onto the cool tile and made my way to my dresser to grab a pair of sweatpants. My cock was half-mast from a hot dream when I woke, but now hung completely flaccid as I raked a hand down my face and made my way into the pitch-black hallway.

As I entered the living room, I could see my father's legs perched on the couch while his upper body laid on the end table, illuminated by the moonlight coming through the broken curtains. A smashed bottle of vodka was on the floor below him, while a broken lamp hung between his grasp, dangling less than an inch from the shards of glass below it.

"The fuck, old man?" I growled into the room, knowing my words were to no one—he was out cold.

Taking my time, I walked into the kitchen and grabbed the broom and dustpan, carrying it back with me to my bedroom so I could slip on a pair of flip-flops I owned for situations like these.

Once back to where my father laid snoring, I removed the broken lamp from his hold and unplugged it, setting it down on the floor behind me before I cleaned up the glass. I didn't bother trying to wake him up or move him, but I would clean up the glass fragments so he wouldn't get hurt when he inevitably fell off the table and couch.

He needed help. Over the years, I had tried everything, but we couldn't afford rehab centers, and the resources the city offered were worthless. He tried and failed more times than I could count. His sponsor quit on him, my mother left him, and I... Well, I'm still here, but evidently am not enough of a reason for him to get sober.

CHAPTER THREE

ISLA

I went back to the library every single day at the same time, hoping I'd run into him again. It had been a week, and I hadn't seen him. The table I sat at offered a view of pretty much the entire library. Yet, he hadn't been back.

Forcing myself to focus on my mock advertising portfolio, I spread out my textbook, notebook, and laptop and dove in. The semester-long project was due in just two weeks, and I really needed to stop having my head in the clouds if I wanted to keep up my 4.0 GPA, which I did.

"Did you purposely take up this entire table with all of your things, or can you make space for one more?"

My pen clanked against the table as I dropped it. The air caught in my chest at the sound of his voice—a voice I wasn't sure I'd ever hear again.

"You... No, please, sit," I encouraged, pulling my textbooks closer to me and freeing up the table space across from me.

He tilted his head to read the spine of my book. "What are you working on?"

"A sample pitch for a running shoe campaign. My mock advertising portfolio is due soon. Business major."

"That's a safe choice," he crooned. "What do you *actually* want to study?"

My eyes widened at how bluntly he asked that question. No one had cared enough to ask. My palms were sweaty, and I fought the urge to wipe them against my jeans. Lifting my chin, I countered, "How do you know business isn't what I want to study?"

He assessed me through narrow eyes, and I counted each painfully long second he stared at me. All forty-two of them. "Business is a major you're forced to study, but you have no passion for. Based on how you carry yourself and the quality of the clothing and items you carry, I'd say you more likely wanted to go into art or fashion but were pushed into business by your family. Am I right?"

"Yes and no," I told him without hesitation, my confidence growing. "I was pushed to study business, yes. It was the only way my father would allow me to attend Ridgewood U. But it's not art or fashion I wanted to major in..." my voice trailed off and I looked out the window, feeling irritated with myself for being so candid, and still so angry with my father for forcing my hand with this decision.

He said nothing, and I appreciated the time he gave me to linger in my thoughts.

"Veterinarian," I blurted, my head snapping back toward him and meeting his gaze. "I want to be a veterinarian, but my father won't allow it."

"Why do you need his permission?"

"He has the money..." My voice was soft, embarrassed. It was the truth, but at twenty-two years old, I hated I still relied on his money, if only a small allowance of it.

"You don't need his money," he said firmly, his voice a low rumble—almost like a growl. I stared at him, wondering if he had really just made that sound.

"You know, you never did tell me your name."

"You don't need to know it." He stood suddenly, pushing the chair from beneath him.

My spine tingled from the anger in his tone. As he moved to the back of the library, I hopped out of my seat and followed him. "You're the one who sought me out, my friend. Why won't you tell me your name?" I questioned, whisper-shouting, as I practically jogged to keep up with his huge strides. Rounding another corner, we were almost at the very back of the library, the section hardly anyone used.

Hidden in their own little world, behind the last long bookshelf, stood two tables—lopsided from broken legs— and a row of computers that looked like they were from the first batch of computers ever made. I don't think I had ever ventured to this part of the library. It seemed as though it was completely abandoned and used for broken storage.

Why had he come back here?

A tattered backpack laid on one of the tables, a textbook pulled out next to it, and a water bottle sat on the floor by the chair. I was so confused and stopped without fully entering the space.

Watching me closely, he took a seat where the items were. He leaned back with his legs stretched in front of him and his hands clasped behind his head, elbows outstretched.

"We're piss poor." His gaze met mine, and a smirk played on his lips. "My dad is an alcoholic. My mom left when I was younger. Same sob story you've probably heard a thousand times. I applied to every school I could think of and got into most of them. Know why I didn't go to any?"

My heart hammered in my chest as I listened to his words, not sure what to say, or if I needed to say anything at all.

"Because I didn't get a single scholarship. But I didn't let my lack of money stop me. I go full-time, even though it's adding up a crippling amount of debt. All I need is that expensive piece of paper and then I can do what I want. So don't use daddy's money as an excuse to hide behind, Starlight, because you sure as shit don't need him or his money to make it on your own."

I let his words sink in and a slight tremor ran through my body. He was right. But who was he to talk to me like that?

And why was I so turned on by it?

Ignoring the desire pooling low in my belly, I marched up to him, head held high, and pointed my finger at his chest. "Listen here. I don't know who you think you are, but you don't get to speak to me like that. You don't get to assume just because I wear nice clothes or have designer purses, you have me and my life all mapped out."

His eyebrow quirked. "Don't I?"

"No, you absolutely do not." I resisted the urge to stomp my foot in protest, knowing it would only further solidify his assumption of me. I could feel my cheeks heat. My stomach flipped under the intensity of his gaze, and I was finding it hard to breathe.

Without warning, his hands flew to my waist, and he gripped my hips tightly, pulling me down onto his lap. I gasped realizing the precarious position he had pulled me into, suddenly hyper aware of every part of his body. The softness of my thighs touching the hard muscles of his. My hands had come to rest on his chest and with a small adjustment of his hips, I could feel the ridge of his cock beneath me, just a few layers of fabric separating us. It took everything I had in me not to rock against it and chase the relief it would give to my aching pussy.

I swallowed thickly, unsure of how to handle myself in this situation.

Here, in the back of the library, I was straddling a stranger.

As if he could hear my thoughts, his fist circled around my hair and he moved his lips to align with my ear. "The blush that's creeping up your neck and the way you're squirming against my dick right now says otherwise, Starlight. I think you like how bluntly I speak to you. I think you like it a fuck ton."

My chest rose and fell with heavy breaths and he was right; I was squirming in his lap. Arousal flooded my body. I was desperately in need of friction. It'd been too long since I had been with anyone but my pretty blue vibrator, and the hard cock below me was a feeling my body craved. My pussy clenched in anticipation.

"Tell me your name," I breathed, my voice raspy and strained. His hand was still fisting my hair while the other gripped my hip, lightly guiding my hips to rub against him. He may have been encouraging it, but I sure as hell wasn't stopping it. Instead, my body welcomed the touch of this stranger.

This stranger who I was full on dry humping in the back of the library.

Were there cameras?

Oh god, what if someone was watching the security system right now? They'd be getting quite a show, seeing me rub against this random guy. But maybe they'd just assume he wasn't random, and we were just another horny couple who couldn't keep their hands off each other.

Or maybe no one was watching, and I was being paranoid.

His nose softly ran against my collarbone, breaking me out of my thoughts and turning my attention to his movements. "Why do you want to know so bad?"

"Why do you not want to tell me?" I breathed, my eyes closing, getting lost in the sensation. He was setting my skin on fire with the simplest of touches.

"I'll fuck up your life, Isla. I'm not good for you. I'll ruin everything."

"Maybe I want you to ruin me."

His growl vibrated against my skin. "You have no idea what you're asking. Don't say things you don't mean, Starlight."

His words struck a chord, pulling me back to the present. Yet another man, assuming the words I say aren't my truth. I could think for myself, but for some reason, people didn't believe I could. It was infuriating.

With nothing to lose, I scooted my body further up his lap, pressing my chest against his. "Can you feel my heart beating?" I demanded.

His chest pushed into mine as he straightened his spine, his chest flattening against mine. He grew still, tightening his grip on my hip. "Yeah."

"It's never beat like this. You do something to me. I don't know what, or why, but you're driving me wild."

"I'll fuck up your life," he repeated, shaking his head. "We're worlds apart."

"We don't have to be."

The words were barely off my tongue before he crashed his lips to mine, consuming me in a kiss so intense we were breathing as one. His hands began to roam my body, taking their time exploring every exposed piece of flesh and lightly trailing across my clothes. A ravenous hunger grew within me and I deepened our kiss. The background faded away, and I got lost in the moment, happily letting myself get pulled deeper into the web he had drawn me into.

A moan escaped my body, and he sucked it into his mouth, matching it with a low rumble from within his chest. "Careful, keep making noises like that and I'll have no choice but to make you swallow your screams."

"Is that a threat or a promise?" I asked, growing bold as my fingers pulled at the hem of his shirt and dipped beneath to feel his skin. As my fingertips wisped across his stomach, I felt his abdomen tighten against my touch. He captured my mouth again, kissing me so hard I was sure my lips would bruise.

Without breaking our kiss, he stood, holding me in his arms before my back suddenly met with the firm surface of a table. The wood was cold beneath my back, a stark contrast to the heat of his body. Leaning forward, his body engulfed mine, pressing into me easily from the incline caused by the broken table legs.

"I shouldn't be doing this," he murmured when he pulled away slightly. His lips hovered so close to mine, yet he was clearly at war with himself. "I should be restraining myself and walking away."

"Is that what you want?" I panted into his mouth. "Because it's not what I want."

He groaned, pushing his erection between my thighs.

Even with us both fully clothed, I could feel him every-where. "What I want is to rip your clothes from your perfect body and worship every inch of your skin. I want you screaming, panting, and so crazy with need that every time you're with another man, you'll picture me. I want you to come so hard you see stars—and I want that right here in this library, right fucking now."

I moaned through the feeling of his hips rocking into me. "So take it. Take what you want."

What on earth was I saying? I couldn't believe the words had just floated from my lips, but my brain was so clouded with arousal it didn't matter. I'd let this man take me, sprawled out across a table right in the middle of the library, if he told me that's what he wanted.

The movements of his hips stopped and he looked over both shoulders toward the shelves filled with old, wrinkled magazines. A look of hesitancy passed through his gaze when his eyes met mine again, before he reached into his back pocket. I licked my lips, transfixed on his hands while he pulled a condom from his wallet.

My heart hammered in my chest as I questioned my morals. Was I really going to let him fuck me against this table in public? My head screamed *no*, while my heart and my pussy begged *yes*. Panic began to rise, heating my chest and cheeks.

"This is a bad idea," he told me, standing up straight and fisting his hair. "I'm sorry, I got carried away."

Before I could think it through, I leaned up and grabbed the fabric of his shirt with my fist, pulling him back down on top of me, and reconnecting our kiss. I was trying to convey everything I couldn't put into words. Yes, this was a bad idea, but I didn't care—I wanted it. Him. *"Please,"* I whispered against his lips.

He pulled back slightly and searched my eyes. Whatever he saw in them snapped the last of his willpower. "Fuck it," he growled, slamming his lips back into mine.

Frantically, we began to tug at each other's clothes, pulling off layers as quickly as possible. As he worked the buttons on my jeans, I pulled the hem of his shirt up, desperate to feel every inch of his skin. Reaching behind him, he pulled it up and over his head, dropping it to the table beside me and giving me a front row view of the planes of his chest and the taut muscles that were hidden beneath his shirt. He wasn't overly muscular, but rather he had the muscles someone earns from hard work and manual labor. I practically salivated at the sight.

Once his shirt was off, he began tugging my unbuttoned jeans down until they hung right below my knees. He stared down at me with a hunger in his eyes that made me shiver.

"Tell me your name," I demanded, though my tone was soft.

"Telling you my name will only make it harder for both of us to walk away," he groaned, unbuttoning his jeans and tugging them down slightly to pull himself out. Fisting his cock, he slid his hand from base to tip and back down, never breaking our gaze. "I told you, Starlight, I'll fuck up your life. You don't want me hanging around messing things up. The less you know about me, the better it is for you."

"No, the better it is for you. And you think walking away is going to be easy for either of us? We just met, but for some reason..." my voice trailed off, not wanting to finish the thought. If he was determined to make this no strings, then *I* needed to recognize it was no strings too.

The problem with no strings was that I didn't think I could do it. I couldn't explain the magnetic pull I had for this man, despite having just met him, but it was real and tangible, and I could *feel* this could be something.

CHAPTER FOUR

CALEB

My cock was painfully hard as I held it in my hand and stared down at the absolute goddess in front of me. I was driving myself crazy, debating on if I should fuck her senseless or tuck myself back in and walk away. The sight of her laid out in front of me. Only a thin triangle of black lace covering her bare pussy—the *sexiest* thing she could have possibly been wearing—pushed me to the brink of insanity.

Time stopped, and it felt like hours since we had snuck away to the deserted part of the library, but it had been less than ten minutes. I could still salvage this for both of us. Walk away now and do everything I could to forget about her, her perfect body, and the way every atom in my body knew this would wreck me. She would wreck me.

And I'd wreck her.

Her perfect life, her pure heart, her image.

She didn't deserve a man like me fucking up her life. The son of a drunk, the outcast, the one that would always have to work harder than any other bastard in the room just to get where I needed to be in life. Although I didn't know much about her, I knew enough from what she had just told me. Bottom line, she was the daughter of a powerful man with a lot of money.

Devastatingly beautiful with her dark hair, creamy skin, and stormy eyes. She could bring me to my knees from just her looks alone, but as my luck would have it, it seemed as though the woman had the personality to match, too. Isla had goals, dreams, ambitions. She was going to excel in life. I had my own goals and dreams, but Isla—Isla was different. Everything she wanted was within reach if she just allowed it to be, whereas I would have to fight.

I'd slow her down.

And I didn't want to be the man that slowed her down, but I'd be damned if I didn't want just a little taste, too.

With one final mental debate, I threw all resolve out the window and sheathed my cock with the condom I had tossed onto the table. Isla watched my movements the entire time, and against all odds, my cock hardened even more.

I was so fucked.

Leaning back down, I pressed my lips against hers and coaxed her mouth open with my tongue, memorizing every inch of her kiss. Moving my fingers to the thin lace that covered her pussy, I pushed them aside and plunged two fingers inside, finding her exactly how I wanted her: dripping wet and ready for me.

Finding a rhythm that had her writhing beneath me, I momentarily lost myself in the ecstasy of her pussy. Her warmth radiated around my fingers, and as she contracted her pussy walls around them, I nearly came on the spot.

Releasing her mouth from mine, I licked my way to her chest, pulling her tank top down before latching onto her nipple, flicking the hardened peak with my tongue. Within a few swirls around it, I was able to draw out a wanton moan from her greedy lips.

I needed to be inside her.

Pulling my fingers out, I took her by surprise when I reached up and pushed them past her swollen lips, inserting them into her mouth. I groaned, feeling her lapping up her taste with a look of ferocity and determination within her gray-blue eyes. Maybe I underestimated her.

Without risking the chance of changing my mind again, I pulled my fingers from her mouth and moved her panties aside, lining myself up with her center. The tip of my cock nudged her entrance. "Last chance to call this off."

She shook her head. "I'm all in."

Her words were all I needed to snap my last thread of morality. Slamming into her in one thrust, I was met with her lustful moan when I filled her to the hilt. My eyes practically rolled back in my head with how good she felt, wrapped around my cock perfectly.

The flutter behind my rib cage made me pause, wondering what the fuck was going on. Our bodies were fully connected, but it felt like more. Deeper.

I knew this was a bad idea.

I stood unmoving, committing to memory the way her eyes were hooded, how she bit her lip, and the way she started to squirm from the fullness of me being inside of her.

There was no way I could walk away from this woman after this, no possible way. And the thought absolutely terrified me. I had to force myself, but I knew I needed to at least give her a small piece of myself before I tossed both of our hearts aside. "Caleb. My name's Caleb Hart."

She giggled at my admission, but it wasn't the sound I wanted to hear from her, so I quickly transformed her giggle into a loud breathy moan, drifting my fingers over to her clit. I rubbed it in precise circles, applying a moderate pressure as I did. She whimpered beneath my touch, and I drew my free hand to clamp down over her mouth, stifling her noises.

"You're in a library, Isla," I chastised, rocking my hips into her slowly. My thrusts were deliberate, taking my time to pull out almost fully before gliding back in. "You wouldn't want to disturb others in the building, would you?"

She shook her head no from beneath the hold I had on her mouth.

The table began to move beneath us as I slammed into her, increasing my pace while I continued to rub her clit. Her body felt in sync with mine—I could practically feel her orgasm building, getting closer to the point of shattering beneath me.

I wanted nothing more than to see the look in her eyes when she came all over my cock.

Still aware of our surroundings, I slowed my pace to dull the slapping of our skin, hearing a pair of voices draw near. Isla heard them too and her eyes widened, a hint of fear flashing behind them.

Leaning closer to her ear, I whispered, "Shh, I've got you."

The change in angle pushed me deeper, hitting the sweet spot deep inside her, drawing out an indescribable sound from her. It was something between a moan and a squeal, and my new favorite sound. Rolling my hips into her, my cock stroked her while my hand still covered her mouth, hiding her sounds. I could feel her hot breath panting into the palm of my hand.

The idea of being caught gave me a mix of fear and exhilaration, and while I hoped they'd fuck off to where they came from, I was slightly curious to find out what would happen if they came a little closer.

Applying a little more pressure to Isla's clit, she came without warning, trembling beneath me as her juices drenched my cock, coating me in her desire. Watching her writhe beneath me, fighting against the hold on her mouth that kept her quiet because she wanted to be loud, was enough to bring me to ruin right behind her.

Grunting through my release, I moved my hand to grip the back of her neck, holding it tightly as I filled the condom. A wicked, fleeting wish that I was bare so I filled her instead, infiltrated my thoughts.

As we both came down post-release, she lay beneath me, her chest rising and falling, catching her breath with a lazy, satisfied smile on her face.

"You look fully satiated now," I mused, pulling the condom from my dick that was still half-mast, simply from the sight of her. Tucking myself back into my pants, I tossed the condom into the trash can nearby before grabbing her hand and tugging her upright. My fingers slipped into the belt loops of her jeans and I tugged them back up her legs and over the curve of her ass.

"Satisfied yes, satiated no. We might need to do it a few more times before I'm satiated."

Slipping the button through the hole in her jeans, I looked down at her with what I hoped was a serious expression. "There won't be any more times, Isla. That was a one time thing. Like I said, I won't be the man who fucks up your life."

"I already said I didn't—"

"It doesn't matter. You deserve better than what I can give you. You deserve better than a man like me."

"What does that even mean? A man like you?" she questioned, taking a step closer, although we were only inches apart.

I ran a hand down my face, suppressing a groan when I smelled her scent on my fingers. My mind was screaming at me to get the fuck out of the situation, while my dick was straining against my pants again, begging for me to spin her around and bend her over this table for round two. "Just trust me, Starlight. I'm not the man for you."

My fingers twitched by my sides, dying to reach out and tuck the deep chocolate lock of hair that'd fallen over the side of her face behind her ear so I could get a look at her stormy, gray-blue eyes one last time. Walking away after fucking her was a dick move, and I was fully aware of the consequences of my actions, but I had no other option. She'd either hate me now for being an asshole or she'd hate me later for ruining her life.

I'd rather be remembered as the guy she had sex with in a library than the one that cost her everything. Because that's what I'd end up being to her, the guy who ultimately screwed everything up.

Just as the people who'd been walking near us came into view, I snatched my old-ass backpack off the table next to her and hightailed it out of there, knowing I'd never be able to show my face in this damn library again.

CHAPTER FIVE

ISLA

In life there are things that suck, things that hurt, and things that cut you deep into your core. Unforgivable, inconceivable, soul-shattering things that hurt you so badly, you're not even entirely sure you'll ever fully recover.

I'd had boyfriends growing up, and my share of heartbreak. I'd experienced one-night stands and had the walk of shame once or twice. Being ghosted was a normal thing these days, and I had done the ghosting too. I knew it sucked. I'd felt the frustration.

What I hadn't yet experienced with dating, though, was handing my heart to someone I literally knew nothing about and having it handed back, tattered and bruised after sharing something so spontaneous and intimate. Until now.

I hadn't purposely given it to him—it wasn't as if I had put it on a plate with a neon sign over it that read 'you can break this'—but somehow, that's exactly what happened.

Like a desperate little girl, I spent the days that followed camped out at a table in the front of the library, hoping he'd walk back in, apologize for stomping on my heart, and beg for a do-over. I practically spent from open to close inside of those four walls, skipping my classes and doing busy work on my computer.

I created a resume, *a freaking resume*, despite having never worked a day in my life. It was the saddest resume ever, but creating it made me realize maybe I should get a job. I started looking around online and applying to places to work part-time, unsure of how I would even swing it with a full load of classes, but I had decided it was time to bulk up my nonexistent work experience.

Just when I had convinced myself Caleb would never come back to the library, instinct told me I was being watched. A spine-tingling sensation radiated down my spine and caused me to look around, searching for the source of the inkling. I made eye contact with a few library patrons, but none of them gave me an ah-ha feeling. None of them was the person who had me on high alert.

Slumping back down into my chair, I continued working on the email to a veterinary clinic hiring for a part-time receptionist, attempting to make myself sound more knowl-edgeable and enticing. I was failing miserably. I could feel the tears welling up and lining my lashes, threatening to spill over.

My heart ached.

I was pathetic.

Twenty-two years old and I had never felt more like a child.

Is this how I was going to let life pass me by? Feeling reliant on my parents, who were determined to keep me in a gold cage my entire life? I couldn't even go to veterinary school like I wanted to, all because my father wouldn't allow it.

Why was *I*, a grown adult, allowing *him* to make my decisions, like I was still under his roof?

Because without him, you have no money.

The intensity from the feeling of being watched still had my spine tingling, but with more determination I returned my focus to the email in front of me and set to work on making myself sound like I knew my worth, even though I was still adding up all the pennies in front of me.

CHAPTER SIX

CALEB

Standing in the middle of the bread aisle, I looked down at the pathetic excuse for groceries I'd stacked in my hand basket. As a grown man, I should have eaten healthier than I did when I was a preteen boy, but processed junk was less expensive than healthy foods. So, there I was with a basket full of instant soup, granola bars, chips, pre-packaged pastries, and a package of hot dogs, longing for a home-cooked meal. I made a mental note to watch some cooking videos online and teach myself some easy recipes.

Without looking up, I continued down the aisle in the direction of the produce section, on a mission to add something green to the pile.

What did I need to make lasagna? When I was younger, my grandmother would make lasagna for us, and my stomach would be full for days. She packed it full of cheeses, meats, and spinach. Seemed easy enough, maybe I'd—

"Caleb!"

My head whipped down the aisle I had just meandered through, toward the shriek of her voice. I felt my blood run cold when my gaze landed on her. Over the last couple weeks I had tried to convince myself she meant nothing and I'd never see her again, knowing as much as I wished otherwise, it was for the best. I hadn't anticipated how it would feel to actually see her again.

With fury in her eyes, Isla stomped down the aisle, not stopping until we were chest to chest. I had to admire her tenacity. She certainly wasn't afraid to back down, and by the looks of it, she was currently out for blood. My blood.

With a loud clunk, her hand basket hit the floor. I couldn't help but glance down at it, stuffed to the brim with *healthy* food. Things that could make a full meal.

Taking my time, I slowly raked my eyes up her body as I figured out what to say to her. I had hoped to avoid a run-in like this—and after two solid weeks passing, I thought I was in the clear—but I should have known better than to continue shopping at places that were near the library.

I guess it was only a matter of time.

"Isla," I stated, trying to remain aloof, even though my stomach was doing backflips. The *need* to reach out and touch her clawed at me, but I refused to let myself.

"We need to talk."

"We don't. There's nothing to say." I watched her face fall, and I gritted my teeth, hating I was the one contributing to that look. I should have no feelings for this girl, yet somehow the pain I had just caused her physically hurt me, too. Against my better judgment, I twisted the knife I had just stabbed her with. "We had a little fun. It wasn't a big deal."

Her sadness transformed back to anger before my very eyes, her features morphing into the fiery look she had walked up to me with. "That's bullshit, Caleb, and you know it. It wasn't one-sided. If it were, you wouldn't have told me your name."

Shit. She wasn't wrong.

"What is it exactly you want from me, Isla? I have nothing to give."

Her gaze cast down to the basket sitting beside her feet, seemingly lost in thought. I wasn't sure what she was going for when she marched up to me, looking for a fight, but I wasn't going to give her one. She wasn't my girlfriend.

She could never be my girlfriend.

We stood in silence for a moment before she finally answered my question, avoiding my gaze. "I just want to talk."

Her melancholy tone of voice sent a frigid blast through my veins. What was it about her that made me give a damn? Letting out a huff of air, I bent to pick up her groceries. "Then talk."

Weaving through the aisles, I made my way to the check stand, not turning to see if Isla had followed. I knew she was right behind me, keeping up with my long strides. Removing the items from my basket and hers, I placed them onto the conveyor belt without placing a divider between. The desire to take care of her and pay for her groceries consumed me, regardless of whether it drained my bank account to do it.

I refused to turn and look at her and instead directed my focus on the cashier, who began scanning our items. The incessant beep of each item being scanned grated on my nerves as I watched the dollar signs climb.

Once he finished and totaled out the transaction, Isla's attention shifted from the floor to her surroundings, and she frantically waved her arms at the cashier, trying to pull his attention to her. "Oh! No, wait," she exclaimed as she dug through her purse, looking for what I assumed would be her wallet.

"I've got it," I grumbled, swiping my debit card through the card reader. From my periphery, I could see her cheeks redden, and I fought against a smirk.

Thanking the cashier, I picked up Isla's bag of groceries and thrust it into her arms before grabbing my own significantly lighter bag.

"You didn't have to do that, Caleb. I can pay for my own groceries," she argued, falling into step beside me as I exited the store.

"Where are we heading?" I asked, looking around for a place we could go.

Isla did the same before she wordlessly started walking to our right. I shook my head with slight annoyance, following behind her and admiring the view. She wore a pair of jeans that hugged her ass perfectly, and a loose fitting burnt orange shirt with a deep V cut down the back, giving me a view of her creamy skin and the luscious curves hiding beneath. My cock strained in my pants at the sight, and the memory of how she felt crumbling blissfully beneath me played like a movie in my head.

She stopped at the steps of the library, climbing a few before she settled down on one and placed her grocery bag beside her. I did the same, letting my legs stretch wide in front of me, while my elbows sat on the step above me. Conflicting feelings brewed within me—I wasn't sure how I wanted to handle this. I couldn't deny the attraction I had toward her and all the things she made me *feel*, but the self-destructing side of me knew I shouldn't make her a part of my life.

In my eyes, Isla was the definition of perfection. Rich

family, supermodel looks, killer curves, and from the brief interactions I'd had with her, the most breathtakingly genuine personality. A guy like me didn't deserve a girl like her.

I needed to stomp out the flicker of hope she had. There was no other choice.

Swallowing my morals and the lump in my throat, I stepped into a persona I reserved only for very rare occasions.

"I'm not sure why you think there's anything to talk about. You were a warm pussy for me to slide into, and nothing more. I warned you of that before I fucked you, did I not?" I crossed my arms over my chest and schooled my expression into what I hoped was disinterest, feeling nauseated at my own words.

"You're so full of shit, Caleb. I may not know you all that well, but I have been around liars my entire life. People who use others to get exactly what they want. People who do anything it takes to get what they want. That's not you, and I know what I felt wasn't one-sided."

"And what exactly did you feel, Starlight? Because the only thing I felt was your pussy as it gripped my cock and swallowed it whole."

Redness slid up her cheeks as she stared at the steps below us. The words tasted like bile on my tongue and the moment they passed my lips, I wished I could take them back. There was no truth to my statement, but she needed to think there was. "Look, I told you already. There's nothing I can give you. Getting involved with someone like me won't do you any favors."

"And what if I don't want anything?" she asked quietly,

still staring down at the concrete of the stairs. "What if all I'm asking for is a little fun?"

I turned my head to face her, the words falling out of my mouth before I could stop them. "We both know that's not all it would be."

She snapped her gaze to me, our eyes connecting like magnets. "So you admit you feel something, then?"

"Like I said, you were—"

"I know, just a warm pussy to slide into, right?" Tears formed as she repeated my words, and I felt like the world's biggest jackass.

My entire mouth went dry, and I jutted my tongue out to wet my lips, wondering if there was any way to salvage this so I wasn't coming across so harshly. Why was this so hard to do? I hardly knew the girl and had slept with her one time. I forced the lump in my throat down with a thick swallow. "Right," I told her, nodding once.

"I don't believe that," she seethed. She wasn't letting up, as though she could see right through me. And maybe she could, because it sure as hell felt like she could see me, deep down in my soul.

"What part of this are you not comprehending? You come from money and privilege. I come from pain and suffering. This idea you've painted in your head about us riding off into the sunset and a white picket fence, it'll never happen."

"Gaslighting me, Caleb? Really? I never asked you for any of those things. I never even alluded to it. All I want is a chance to get to know you, but you know what? Forget I even asked. I'm not going to beg for your time. I may be trying to pave my way and break apart from my father's control and my life of *privilege*, but I know my damn worth, too."

My heart slammed behind my ribs, loving the ferocity this woman exuded. Pride bloomed in my chest as I watched her stand, bending at the waist to pick up her bag of groceries. I had no right to be prideful over this woman and the strength she harbored, but I was, and I couldn't explain why. My brows furrowed with my conflicting emotions, confused at what to feel.

I would let her go, here and now. She wouldn't find me again after what I said. Isla didn't seem like the type to give a second chance after she was burned, and the look on her face told me my words had scorched her.

Whoever came up with that 'sticks and stones' line was fucking lying when they said words couldn't hurt you.

My words hurt *me*. Everything I said was bitter and ugly, with not even an ounce of truth behind them. But that's what I wanted, right? I wanted her to go. To leave me alone and never come back. For her own benefit.

Right?

She gave me her back and floated down the stairs, not sparing me a glance as she turned left and headed back in the direction we had come from.

Fuck.

CHAPTER SEVEN

CALEB

My body reacted before my mind and I raced down the steps, chasing after her. The sound of my shoes slamming onto the sidewalk as I jogged after her echoed in my ears, along with my heartbeat. I was completely backpedaling on everything I just said, but I'd be damned if the sight of her walking away didn't kill me. She wasn't far ahead, but the head start I gave her before coming to my goddamn senses was enough to make me hustle to catch up.

"Isla, wait," I yelled from behind her, but she either didn't hear me or ignored me. Likely the latter. Not that I didn't deserve it.

I caught up to her and thrust my arm forward, encircling my fingers around her bicep. She stopped instantly, spinning to face me. Malice laced tears pooled in her eyes, and I reached up to wipe a fallen tear with the pad of my thumb. She recoiled from my touch, and my heart sunk into the pits of my stomach. Still, I held my hand against her face, not wanting to let her go.

"No," she said, her voice strong despite the quiver in her lower lip. She put her hands on my chest as if to push me away, but didn't.

"I'm sorry," I breathed, leaning my forehead against hers. An overwhelming weight of anguish sat on my chest. I rubbed my thumb against her cheek, my head spinning. I was so incredibly stupid.

Stupid to think I could let her go. Stupid to think I could keep her.

This would never work. I couldn't pinpoint what changed for me so suddenly, but watching her walk away knowing she wouldn't try again... I decided right then and there, losing her forever wasn't a risk worth taking.

She shook her head, pulling away from my touch—away from *me*—and took a step back. "No, Caleb. You don't get to cut me down with your words then instantly change your mind. I heard you, okay? Loud and clear. Warm pussy. Easy lay. No strings. You drove your point home and now *I'm going home*."

"Isla, please."

"I'm not interested in anything else you have to say. It was interesting to meet you, Caleb. Have a nice life."

Once again she began to turn away, but I caught her arm, sliding my hand down until my fingers laced with hers. She stared down at our connected hands with confusion, and I stared at her face, studying the rosiness of her cheeks and the fullness of her lashes. Different emotions danced across her face as we stood silent, connected but miles apart.

"I was an ass," I started, still conflicted on if this was the right thing to do. "Isla, I have nothing to offer you. My life is a joke. I work a shitty job just to put food in my stomach, and I live at home with a man who's been consistently drunk for the last thirteen years. I go to school to evade this life, but the truth is, I'll never leave. Not when my two choices are to care for my dad or have his death on my hands. That's what I'm looking at, Isla. I either stay or kill him because there will be no one to keep him from drinking himself to death. Why would I bring you into that life?"

Her brows laced together, and she raised her chin. "Did I propose to you, Caleb?"

Now it was my turn to be confused. "What?" I asked. "No? What are you talking about?"

"I didn't propose, so this idea you have, thinking you're locking me into a shitty life, is ridiculous. I never asked for commitment, Caleb. I literally only asked to get to know you. I like you. I don't know why, especially after the way you've treated me, but I do. You make me feel something I've never felt, and it's a feeling I'd like to explore. I've lived a sheltered, privileged life, but it's not who *I* am. I'm so much more than the girl you think you see. Spending time together and hanging out doesn't equal wedding bells and my stomach swollen with your kid. It's just two people, exploring a feeling and having a little fun for a while."

"You think I'll let you go? That once we've 'had some fun' I'll say goodbye and we'll go our separate ways?"

She threw her hands into the air, letting out an exasperated groan. "Haven't you already? Is that not exactly what you did? Had your fun, then instantly pushed me away."

"I'm trying to do what I think is best for you, Isla." A low growl ricocheted through my body, hating that she was right.

"Why don't you let me decide what's best for me? This is the twenty-first century, is it not?"

A smirk pulled at the corner of my mouth and I reached up to brush away the hair that'd fallen into my eyes. "You're sexy when you're standing up for yourself."

"Yeah? Well, you're still an ass even when you apologize." Her eyes drifted back down to where our hands were still connected and she loosened her fingers, attempting to unlock our hold on one another, but I tightened my grip, not letting her walk away.

"Want to get something to eat?" I asked quietly. My confidence was starting to wane, unsure of what her next move may be. I waited with bated breath as her eyes bounced to mine.

She shook her head no. My heart sank, and I dropped my head, feeling defeated, although I knew I had no jurisdiction to feel that way. I had burned my bridge with her, and in the moments it took me to come to my senses, she had also come to hers, realizing I wasn't worth it.

The realization stung, and I released her hand quickly, as though it had burned me.

She read my features like an open book written in large font. Smiling, she rolled her eyes at me. "I don't want to get something to eat, because you just bought me a huge bag of groceries. Do you want to come to my place and I'll make you something?"

I beamed at her, my chest inflating with excitement. A giant, dopey smile overtook my face, and I practically felt my stomach rumble on the spot. "You cook?"

"Not very well... I was hoping you had an unrevealed talent of mastery in the kitchen."

I tipped my head back and hearty, genuine laughter erupted from my chest. I shook my head. "No, Starlight, I don't cook, but we can figure it out together."

Bending over, I picked up the two bags of groceries and cradled them in my arms before tipping my chin at her. "Lead the way."

She did, spinning on her heel with a small pep in her step I couldn't ignore, giving me the most perfect view of her ass as she led me to her apartment.

CHAPTER EIGHT

"Well, it's safe to say it's inedible," Caleb said as he pushed burnt hot dogs into the trash can. A flurry of black char floated into the air as they rolled off the plate he held.

I laughed as they made a soft thump into the bottom of the trash. "I don't know how you forgot about them!"

Caleb had insisted on cooking the hot dogs in a skillet with oil to crisp them up, claiming they were way better than when you boiled them. I inwardly shuddered as he explained his reasoning. Hot dogs grossed me out, but I was prepared to suck it up and eat one.

"I do. It's your fault."

"My fault?" I questioned innocently, turning back to stir the pot of pasta. It was the type you just added some milk and a seasoning packet to once the noodles were cooked. A step up from mac and cheese. A little more sophisticated— or at least that's what I was telling myself as I silently prayed it wouldn't boil over and burn too.

My breathing hitched when Caleb's body pressed against

mine. I hadn't heard him move toward me and suddenly I felt him everywhere, making it a struggle to simply fill my lungs with air. His hands brushed down my shoulders and situated on the outside of my upper arms, before he reached out and pulled my hair aside, exposing the right side of my neck.

Leaning in closer, his mouth grazed the shell of my ear. "I'm having a hard time not touching you right now. I'm trying to be a gentleman, to treat you respectfully. But right now, all I want to do is shove you to your knees and disrespect the fuck out of you."

I stopped stirring the pasta, abandoning the wooden spoon in the boiling water. Spinning, I faced him and tilted my head to look into his eyes just as he dipped his head down lower. Our noses brushed together, our breath mingling. My heart raced and threatened to run right out of my rib cage.

"What's stopping you?" My voice was barely audible as I swallowed down a lump that had formed in my throat.

He rubbed his nose lightly against mine, his lips slightly parted as he caught the air I was expelling. My eyes shut in anticipation, and I tried to control the way the arousal was sparking through my body, sending tingles throughout.

"You deserve better than me. I plan to give you better."

Sexual tension filled the air and I was so tempted to close the almost nonexistent distance between us and press my lips to his. We both stayed unmoving, in the moment as time ticked by, and with each passing second, more magnetism pulsed between us.

Rising up on my tiptoes, my eyes fluttered closed as I seemed to move in slow motion toward him. I could *feel* our lips about to meet when the sizzle of water boiling over startled us both, pulling us from the moment. Caleb took a step back, giving me space to turn, as I turned my attention to the stove. A plume of steam had risen up into the range hood, and I lifted the pot quickly to remove it from the heat.

"*Shit*," I muttered to myself, setting the pot on the neighboring burner and grabbing the towel hanging from the oven's handle. A foamy liquid had already started to burn onto the glass stovetop, and I knew it'd be a complete bitch to clean. "We're disastrous chefs."

"This is why I only buy pre-made crap," Caleb said, chuckling to himself as he ran a dish towel under a stream of water. He rang it out and handed it to me so I could better clean up the mess. "Do you want to order a pizza instead?"

"Hell yes. My treat, since you bought all the groceries. But, I'm also going to finish this pasta since it's almost done. We can eat it too, or I'll save it for dinner tomorrow."

"Sounds good, Starlight," he told me, pressing a kiss to my hair. "What do you like on your pizza?"

"Pepperoni and black olives."

He outwardly shuddered, clearly poking fun at my expense. "Black olives? Gross. You just lost a few points in my book, but we'll see if you can't redeem them later." Reaching into his back pocket, Caleb pulled out his cell phone.

Thank goodness for technology and the ability to order food at the touch of a few buttons.

MY SMALL IKEA coffee table was littered with the trash from our impromptu pizza and movie night, and I sank back into my couch in a lazy food coma as the closing credits rolled from the rom-com we had just watched. The night turned out to be unexpectedly perfect. Spending time with Caleb felt as natural as breathing, yet there was something so closed off about him, so guarded. I couldn't pinpoint what and I suspected he wouldn't be revealing it anytime soon, but I desperately wanted to know the piece of him he was keeping hidden.

It was unreal to believe this was our first time hanging out. In our few interactions, it felt like so much had happened between us, and I was finding it hard to comprehend exactly how it felt so easy to be in his presence. There was so much I didn't know about him—so much he didn't know about me.

I ached to dive in and start asking him tons of questions about himself, wanting to absorb any bit of information he'd give me, but instead, I decided it was probably better to keep the conversation light. "So, was it as bad as you thought it'd be?"

Caleb laughed at my question. He put up the most pathetic protest on not wanting to watch *The Proposal*, giving in to my request almost immediately. "My favorite part was the chick chanting Lil' John lyrics with the guy's grandma around the bonfire. That was hilarious."

"That's my favorite part too," I told him, turning slightly on the couch so I could face him better. "I'll admit, I actually channel my inner Sandra Bullock and Betty White whenever I'm having a bad day. It always makes me laugh and helps improve my mood."

"Maybe I should give it a try. I have a lot of days where my mood could use some improvement." Caleb's face darkened, and he looked down at his lap. I could feel the energy change, becoming raw, like an open wound.

It clawed at me, making my empathetic heart bleed for him. "I know we don't know each other well, but you can trust me, Caleb. If you need someone to talk to—a friend—I'm here. I'm a pretty good listener." I reached out and placed my hand on his.

He snapped his eyes to mine, and I braced myself for him to move his hand. His walls were up and although his face still showed a semblance of vulnerability, I could see him shutting down.

"Look, I know we've had a weird beginning to—" I waved my other hand between us, "—*this*, but I like you. I don't know why, since you've been a total ass to me, but I do. I'm not expecting you to lower your guard and tell me every-thing, but just know if you need to talk, you can. I won't push it or force you to though."

Quiet filled the room and his eyes bounced between me, his hands in his lap, and the now darkened TV. He was lost in thought and I let him be, sitting in a comfortable silence while he processed whatever it was he was thinking about.

"I don't want to be that guy with the sob story, Isla, but unfortunately, that's my life," he said, staring down at our hands. "I don't want to project my problems onto you. I keep telling you I'll fuck up your life." He turned his head to look at me, his dark brown eyes pinning me with a saddened look. "Aren't you curious as to why?"

"I have my suspicions why," I stated matter-of-factly, watching as he guided my hand to his mouth and kissed my knuckles. The sweet gesture made my heart flip. "You think there's something you can't give to me? Something I'll be missing if you and I were to become a thing."

He grunted, setting our hands back in his lap and unlocking our fingers, separating our hold from one another so he could pick at a string on the seam of his jeans. "I'm just going to say it, Isla. I'm not good enough for you. You come from a life of luxury and even though you say you're trying to evade that lifestyle, you'll want it back eventually. If things work out between us, I will *never* be able to give you a life of luxury. You'd be living a lower-class life until I'm able to get my career on the police force going, but even then, law enforcement doesn't pay very well. Not like what you're used to. We'd be living middle-class, at best. I'll never be able to provide you with the life like what you grew up with. Fancy cars, lavish vacations, mansions, and a full staff. It'll never happen."

My entire body trembled with anger, a pent up rage I wasn't even aware I was harboring. Anger, and hurt, and absolute disgust. Logically, I could recognize I shouldn't have been so upset that he judged me so wholly, assuming my upbringing would be indicative of what I wanted in life, but I was so tired of having people decide my fate for me, I let the anger spike. "How fucking dare you."

I stood and began cleaning up the paper plates we had used with our pizza and gathered the empty water bottles, needing a distraction. Caleb's eyes trailed me as I went to the kitchen, dumping everything into the trash.

"You know," I called, grateful for the distance between the rooms. "That's an awfully big assumption for a guy who has never actually bothered to ask how my life was growing up with that kind of money. There's a reason I left it, Caleb. There's a reason why I'm out here paving my own way. Did you ever consider that?"

"Of course I did—"

"No, you fucking didn't." My tone shut him up and as I walked back into the living room, he rose from his spot on the couch. "You don't know shit about my life. You think you do, but all you think you know are assumptions about what a rich girl's life would be like. Did you know growing up, I spent more time with my nannies than my parents? Yes, *nannies*, plural. I had a new nanny every six months because my father didn't know how to keep it in his pants and my mother fired them every time she caught him with the newest one. My parents ignored me and fought about my existence constantly. I went to private schools, where I had to defend myself against children who thought they were men as they sexually harassed anyone they wanted, because it'd just get swept under the rug. Throw enough money at something and the problem becomes a solution."

I laughed, anger continuing to spill over. "And don't get me started about the petty bitches who spewed hate because they were *jealous* their predator of a boyfriend was giving unwanted attention elsewhere. My home was my solace, but not in the way you might think. It was my sanctuary because it was the lesser of two evils. My mother kept to herself, hopped up on pills to dull the heartache caused by my father's transgressions. My father locked himself away in his office, throwing himself into his work or whatever nanny was on staff that month. And then there was me. Daydreaming about the day when I could walk out of the door and never look back. Do I love my parents? Of course I do. They're my parents. Do I rely on the minimal financial help I receive from them? Unfortunately, yes, because I am a broke college student who desperately wants to follow her dreams but is still partially living under daddy's thumb. So don't sit here and assume you know anything about me and the life I want,

Caleb. You don't. I'd cut myself off from my parents and never look back if I had any job experience under my belt to get hired with, but I don't. I'm trying, but I'm not there yet. Okay?"

I was shaking. My body quaked with adrenaline and I realized I was standing toe to toe with him, chest to chest, and I couldn't even remember moving. For several seconds, we stared at each other: me with an anger I desperately was trying to fight off and him with emotions so mixed I struggled to read them. Without saying a word, Caleb wrapped his arms around my shoulders and buried his nose in my hair.

All the air in my lungs deflated as I took comfort in his embrace, letting myself melt into his chest as a sense of calm whooshed over me. I had been waiting years to get all the pent-up frustration off my chest, but the opportunity to express it had never presented itself. Until Caleb opened his mouth, baiting me to the point where I couldn't help but explode. I felt a little guilty, yet I couldn't bring myself to apologize. I wasn't sorry.

"I will never question you again, Starlight. Your choices, your path, your experiences. They're yours, not mine. I'm sorry." He placed a soft kiss on top of my head, tightening his already firm hold on me. His voice lowered to a whisper as he apologized again.

I don't tell him it's okay, even though it's at the tip of my tongue. Because it wasn't okay, and I was tired of people walking all over me. But in reality, I'd already forgiven him. It wasn't his fault he assumed. Most people do.

It also wasn't lost on me that he apologized several times in the short time we'd known each other, but I let it go for now, hoping it was just a learning curve as we figured each other out. Like me, Caleb had been dealt a shitty hand in life. The only difference between us was I had the money to use as a crutch and bury my sorrows with materialistic things. Or at least I used to.

Moving my head to the side, I rested my cheek against his chest rather than my forehead and looked around at what I could see of my apartment. The only evidence of the affluence in my past was the Louis Vuitton sitting on top of my entryway table. The same entryway table I bought on clearance at TJ Maxx for $39.99 because it had a huge chip on the side and one leg was cut slightly shorter than the rest, causing it to tilt. I could see the bent cardboard beneath said leg to level it from where I stood, nestled into Caleb. The art on the wall was from the Goodwill. Most of the apartment's decor was from the dollar aisles at Target.

Very little had been brought over from my parents' house, not including the clothes in my closet. I couldn't afford to leave those behind and as much as I wanted to deny it, I wouldn't have left them, regardless. I loved my clothes, and while I may not be able to afford their price tags now, that didn't mean I couldn't take care of what I had and incorporate them into my wardrobe for years to come. Except for replacing my underwear every six months like you're supposed to, the rest would likely outlive their style.

"I shouldn't have exploded like I did," I murmured on a deep inhale, my shoulders sagging as I released the breath.

He kissed the top of my head again before saying, "I understand why you did. I was wrong."

"Where do we go from here, Caleb? We barely know each other and we've both screwed up now. Should we start fresh? Pretend like all this didn't happen? Maybe we *should* just wash our hands of this whole thing and part ways. No harm, no foul." I knew I was rambling again, but I couldn't help it. Nerves had reared their ugly head and began gnawing on my insides, my insecurities becoming present once again.

"No," he stated simply, causing me to pull back and look up at him.

"No?"

"No. We're not parting ways. We're not pretending like this didn't happen, and we're not starting fresh. We've done a damn good job of proving to each other that we're humans. We have flaws, we judge, and we make mistakes. The only place to go from here is up, so we'll do just that."

His response did something to my tummy, sending the butterflies into a frenzy. "You're more than what meets the eye, Caleb Hart. Who knew you were so philosophical?"

His eyes rolled, and a playful smirk dusted his face. "I like you, Isla. And just because we've had a really rocky start doesn't mean our story will continue to be full of obstacles."

"Our story? I thought you wanted no strings."

"I think we both know that was bullshit." He lowered his arms, dropping them to my waist before trailing the tips of his fingers down to my ass, roughly cupping it through my jeans with his entire hand. A squeak of surprise spilled from my lips, and my body spasmed, causing my hips to push forward into his. "What do you say, Isla? You want to jump in feet first with me and see where this takes us?"

Caleb slid his opposite hand down to match the other, gripping my whole ass tightly as he hoisted me into his arms. I wrapped my legs around his middle and slid my arms around his neck.

"You're giving me whiplash and I can't keep up. Earlier today you were insistent about not wanting anything with me. Now you're asking me to jump in and see where this goes." My smile slipped as my own words radiated through my mind, replaying themselves. "How am I supposed to trust you won't wake up in the morning and change your mind again? Or just be gone?"

Carrying me over to my small desk, he sat me down on top of it, placing one hand on either side of me. "You don't know either of those things won't be true until we wake up tomorrow morning and I'm still here, still wanting you. But Isla, the power is also in your hands. You could just as easily wake up tomorrow with your mind changed."

Holding his gaze, I lifted my chin as a smile pulled at my lips. "Well, then, we better make the most of tonight. Just in case."

CHAPTER NINE

CALEB

I barely had the chance to process her words before her hot lips were pressing soft kisses against my jawline while her hands worked to unlatch the buckle on my pants. The chill of her fingertips against my lower abdomen left a ripple of goosebumps in their wake. I couldn't bite back the sharp intake of breath when her soft hand wrapped around my cock, setting it free from my briefs. Her urgency took me by surprise and clearly my brain struggled to keep up as I stood before her, hands by my side, unmoving.

Her stride never broke as she began pumping my length from base to tip as she licked and nipped at my neck. A deep groan emulated from my chest, my mind racing to catch up, and I wrapped a fist around her long hair that fell loose at her shoulders.

Yanking her hair back, I met her lips with mine, kissing her recklessly and shaking all thoughts of being a gentleman away.

"I like that you don't treat me like I'm some fragile little doll, Caleb." She reached around and placed her hand on top of my hand that firmly held her hair. "I like *this*."

She spread her legs further apart, and I stepped into the curve of her body, filling her space with my form. The heels of her feet pressed into my calves as her back arched. My breathing shallowed at the sight of her body in a perfect bend, and I growled, pulling her hair back harder to allow me access to the side of her neck. I licked it first, then began raking my teeth against the soft skin as I made my way to her jaw. "You like things a little rough, Starlight? I think I can handle that."

"Can you?" she questioned, floating her hand up my chest. Her fingers braced the column of my neck, wrapping around its front before she dug her nails into my skin. The pressure was just enough to cause a slight tinge of discomfort. Isla pushed her palm deeper into my throat, compressing my Adam's apple and causing me to release a small cough.

There had never been a time in my life where I could remember being wholeheartedly shocked by something a woman did to me during foreplay, so this was a new experience. The way Isla's eyes twinkled with mischief as she looked up at me from below her lashes, and the way her fingertips flexed into my flesh as she strengthened her grasp went straight to my dick she stroked with her other hand. I hadn't come from a hand job since I was a teenager, but I knew with certainty if she kept going, I'd explode like a firework on the Fourth of July.

Slamming my lips back to hers, I traced the seam of her mouth with my tongue and swallowed her small gasp as I took entry, exploring with swift determination to learn everything that made this woman moan, gasp, whimper, and sigh. Her pleasure was mine and I would learn her body inside and out for even a minuscule fraction of the attention she was currently giving me. I had never been so wound up, so turned on, by a simple touch, but I wasn't thinking about her touch from the hand holding my cock.

The power she emitted as she wrapped her hand around my throat had the ability to bring me to my knees simply because, through her touch, she showed me everything I had missed when I looked at her initially. I *felt* her strength, her determination, her independence. I was catching sight of the real Isla, not the Isla who had been presented to the world on a prim and proper platter. I was seeing the woman behind the facade.

I had been wrong about her. So fucking wrong.

Breaking our kiss, I grabbed onto her wrist and gently pulled it away from my cock as I began to lower myself to my knees in front of her. Her grasp remained firmly on my throat as she watched me through curious eyes until I was fully kneeling on the floor. Her body tilted with mine as she watched, finally letting go and placing her hand on the desk beside her.

"What are you doing?" she asked, her eyes trained on mine as she looked down at me from my position on the floor.

"Admitting my wrongs."

"Didn't you already do that?"

I nodded. "Yes, but the realization of my mistake is like a neon sign in my face now. I should have never assumed anything about you."

She looked at me with confusion, her eyebrows shooting up as she peered at me through narrowed eyes. "Huh? Caleb, seriously, I feel like you're over exaggerating the situation a little. You misjudged, you apologized, and that's that. Now, get up. You're being so extra right now."

"No. I won't make the same mistakes my father did in thinking he could get away with treating women like shit, like they're inferior to a man. This is me, on my knees, showing you I haven't treated you fairly and I recognize it. You deserve to be treated like a queen."

Once again, her eyes narrowed as she stared at me quietly. Then, before I knew what was happening, her hand whipped out and smacked me upside the head, catching my ear in the process.

"Get up, you overdramatic psycho. Seriously, stand up." She grabbed my biceps, tugging my upper arms so I had no choice but to follow her lead and stand as she slipped off the desk and stood in front of me. "What is wrong with you? You go from 'I want no strings, let's just have some fun' to 'let me bow on my knees like a pussy ass bitch.' Can you just... Be you? Truly. The guy I met in the library who made me think and pushed my limits in a fun and spontaneous way. Bring him back."

"I... Yeah." I tucked myself back into my jeans before turning to face the couch, fisting my hair, as I stomped over to it and slumped down. She followed, bouncing down onto it next to me.

Frustration brewed inside me, and embarrassment trickled through my bloodstream. She was right. What was wrong with me?

Truth was, I was absolutely fucking terrible at this. My last girlfriend—my *only* girlfriend—had been junior year of high school. The relationship had been your typical high school boyfriend-girlfriend situation which went absolutely nowhere. Since then, I had thrown myself into working whatever dead-end job I could and focused on school so I could make sure I started earning a living. I didn't know what I was doing with Isla, not one goddamned bit. I've been so hot and cold—all over the place—in the excruciatingly short time I've known her. I was surprised she hadn't kicked me out of her apartment solely based on my erratic behavior.

I was acting like a fucking crazy person.

Running a hand down my face, I massaged my jaw for a moment before turning back to her. "I think I'm just afraid of ruining the one thing in my life that could be good. We could be good, Isla. I'm not used to things going good for me."

Her eyes flared with heat at my admission, and I decided at that moment we were finished talking. I had ruined the moment earlier, but I wouldn't make the same mistake twice.

"Take off your pants, Isla," I commanded, my voice low and thick with a promise. My cock strained against my pants as I watched her tongue dart out to wet her lips before she did as I asked, standing to remove her pants.

I followed her movements as she unlatched the button of her jeans from its loop and slowly pulled down her zipper. From the widened opening of her jeans, cream-colored lace panties peeked through and made my mouth water. She tugged the jeans down her thighs and used her feet to press the legs down further before stepping out of them. The rust-colored shirt she wore draped from her tits as she bent to move the pants, revealing what I had to look forward to seeing fully tonight.

Tonight would be vastly different from the day in the library. Tonight I planned to take my time.

Once free from her pants, she sat back down on the

couch beside me, looking at me coyly, waiting for me to do or say something. I didn't hesitate before I reached over and grabbed her thigh, squeezing the supple skin roughly. My calloused palm contrasted the softness of her skin and somehow the touch alone radiated heat straight to my dick. I wasn't gentle when I pulled her by her thigh, laying her leg over mine so they spread out, the side of her body pressed against mine.

Shifting my weight, I leaned into her, leaving my hand on her thigh while I reached around with my other hand and wound my fingers through her hair, bringing her face toward me. Her lips instantly found mine, and she sighed into our kiss, letting me take the reins. I guided her into a heated kiss, only breaking apart when I could physically feel her need to breathe.

Isla's chest rose and fell hard as she looked at me through hooded eyes, her cheeks stained pink with arousal. She bit her lower lip, fighting a smile as she leaned her head back against the couch.

"Grab that blanket for me, would ya?" I asked casually, reaching forward and taking the remote off the small coffee table in front of us and clicking the power button. The TV came to life and one of my favorite comedies was already playing. Convenient, since it was now my turn to choose a movie.

Isla whipped the blanket at me, its soft knit covering my face as it hit me and dropped into my lap. I reached to reposition it over us, and she went to move her leg off of mine.

"Absolutely not," I growled, snatching it back before it had even really moved.

Her warm laugh filtered through the air. "Alright, have it your way." She shrugged, snuggling in closer to me.

As I finished spreading the blanket over her lap, my eyes caught on a small wet spot seeping through her panties and I dipped my finger down to rub over it, feeling the evidence of how our kiss had made her feel. Isla's breathing hitched at my touch, so I left my hand, continuing to lightly rub up and down the small stretch of fabric. She finished laying the blanket over her lap and let her eyes fall on where my hand slowly moved beneath the blanket.

"Watch the movie, Isla."

Her eyes immediately snapped to mine before moving to focus on the TV. Satisfied, I also turned my attention to the TV, leaving my hand pressed against her panty-covered pussy under the blanket.

I let her squirm against the side of my hand, knowing that with every passing minute, she was getting more desperate for my touch. My attention was on the movie—laughing at all the appropriate parts—as I let her grow more desperate for me. It'd only been a few minutes—maybe twenty—but the way her hips subtly moved in a silent plea to be touched, had encouraged my dick to grow impossibly hard. It was getting more difficult to pretend like I wasn't eager to give her exactly what she wanted. And she showed incredible restraint too, as she pretended to watch the movie I had put on for us.

As fun as this was, I knew something else we could be doing that'd be a lot more enjoyable.

Slowly, I trailed my fingers over her center, my touch featherlight as I made my way to the top of the lace trimmed cotton fabric. She kept her lips pressed firmly together, trying to steady her breathing while anticipation and arousal both ran at full speed through her veins.

My hand dipped below the fabric and I pushed it lower until my fingers skated across her clit, sending her body into a sharp jolt.

"Mmmm," she hummed, her eyes fluttering closed as I rubbed slow, lazy circles on her clit. I kept my pointer finger on her nub as I shifted my hand to allow my middle and ring fingers to dip into her wetness, staying right on the surface.

She was *soaked* and heat radiated from her, so ready for me and me alone, reminding me of our first time together. On instinct, her legs spread wider beneath the blanket as she opened herself up for me. But I kept my hand unmoving, simply enjoying the soft, wet feeling of her bare skin.

"Please, Caleb," she begged, moving her own hand beneath the blanket to rest on top of mine. She tried to push my hand down more, but I held firm, unmoving. "Touch me, Caleb. *God*, I need you to touch me."

Ignoring her pleas, I turned my head to the side and allowed my mouth to find her jawline, pressing soft kisses just beneath it while moving to her ear. I nuzzled it with my nose, inhaling her scent while she squirmed again. Hot air floated past my parted lips as I panted, my own arousal heightening the anticipation of the moment.

"I'm going to treat you like a queen while we're in public, Isla," I murmured against her skin. "A queen who is deserving of much more than a lowly boy like me."

She whimpered as I slowly dipped my fingers into her, moving the heel of my hand against her clit as I did. Scissoring my fingers in an opening and closing motion, I stretched her and watched as she bit her lip in an effort to hold in her moan.

"But, Isla?" I asked, curling my fingers up to caress her G-spot.

All sound faded away except for my fingers moving inside of her wet pussy, my question left unanswered as Isla succumbed to the pleasure. I took the opportunity to suck the supple skin of her neck into my mouth roughly, not caring if it left a mark in my wake.

"In private, I will treat you like the slut I know you are. Your pleasure is mine. Your orgasms? Mine. Any objections, Starlight?"

"None whatsoever," she moaned as her hips rolled against my touch.

That was all I needed to withdraw my fingers from her pussy, moving my hands to her hips to pull her onto my lap. My fingers gripped the hem of her shirt and I pulled it up over her head, her arms lifting to help it glide off her. As I tossed the shirt to the side, I caught her lips with mine, kissing her like my life depended on it. Isla melted into me, wrapping her arms around my neck as I took my time exploring her body with my touch and my tongue.

Gripping her ass, I flipped her, laying her down on the couch and kneeled between her legs, looking down at her. She looked like a goddess, laid out wearing only thin layers of lace and cotton, her skin flushed and her hair wild.

"Time to take these off too, Starlight," I told her, hooking my thumbs into her panties. She lifted her hips, and I slid them past the curve of her ass and down her thighs before I had to stand from the couch to pull them off completely.

Through half hooded eyes, she caught me by surprise when she asked a question I wasn't ready to answer truthfully. "Caleb, why do you call me Starlight?"

My mind spiraled, caught between wanting to ignore the question, lie about the answer, or answer her truthfully. It was a loaded answer, with far too many emotions laced through it.

The nickname came to me one night as I lay in bed, staring up at the dark ceiling, unable to sleep. I had seen her a few times at the library by that point, watching from afar and wondering about who she was. She had never noticed me, but I sure as hell saw her. For nights I'd lay awake, my mind too focused on thoughts of her to rest. With so many questions about her burning in my mind, begging for me to gain the answers. I'd been so torn between wanting to approach her and wanting to keep my distance, knowing she was way out of my league. Still, I wanted to know everything I could about the mystery woman. She had become my light in the dark. My starlight. The one thing that burned bright when everything else felt draped in shadow.

This was the longest we'd spent in each other's presence. I was terrified that by telling her the truth behind the nickname, we'd be past the point of no return. But weren't we already heading down that path? I wouldn't let her go after this. I couldn't. It may have been an obscenely short amount of time since we'd agreed to give each other a chance, but the organ locked up tight behind my rib cage knew there'd be no one else in this lifetime like Isla. I could *feel* it, and at the risk of sounding like a complete sap, she made me want to make sure I got myself out of this shit life.

And I would. I might have been young and still in college, literally figuring my life out day by day, but I knew without a shred of doubt I'd do whatever it took to give her an amazing life.

Whatever she wanted.

I owed her a truthful explanation, even if it made me feel vulnerable. "Because even before we had met, I knew you were like the stars in the night sky. You were made to shine through the darkness in my life and guide me to the sun."

Leaning forward, I dropped a featherlight kiss to her mouth and urged her lips to part for me. I didn't want her response, not now. I wanted *her*.

She let out a soft sigh as she sank into the kiss, her fingers curling around my biceps, holding me in place as I kissed her harder.

"Spread your legs for me, baby. Let me see all of you," I rasped, my voice thick as I reached down to palm my aching cock, repositioning it within the confines of my jeans. Pulling away from her, I leaned back on the couch as she let her legs drop to the sides, giving me a perfect view of her pussy. It was glistening. I brought my fist to my mouth and bit down, groaning at the sheer perfection of her body. "Fucking perfect."

"Well, are you going to do something? Or just stare down at my pussy and wait for it to beg you to eat it?"

I smirked, shaking my head slowly before tsking. "I knew I was right about you. Such a dirty slut. *My* dirty slut."

"The 'my' is debatable. We'll see if you pass the test and deserve me."

"We both know I don't."

"I'll be the judge of that." Her legs floated upward to close, but I caught her right knee in my hand, pushing it back down.

She quirked a brow before dropping the other knee to hang off the side of the couch.

"That's *my* good girl," I praised. "I wasn't done admiring the view."

Before she could even try to respond, I stood from the couch, bending toward her, and slid my arms beneath her. I scooped her into a bridal hold and clutched her against my chest, carrying her to her open bedroom door.

Walking through the threshold, I didn't bother turning on the lights before I tossed her down onto her bed and crawled up the length of her, my knee landing between her thighs, my body completely overtaking her frame as I settled above her.

Bringing my lips to the soft skin of her throat, I kissed my way down, letting my fingers find their rightful place between her thighs as I started my descent through the soft tuft of hair and dipped into her warmth. Isla gasped, her fingernails digging into my shoulders while I curved my fingers to stroke the sweet spot inside her.

I dragged them slowly, bringing her wetness to her clit and massaged it, before driving my fingers into her again. She squirmed beneath me, soft moans escaping her lips as her chest rose and fell in perfect harmony. The sight of her was exquisite, her body igniting beneath my touch.

"Fuck, Caleb, *yes,*" she moaned as my fingers scissored within her.

Removing them, I brought my hand to her perfect tits and yanked down her bra, rubbing her juices over her hardened nipple. Leaning forward, I sucked it roughly into my mouth, tasting her as my tongue lapped against the peak. A groan rumbled through my chest at the flavor, and my cock strained painfully against my jeans.

As though she could read my thoughts, Isla reached her hands down and lowered the zipper—the button still unclasped from earlier—and pushed her hand inside to free my cock. Her hand wrapped around my length as her thumb found the bead of precum that had leaked from the tip. She smeared it around before bringing her thumb to her own lips, sucking it off of her.

"Fuck," I muttered.

"Take them off," Isla breathed as she pushed the jeans off my hips. I stood from the bed, pushing them down and stepping out of them. As I took off my pants, Isla sat up slightly, reaching around to unclasp her bra, tossing it aside while I crawled up her body, repositioning myself above her as I was.

"I'd like to fuck you now," I told her playfully.

I licked my lips as I gazed down at her, taking my cock in my hand and rimming her entrance. "I want to fuck you bare so bad. I've never fucked without a condom and I just got tested last month—I'm clean. The only person I've been with since I tested is you."

Her hips rocked into mine, nudging the head of my cock against her slick pussy and it took every ounce of restraint I had not to plunge into her.

Using my cock, I rubbed against her clit, and drew a moan from her before she answered. "I'm clean too. I just had my yearly doctor's visit, and they tested me, as well."

Relief poured out of me at her words, but there was one last thing to check before I took the risk. "Birth control?" I asked, praying to the heavens above she was on something.

"IUD," she confirmed, rocking her hips again, her eyes fluttering closed. "Please—"

One thrust is all it took to drive into her fully, the walls of her pussy contracting around my cock, squeezing it as she adjusted to me inside her. I gave her a moment before I leaned forward and bit down on her shoulder, my hips beginning to rock.

"Fuck, your pussy is so damn tight, Isla," I growled

against her skin, relishing in the way her pussy stretched around my cock, grasping me like a vise. Completely seated inside of her, I pumped with shallow thrusts as I kept myself in her depths completely.

She groaned and tilted her face to capture my lips. Our tongues met and lapped against each other as she rolled her hips to meet my every thrust. "You feel so good."

I pumped into her faster, my cock slipping in and out at a perfect rhythm. Her tits bounced against my every thrust as I pounded into her roughly. Bringing her leg up, I held it in the crook of my arm as I adjusted our angle.

My entire body was electrified, building and tingling from the absolute euphoria. Over and over I rutted inside her, my release simmering as I pistoned in and out of her perfect body, her moans encouraging me to keep going.

"Come for me, baby, let me hear you scream this time."

Her eyes snapped open and locked with mine, and I saw the exact moment her face fell—a look of embarrassment coating her features. I slowed my pace, slowly rocking into her as I pushed her hair away from her face.

"What's wrong?" I asked, stilling inside of her. "Do you want me to stop?"

Isla shook her head quickly and bit down on her lower lip, shifting her face to look blankly at the wall. "I... It's just... I can't just come from penetration alone. I need... *More*. I need clit stimulation to come."

Oh, thank fuck.

"I got you, Starlight," I told her, immediately pulling out of her and shifting down her body. Sucking her clit into my mouth, an unrestrained hunger pulsed through my veins as I devoured her fully. I'd been dying to taste her.

Her thighs slapped against the sides of my face as she

yelled out a deep moan, her hips lifting from the bed. She fucked my face, and my tongue prodded the soft flesh, pushing inside her as I brought my fingers to her clit and rubbed her relentlessly.

"Oh my god, Caleb. Fuck... Yes! Don't stop. Please keep going." She rode my face, and I brought my tongue back to her clit, sucking it and swirling my tongue. My fingers made their way back inside her and I curved them, quickly finding her G-spot as she screamed out again. She bucked against me, but I didn't slow my assault, lapping up every delicious drop of her as her body continued to beg for release.

It took one rough suction on her clit before her body roared with release, her hands flying to my head as she pushed my face further against her pussy. My tempo never wavered, continuing to lick and suck at her as she rode out her orgasm before falling back against the bed. Her chest heaved as she caught her breath—but I wasn't done with her yet.

My cock found its way back between her legs, and I hooked both of her legs under my arms and I scooted her hips up. I drove into her, my eyes closing with the overwhelming feeling of pleasure. The angle, along with how perfectly wet Isla was, allowed me to fall to ruin impossibly fast, chasing my own release. I came with a boom of ecstasy —spurts of cum lined her walls as I held my body flush against hers—savoring the hardest climax I'd ever experienced.

Lowering her legs, I stayed inside her, staring down at the woman spread out before me, until I felt myself growing soft.

Pulling out slowly, I held my cock and ambled toward her bathroom in search of a washcloth. At my second attempt of opening a random bathroom drawer, I found several folded towels and pulled two out, letting the warm water from the faucet engulf them and then ringing them out. I quickly cleaned myself and tossed the washcloth into the sink before making my way back to the bed where the girl of my dreams was sprawled out, naked and waiting for me to return. After climbing back on the bed, I repositioned myself between her legs, kissing the inside of her thighs, and pressed the warm towel against her to clean up my cum leaking from her body.

A contented sigh left her lips as she smiled down at me. "Thank you," she whispered.

"Anything for my queen," I told her seriously, leaning down and pressing a quick kiss against her pussy. Once satisfied, I moved from the bed to toss the washcloth into the sink with the other before returning to the bed, picking up a blanket that'd fallen to the floor as I sat down next to her.

Draping the blanket over Isla's naked body, I laid beside her and pulled some of the blanket to cover myself. My hands moved to cup the back of my head and I stretched out, enjoying the simplicity of the moments after. The way Isla curled her body close to mine, resting her head against my chest. The feeling of her smooth leg as it draped over mine. The comfort of the silence between us.

A lonely guy could get used to this.

"I still don't think I deserve you," I murmured in the darkness as I wrapped my arm beneath her, pulling her closer.

"You don't," she stated simply. "But I don't deserve you either, so I think that puts us on an even playing field."

CHAPTER TEN

ISLA

I woke with Caleb's arm draped across my chest, his body curled into me, snuggling me as though I was his teddy bear. His soft breaths grazed my shoulder as he continued to sleep soundly beside me and I smiled to myself, replaying the intensity of earlier in my mind.

Without disturbing him, I lifted my head slightly to see the time illuminated on the clock, surprised to see it was only a little past two in the morning. It felt like it'd been hours since we laid in each other's arms and fell asleep.

We hadn't discussed him spending the night, but as he snored lightly by my side, I had no intention of waking him up.

The back of my head reunited with my pillow and I thought back over every fleeting moment shared between us since the first interaction in the library when he paid my overdue balance. Caleb was so adamant in shielding me from his life, but as far as I had learned, it was because he thought he couldn't give me the life I deserved. As my thoughts swam, I realized something still felt off. There had to be more to the story... But, what?

Shifting my head to look at him, I searched his face as though he'd somehow reveal his past, even from his state of slumber. What could be so abhorrent he thought it would scare me off? Because that's what it was about, wasn't it? Scaring me off?

"What are you hiding?" I whispered to the darkness as I brought my hand to his face and gently brushed a piece of fallen hair away from his eyes. Slowly, my fingers brushed against his cheek, down to his sharp jawline, making my insides turn to mush. Caleb was truly a beautiful man despite his efforts to be in the background.

After a few moments, he stirred and pulled me closer, rolling me into him. "Hey, Starlight," he muttered sleepily, cracking an eye open and smiling.

"Hey, yourself." My hand found his beneath the blanket and our fingers laced together. "Have a good nap?"

My heart rate accelerated, and a rush of nerves came over me, making me feel awkward. I drove myself insane internally, questioning if the man next to me was telling me the whole truth about himself.

If he noticed, he didn't act bothered as he answered my question and released my hand to stretch his arms up over his head. "The best. I don't think I've slept that well in years."

"It wasn't even a full night's sleep!"

"Doesn't matter. I never rest easy. Those few hours were great."

I offered no response, staring up at the ceiling as I tried to quiet my mind and convince myself I was wrong about the situation, and he was simply ashamed of his upbringing.

I could relate to that myself, couldn't I? There were so many things about my past I was ashamed of or wished I could go back and do differently. I tried to not let regrets rule my life, but I had a list of them. Maybe Caleb was the same—maybe he feared if I knew too much, I'd be the one changing my mind come morning.

"What's wrong, Isla?"

Looking at him, I could see his brows furrowed in confusion even through the darkness. He brought his hand back beneath the blankets and found my thigh, resting it on top while he brushed his thumb over my skin and waited for me to explain.

Honesty, right?

"I can't shake the feeling there's something more you're not telling me."

"More about what, Isla?"

"About your past. About why you've been so hesitant. Something doesn't add up... It feels like you're hiding something."

Caleb twisted toward me, his hands surrounding my face. "I've told you. My dad's a drunk, we're piss poor, and my mom bolted when I was a kid. There's not much more to know than that."

Kissing me, he coaxed my lips apart before sliding his tongue to meet mine. Gliding one hand from my cheek, he brought it around to cup the back of my head, weaving his fingers into my hair as he deepened our kiss. I felt the way his chest released a sigh as he gave into the magnetism between us, and I knew our connection was undeniable. Caleb was meant to be in my life, as tumultuous as our beginning may have been.

So while his words should have reassured me, and his kiss

should have sealed the deal, I still had a small patch of lingering uncertainty buried within me. I knew I needed to explore it further if I wanted to ever fully trust him.

"TELL me about the life you left behind." Caleb's voice was soft as he drew lazy circles between my shoulder blades while I laid on my stomach. The sheet draped low on my body, exposing my torso as my arms were folded beneath my head.

I groaned into my arm, the aftermath of my last orgasm still lightly pulsing through my body. "You were just buried inside me and now you want to talk about my family?"

"Yep," he chuckled. "Tell me everything, Starlight."

The irony wasn't lost on me that he wanted to know everything about me yet wouldn't tell me everything about him. But I pushed those thoughts aside. Maybe if I opened up more, he would too.

"My father owns Skyline Tech," I said on a sigh, looking up at him for his reaction. Usually once I told people what my father does, dollar signs reflected in their eyes as they mentally calculated how rich I was. I felt my brows scrunch together when Caleb's reaction didn't change with the knowledge. "He founded the company when he was twenty-four years old and soared to the top of the industry. He married my mother shortly after making his first million, and she's been riding his coattails ever since."

I stopped myself, realizing how bitter it sounded. "They love each other, of course. They just aren't in love. I'm not sure they ever were," I added.

Caleb nodded his head in a silent response, urging me to keep going.

"My father wanted an heir. Someone to take over the company. A boy. They struggled to conceive, trying everything they could and coming up short. The doctors told my mother she had an inhospitable womb and would never be able to carry a child, so they turned to surrogacy. And that's how I came into the world.

"But it wasn't good enough for my father. Somehow in his twisted mind, me not being a male and the fact I wasn't born from my mother made me lesser than. My whole life I heard them argue behind closed doors that if I had been a boy, or if she could have carried more children, then he'd have the heir to his legacy. After many years of the same fight, mother convinced him his daughter would be fit to run the company. She'd have the board standing behind her, after all." The words felt filthy against my tongue, sour and vile as I recalled all the times I lay in my four-poster bed, hiding under the duvet as I tried to drown out the sound of their arguments.

A fucking eight bedroom mansion and yet they still chose to make my bedroom right beside theirs.

"The older I became, the more my father warmed up to the idea of me taking over his company someday and he eased up on treating me like a nuisance, but then I also became an asset. I went from relatively ignored to constantly swarmed by an entire team of people. Nanny... Bodyguard whenever I left the house. It's incredible how quickly one person's entire demeanor can shift when selfish intentions shine through."

Silence hung between us as I finished my sentence, the

venom bursting through my words as I relived the bitter memories of my past.

"Fucking prick," Caleb growled as I flipped over onto my back. Without sparing a thought, his arm slipped beneath my shoulders, pulling me close.

"Want to know how old I was when he told me I'd take over the company one day and I had no choice in the matter?" I asked, snuggling into his side so I could steal his body heat—a comfort I craved in order to push back the negative emotions that'd radiated through me. "I was eleven, Caleb. Aren't fathers supposed to tell their little girls they could be anything they wanted to be when they grew up? Mine told me I had no choice, and I'd run his company whether I liked it or not. Then he proceeded to remind me of it every single birthday. 'One year closer to business school, Isla. Soon you'll learn all there is to know so you can take over Skyline. With any luck, you won't run it into the ground your first year.' What I never understood was if he was so worried about me ruining the company, why was he so hell-bent on making me run it?"

"So how did you end up here and not at an Ivy league?"

"Ridgewood University's business program is just as rigorous as many of the Ivy's. I convinced my father that by allowing me to go to school here, he'd be saving an obscene amount of money on tuition. Once he had his assistant look into it and confirm, he allowed it."

"Why would you choose here, though? Why not go anywhere else?"

"He still pushed for me to go to Ivy, but I just wanted to live a normal life for once. I wanted to be like a normal girl who could just get away from her parents and forget where she came from. Ridgewood University was one step closer to leading a normal life and breaking free from his grasp for a while. Running Skyline is something I'll eventually have to do, but these last few years, I've had the chance to get to know myself. I've lived how I want to. The agreement was, if I wanted to live a normal life, I'd have to live with normal finances. He pays my tuition because it benefits him, but as far as everything else, we agreed on a specific allotment to be transferred into my bank account every month to help me with the rest. He's waiting for me to break and come crawling back to his checkbook."

"So he still pays your bills?" Caleb asked, and I couldn't help but hear the skepticism in his tone. It was a lot to process, but I knew somehow within my explanation I had dug myself into a hole and made myself look bad in the process.

My head bobbed in a nod. "Yes, he covers the very basics, though barely. With the amount he gives me—the amount we agreed on—there are many months where I have literal cents in my bank account. Like when we met... I was on my last couple dollars and had left my wallet at home so I wouldn't spend it on something stupid. I knew a couple dollars could cover two night's worth of instant ramen if I needed it."

Embarrassment swept through my body at the admission, making me feel small. Tears pricked the back of my eyes and I wondered if I was making the right choice after all. My life was mapped out for me... It was my path. Maybe I should accept my father's plans and embrace them. I wouldn't have to struggle like I was and I wouldn't have to pretend I was the woman I wanted to be. Instead, I could just pretend to be the woman everyone else wanted me to be. I'd be rich, automatically successful. Life would be easy.

Caleb's voice pushed through the fog my mind had weaved with self-doubt. "But you want to be a veterinarian?"

"Yes," I whispered, my voice barely audible as I choked back a sob. I wouldn't let him see me cry.

He wiped away a traitorous tear that escaped and began peppering my face with quick kisses. It was so adorable, I couldn't help the smile that appeared despite the storm cloud of emotions living in my chest. "Then my girl will be a veterinarian. Fuck your dad's money, you don't need it."

"I kind of do," I retorted quickly. "I don't have a job, remember? No one wants to hire a twenty-two-year-old with no work experience."

"If there's a will, there's a way," he said, dipping his head down and pulling my nipple between his teeth. He used his tongue to roll it around, hardening it into a stiff peak before abandoning it completely. "First, we'll find you a job. Any job, so you can start gaining experience. Then you'll keep going to school until you get your degree finished. That's not much longer, right? I think we will graduate around the same time. And then my girl's off to animal doctor school."

"Animal doctor school?" I laughed, but the laughter quickly turned into a sharp gasp as he found my other nipple and began using his tongue to play with it.

With my nipple clasped lightly between his teeth, he exhaled a deep breath, blowing air on to the sensitive flesh before licking it with the pad of his tongue. When he removed his mouth, he said, "Yep. My very own Doctor Dolittle."

"That dream seems out of reach," I sighed, racking my brain for any and all possibilities of making the idea actually work when in reality, the moment I graduated my father would swoop in and begin my training at Skyline Tech where

I'd work until he was ready to retire. The path was already paved.

I was lost in thought and hadn't noticed Caleb moving down the length of my body and settling between my legs until the warm flat of his tongue ran up the seam of my pussy. He groaned against it, as though he was bringing himself pleasure, and swirled the tip of his tongue against my clit. An unrecognizable slur of words fell from my mouth at the delicious intrusion and I welcomed the way it made me forget all other thoughts.

Right before he began to devour me whole, he looked up from between my legs, and with complete sincerity told me, "Your dream isn't out of reach, Isla. It's as close to you as the stars you're about to see."

CHAPTER ELEVEN

CALEB

The sound of muffled metal music seeping through the headphones of a guy studying at the table behind me acted as a backdrop as I peered around the corner of a shelf of books, watching Isla from afar as she studied. Everything about this girl intrigued me, from the way she chewed on the cap of her pen in between writing notes to the way her fingertip moved across the pages as she read, following the sentences as she took every word in. It had been almost two weeks since we decided to give this thing between us a try, and we had practically been inseparable, barring the times I was at work or we were in class.

Isla still hadn't found a job; she hadn't even been called back for an interview for any of the eighteen places she had applied to around town and online. I could see the defeat behind her eyes as she skimmed her emails and checked her phone for missed calls, and I knew it was from lack of responses.

It killed me. Physically hurt me to see her frustration

overshadow the determination she had. I had even asked my boss if we could hire one more person, only if part-time. The rush of endorphins that had her saying 'yes' was squashed immediately, when she followed it up with *but only if it means you're okay with being taken off the schedule.'*

I'd gladly give up my job if it meant seeing a smile on her face, but it wasn't truly an option. I was almost done with my degree in forensic science, which meant I was one step closer to the police academy. My goal was to be hired onto the force beforehand so I could work part-time hours once my schooling finished for the day.

I knew it'd take me longer to kick-start my career by prioritizing the police academy after graduation, but I needed a safety net to fall back on in case my career in forensics didn't pan out. As soon as I could save up enough money and get my own place, I'd be out of the shithole I called home.

The dude behind me sneezed, pulling me from my thoughts as I looked at him, just as he wiped his mouth with the sleeve of his black trench coat and pushed the headphones that'd slipped back on top of his head. I snorted to myself as the guy continued to look over the papers scattered in front of him and turned my attention back to Isla.

Her back was to me and, given I had been standing there watching her for the last fifteen or so minutes, I decided it was time to greet my girl. Striding over to her, I pulled out the chair next to her and dropped into it, startling her as I did.

"Hey," she blurted, her hand placed firmly in the middle of her chest as though I had given her the biggest scare of her life. I chuckled at the sight, leaning over to press a kiss on her lips.

"Hey."

"How was work?" she asked. Her eyes flicked to her computer screen where her email was pulled up, but met mine again quickly.

"It was fine. I have about thirty minutes left before I have class so I wanted to say hi. How's studying? Any word from the resumes you sent out?"

"Not a peep," she responded solemnly as she cast gaze downward.

I caught her chin, lifting her face and forcing her to look at me. "You *will* hear back from someone," I told her with certainty. It *would* happen. Someone would take a chance on her and see how amazing she was.

Isla offered me a small smile before turning her face away from my grasp and returning her attention to the textbook in front of her. She felt distant today, a little shut down. I didn't like it.

"Do you want to get dinner tonight, Starlight? Carbs have been calling my name, and I just got paid. Let me take my girl out." As if on cue, my stomach rumbled, so I reached down to pat it, tossing a smirk her way as I did.

She laughed and rolled her eyes at me, but couldn't resist the temptation of carbs and a night out. Her head began nodding, accepting my invitation as my smile widened.

DISHES CLINKED TOGETHER as restaurant-goers all around us enjoyed their meals. Fresh baked bread and fragrant scents of garlic and sauces filled the room, and my mouth watered with the promise of delicious Italian food. This place was far out of my budget, but tonight I was feeling spendy. I had yet to treat Isla to a proper date, so this had been several weeks coming. The price tag was worth it, even if I'd have to figure out a way to budget my grocery trips for the rest of the pay period.

"Are you sure this isn't too much?" she asked as she looked around the restaurant and tucked her napkin onto her lap.

"Not at all. Order anything you want, Starlight. Treat yourself."

Looking over the menu, lobster ravioli in a garlic butter sauce immediately caught my eye, but as I skimmed over the price, I kept searching the menu. I may be indulging tonight, but thirty-two dollars for my dish alone was a bit much.

"So what looks good?" I asked, deciding I would get the cheese manicotti instead of the stuffed pillows of lobster heaven, even though my eyes had wandered back to it twice now.

The corners of Isla's mouth curled up into a smile and she triumphantly said, "The lobster ravioli."

My heart ping-ponged in my chest and my eyes must have widened because she started laughing almost immediately after reaching across the table to grab my hand. "Oh my god, Caleb, I'm just kidding! I got you, though. You should get it. Lobster ravioli sounds delicious."

My eyes narrowed. She liked to play dirty. "How did you know that's what I was thinking?"

She shrugged before peering down at her menu again. "Call it intuition. Or call it a lucky guess. I'm getting penne pasta with pesto."

Waiting for our server seemed to take an excruciatingly long time, my stomach turning into an empty cavern the longer we sat. It took several attempts, but I finally managed to make eye contact with our server and he made his way to us, pulling his server book from his apron as he came up to our table.

"Hi guys, my name's Tanner. I'll be your server today." He offered me a nod before turning to Isla. My blood heated as I watched his eyes flare and he stood up straighter, his eyes volleying all over her body while she looked over the wine list, completely oblivious to the attention she was getting.

My hands curled into fists beside me as a wave of fury washed over me. "Hey, man," I said a little too loudly and with a little too much spite behind it. I felt Isla's eyes on me as I continued staring daggers into *Tanner*, his eyes still glued to her.

I cleared my throat and his eyes pivoted to where I was sitting, doing the best I could to hold the rage inside of me. Narrowing my eyes, I glared at him, watching as he plastered a fake smile to his face as he addressed me.

"Are you two ready to order, or would you like me to get you started on some drinks?"

Isla's hand found mine across the table again and she laced her fingers through mine, squeezing in reassurance.

"We're ready," she stated. Her eyes locked on me as she said what I had been thinking but couldn't vocalize. "I'll take the penne with pesto and a house salad on the side, vinaigrette dressing please. I'm fine with water as my drink. And he'll have..."

"Lobster ravioli," I gritted out, my eyes never leaving Isla's even though I was speaking to our server. Fucker deserved to be ignored.

"And to drink, Sir?"

"Water is good for me, too."

"Excellent," he stated, clapping his server book shut. "I'll get your order with the chef and be back with your waters and some fresh bread."

He scampered off, leaving Isla and I alone in our own little world. Our hands were still locked together, eyes never wavering as the candlelight centerpiece flickered between us.

"Lobster ravioli, huh?" she teased, giving my hand another playful squeeze.

"You made it sound irresistible. Don't worry, if you're a good girl, I'll give you a bite."

A sexy shimmer of sin glinted in her eye at my remark, and I smirked as a response. Despite the waiter pissing me off, she had somehow grounded me and the anger dissipated practically the moment he had walked away. Still, I felt like an ass for how I reacted and knew if I wanted to keep from falling into my father's shadow, I needed to know when to man up and apologize.

"I'm sorry for my reaction. The waiter couldn't take his eyes off you and I reacted. Thank you for pulling me out of the anger."

"That server is a pig, Caleb. I'm positive he thought my breasts were the ones ordering my dinner, and not the face attached to the tits. Don't let people like that bother you. Trust me, it's been happening my entire life. Actually, that was mild."

"Well, it wasn't mild to me. I'm not used to—*this*." I gestured between us. "I never thought I'd be a jealous man, but here we are, I guess."

"You have nothing to be jealous of, trust me. I won't call Tanner until you and I are over. Don't worry."

"Very funny," I growled. Standing, I grabbed the side of her chair, pulling her closer to where I sat. The sound of her chair scraping the floor made a terrible noise, drawing the attention of the table across from us. I smiled at the family before taking my seat again, leaning into Isla. I nuzzled her hair with my nose, my lips grazing her earlobe before I whispered dirty promises.

"You're going to pay for your comment later, baby. I'll let you think about your punishment through dinner. Do you want to know your options?"

"Yes," she purred, leaning into me as my hand came up and wrapped around the back of her neck.

I pulled her earlobe into my mouth and sucked on it gently for a moment before releasing it. "Option one: I'll alternate between fucking your pussy and fucking your face like the dirty slut you are, only stopping when you're sputtering and gagging, and your makeup is running down your cheeks like a river."

I bit my cheek to hide my smile as she inhaled a sharp breath and a warm pink flushed over her skin. "And option two?"

"Oh baby, who said there were only two options? Option two: I will worship your gorgeous body, taking my time and edge you to the point of actual tears streaming down your face as you beg for your release, which may never come."

She tugged her bottom lip between her teeth, squirming slightly in her chair. Her hand came to rest on my upper thigh, her fingers brushing against my rock hard cock straining against the fabric of my pants. "And option three?" she asked, running her knuckles across my bulge. I caught her hand, moving it back to my thigh and forcing it to still.

"Option three: you crawl under the table before dinner is done and suck me off. I want you sloppy, wet, and panting beneath the table, holding me off until *Tanner* comes back. Then the second you hear his voice, I'll explode down your throat as I pay the check. You have until I finish my meal to decide, Starlight. The choice is yours."

CHAPTER TWELVE

ISLA

oly shit.

A rush of wetness seeped into my panties from the filthy seduction Caleb whispered—*no growled*—against my ear. My brain couldn't formulate words, so I nodded my head in rapid succession, looking far too eager to get under the table to suck him off.

Our bodies stayed molded together as the rest of the restaurant fell away, making me forget where I was. My full focus was on the man beside me. The way our breath mingled. The feel of his hand over mine as it rested on his thigh. My heart raced, and the excitement of the spicy promises tingled inside me.

Oh my god. Caleb was straight out of a spicy romance novel and I was totally here for it.

Does that make me the main character?

Yesssssss.

An awkward gurgle of a throat clearing had me look up, and I saw our server clutching two glasses of water. His eyes bounced between me and Caleb as he set one water down in front of Caleb, and placed my glass in front of the empty place setting where I once sat.

"Your meals will be out shortly," he muttered, turning away from us as he did, leaving our table.

Caleb reached over the candle centerpiece and grabbed my water, placing it in front of me, since the server didn't. "My guy is salty as hell. So jealous he can't have my girl." He placed a kiss on my jaw before reaching back over and grabbed my silverware.

"He can be jealous all he wants," I said as I shrugged, my eyes fixated on Caleb as he settled back in his chair. He shifted his body slightly, bending his arm over the back of his chair so it draped over, while his wrist rested on the top.

"So, what are your plans for the Thanksgiving break? Do you think you'll start putting the bug in your father's ear about not taking over his company and going to veterinary school instead?"

His words surprised me, catching me off guard. I reached up and twisted a lock of hair around my finger as I thought of how to answer him. Our last conversation on the subject we had tossed around the idea of me beginning to lay the foundation to the ultimately gigantic conversation my father and I needed to have, but I had ended it by brushing it off and telling Caleb maybe I would after the holidays. No need to ruin a perfectly good Thanksgiving dinner by going against your father's only purpose of having a next of kin.

I twisted the hair tighter, the strands cutting off circulation. "Um, no... Maybe after the holidays, remember?"

"Thanksgiving is still three weeks away. Don't you think you'll want to start bringing it up?"

"Why are you pushing it? I told you I would talk to him after the holidays," I snapped, feeling frustrated this is where he steered the conversation.

"I just hate knowing he holds this over you. I want you to follow your dream."

Caleb reached for his water, taking a gulp while maintaining our eye contact. Though I could feel anger fester, it was hard to let it bubble when I could see the sincerity reflecting through his gaze.

But he didn't know my father and the man he could be. There was a reason he scaled to the top of his industry so quickly. My father was a cold, manipulative man, and could turn anything in his favor.

I took a deep breath, exhaling loudly. "I will have the conversation when I'm ready, Caleb. I'd like to have a leg to stand on before broaching the subject. Preferably a job and a plan of action on how to implement my career path. My father likes to see things in motion, not just hear about them. If I want any sliver of consideration from him, I have to play my cards right."

"This isn't—," his voice boomed, causing several patrons to look our way as he lowered his voice and spoke to me rather than the entire restaurant. "I'm sorry. This isn't something your father should have a say in, Isla. It's *your* life. Stop letting him hold the control."

"It's like you haven't heard a word I've said over the last month," I seethed, biting my tongue to keep my voice low. The last thing we needed was more attention. "I was literally brought into this world so he'd have an heir. Someone to take over his legacy once he was ready for retirement. Even before I was conceived he had control over my life. Breaking it won't be easy, and if I want any—*any hope*—in doing so, I have to do things slowly. Calculated. *My* way."

As if he knew I was ready to end the conversation, our server carried over two steaming plates on his left arm, stopping in front of our table to present them to us.

"Pesto penne," he said with gusto as he sat my entrée in front of me. "And the lobster ravioli," he said in a more brisk tone, placing Caleb's meal in front of him with a little more force than needed to set a plate down. "Can I get you anything else at the moment?"

"No thank you, this looks wonderful," I praised. Our server beamed at me and spun on his heel, striding away from our table while Caleb looked at his ravioli with irritation. I placed my hand on top of his as it grasped his fork. "Let's eat. This looks delicious. I'm excited for my carbs."

He huffed a small laugh and cut into his ravioli, placing a bite between his lips before uttering an audible moan. His eyes closed in delight, savoring his bite. As he swallowed, he popped his eyes back open and shoveled another piece of his pasta onto his fork, turning it in my direction. "You have to try this! It's *fucking* amazing."

I laughed and opened my mouth, and he wasted no time placing the fork between my lips. As the flavor hit my taste buds, a moan floated past my lips, too. "Wow, you weren't kidding."

We ate our meal as slowly as we could, sharing bites and savoring the divine flavors, and although we filled the gaps with small talk, our earlier conversation lingered in my mind and I couldn't help but feel tension between us. Tension I didn't want there, but had no desire to amend at the moment. Though, I made a decision about the options he had given me tonight, and knew the clock was ticking on letting him know my choice.

"Look, I know I might have overstepped earlier, but like I said, I just want to see you follow your dreams," Caleb said, breaking the stretch of silence. He set his fork down on his completely empty plate and shifted in his chair to look at me again.

My eyes drifted to my plate, also empty minus a few stray noodles, thanks to Caleb helping me clean my plate. "I don't really want to talk about it right now, please. Tonight's been beautiful, dinner was delicious. Let's just finish our date on a positive note and I'll deal with my future some other time." I offered him a small smile, hoping he'd lay it to rest at this point.

"Ok."

"Thanks."

Our server dropped the check on the table as he passed by, offering us a curt "Thank you" as he moved onto his next table with their drink refills. Caleb reached for it while simultaneously pulling out his wallet. He set the bill down to pull out some cash, and I couldn't help but glance at the total.

"Are you sure I can't pitch in?" I urged, knowing I could barely afford my meal but wanting to help in any way I could.

"Absolutely not." He leaned over and kissed me on the temple while he laid three twenties and a ten down on top of the bill. "This is our first real date, Starlight. I want to take care of you."

Caleb's chocolate eyes sparkled mischievously as he stood, offering me his hand. He helped me shrug on my coat before pulling his own on, reaching down to grab my hand after we were both bundled. Our fingers entwined together as we moved toward the restaurant's double doors.

Once outside the restaurant, he spun me into him and pressed a warm, sweet kiss to my lips, which parted automatically. I sighed into him as he deepened the kiss, his tongue sweeping over mine.

"Did you decide on which option you wanted, Starlight? Not option three, unfortunately, since we're now outside," he asked against my lips, pulling me back into another knee-weakening kiss before I could answer.

As much as one kiss could cloud my judgment, I knew I couldn't let it, and mustered every ounce of strength I could to break the kiss. "I did. Caleb, I choose option four. I'm going home tonight. Alone."

Caleb's face fell at my answer, and I quickly kissed him again. "Tonight was amazing. Well, most of it was," I laughed. "But I have class super early in the morning and honestly, my vagina needs a break from you."

"There's no changing your mind?" He smirked, pulling the hood of my coat onto my head and arranging my hair that lay on top of my chest. He kept a tendril between his fingers.

"Nope," I said playfully, pulling my hair away from him. "I'm going home. You can drive me there, though."

He groaned dramatically, pulling the keys from his pocket with one hand and my hand with the other. We began walking in the direction of the lot where he parked his car, our arms swinging slightly as we moved. "As long as I get a goodnight kiss."

"Deal," I said as he guided me down a row of cars, stopping in front of his beat up sedan. He opened the passenger door so I could dip beneath the frame and drop into the passenger seat.

As he closed the door for me, I heard him say, "A goodnight kiss between your thighs."

"Caleb!" I laughed and his muffled laugh carried through the vehicle as I bent my head back against the headrest.

CHAPTER THIRTEEN

CALEB

It was impossible for me to focus during my anatomy class when the only anatomy I kept thinking about was *hers*. Listening to the professor drone on about whatever we were supposed to be learning about was a lost cause—I couldn't pull my thoughts away from Isla. I think we were studying muscles of the upper body? Or was it lower body? Maybe today was the lecture on blood flow? *Who fucking knew.* My attention span was non-existent today, and I made the decision to skip the rest of my classes early on. There were only two more. I'd just pull the assignments from the student portal and catch up later.

My stomach grumbled, and I leaned back in my chair, pulling my phone from my pocket and swiping to Isla's messages. I had an idea, and after our date last night and our far too innocent goodnight kiss after all the dirty promises I had given to her earlier in the night, she owed me.

Okay, fine, so she didn't owe me shit, but damn, did I want to make her think she did and then happily collect the debt.

I sent off a text, logistics circling my mind as I planned another date in my mind.

> Skip your next class and come on a picnic with me.

A picnic? Where?

> Down by the river.

> C'mon, live a little and play hooky with me.

You're a bad influence. Isn't it a little cold for a picnic? It's the middle of November.

> I'll keep you warm, Starlight.

Text bubbles floated to the screen, then disappeared again. Self-doubt crept in and I wondered if she was about to decline. I couldn't blame her if she did. I knew while she may have hated the degree she was working toward, she still took school seriously.

I mentally fist bumped the air when I saw her message pop up.

Okay, what time should I meet you?

> I'll wait for you outside your class. It ends at 11:30, right?

Sure does. See you then.

I sat my phone down, locking the screen before tapping on it again to see the time. *Shit.* I hadn't realized it was already almost eleven, and if I wanted to pull this off, I needed to get a move on it. I had to run home and get everything we'd need and make it back to campus to grab my queen.

As discreetly as possible, I slid my notebook into my beat-up faded blue JanSport backpack I had been using since the fourth grade. At this point it looked more gray than blue, and had been hand-sewn in a few places to mend some holes that had appeared. I should have replaced it back in high school, but it had always been a luxury I wasn't interested in wasting money on. It's not like I had a ton of it.

Slipping out of my chair, I pulled the backpack strap onto my shoulder and awkwardly shifted my body through the aisle, making my way out the door as quietly as I could, not chancing a look over my shoulder to see if the professor had noticed. His lecture never faltered, so I assumed he hadn't.

When I made it to my car, I practically dove into the driver's seat and flipped the engine, cringing as all the maintenance lights turned on and stayed on. Fuck if this car wouldn't be the death of me someday, not because of a car accident, but because it was liable to explode at any given moment from the amount of things needing to be fixed, replaced, or changed under the hood.

Remember the end goal, Caleb. Degree. Police Academy. Career.

But the thought of driving Isla in this death trap had my knee bouncing as it idled in the campus parking lot. Keeping the car in park, I used my phone to look up auto body shops in town and called the first one with decent reviews. A few of them even said they took good care of their customers, so it seemed promising. The phone rang endlessly and I thought maybe I'd have to move onto the next one, but finally, someone picked up.

"Dave's Auto Repair, Dave speakin'," a gruff older man answered. The owner, it was safe to assume. Unless Dave the owner was so narcissistic he'd hire employees named Dave too.

"Uh, hey, Dave," I began, blowing out a breath from the nerves I was feeling. I hated asking for favors. "Two questions for you. Does your shop give free estimates? And do you offer payment plans?"

Dave grunted on the other line. "Estimates are free, kid. But we don't do payment plans."

My heart plummeted down into my stomach. I knew the amount of work needed on this car would take me months, if not a year, to pay off. But there were other shops to call. I'd keep calling until I found one that could help. Pushing down emotions I wasn't interested in dealing with, I responded, "Alright sir, thank you for your time."

As I pulled the phone away from my ear, feeling defeated by one quick call, I heard Dave again.

"Hey, kid. Just bring your car in for an estimate and I'll see what I can do, dependin' on how much of a bill you rack up. Can you be here before twelve?"

I glanced at the clock, seeing it was now five past eleven. If I brought my car to Dave, there's no way I'd be back in time for Isla, but if I didn't, I might miss this opportunity. Quickly, I weighed my options. Her safety meant more to me than a picnic by the river. I just needed to text her with a quick change of plans.

"Yes, sir," I confirmed to Dave. "I'll head over now and can be there in fifteen. Should I just ask for you?"

Change of plans, Starlight. Head to your apartment and wait for me there. I need to make a quick stop and then I'll be over.

Dave grunted from the other line again before I heard it click dead.

Ok, see you there.

I just need to go see a man named Dave first.

CHAPTER FOURTEEN

I couldn't shake the feeling I was being stood up.

Maybe this was it. Caleb had actually changed his mind about me, or had decided he should have listened to himself to begin with and stayed away. Either way, it'd been two hours since he had originally asked to meet me and I hadn't heard from him since his text instructed me to meet him at my place instead.

So much for a quick stop.

Still, I forced myself to ignore the urge to text him and ask where he was. I didn't want to seem like a needy girlfriend. Or maybe it was just that I didn't want confirmation he was blowing me off.

Shit, I just called myself his girlfriend.

We hadn't put a label on what was going on between us, but I definitely didn't hate the idea of being Caleb's girlfriend.

"Ughhhhh," I groaned, kicking my left leg over the top of the couch and draping my arm over my eyes. Clutching my phone in my hand, I fought the temptation to throw it across the room. How could I be so stupid? *Of course,* he would change his mind. He was so apprehensive in the beginning, I was a fool to think this could be anything, but so hopeful it could be *something*. But I needed to remind myself to get my head out of the clouds. This wasn't a romance novel, this was real life. *My life.* And my life was a fucking disaster of epic proportions.

My phone began to vibrate against my hand, and how quickly I wiped my arm off my face to look at the caller I.D. could have rivaled *The Flash*.

A sigh deflated my chest as I peered at the photo illuminated on my screen. Begrudgingly, I answered the call. "Hello, Father. To what do I owe the pleasure?"

"Why aren't you in class? I expected your voicemail," my father's smooth voice drifted through the phone, his tone flat and businesslike.

"If you expected my voicemail, then why did you call when you knew I had class?"

"Because I wanted to reach your voicemail, Isla. What I have to say does not require a conversation, yet here we are, wasting valuable time."

"By all means, Father, don't let me keep you." My hand slammed over my mouth and my eyes widened at how I was speaking to my father. My stomach immediately fell.

If he noticed, he didn't acknowledge it. "Thanksgiving dinner is at six o'clock sharp. The Bradleys will be joining us this year, so I expect you to arrive no later than four o'clock. Be dressed in business casual, and ready to impress their oldest son, Blake."

"I—what?"

"Oh, don't be daft, Isla. It's unbecoming. Four o'clock."

The line went dead.

For several seconds, I continued to hold the phone to my ear, my mouth hanging open as I replayed the conversation over in my head. My fingers squeezed around the sides of it until they stiffened and I finally brought it down to rest on the couch beside me.

It wasn't enough he wanted to steal away my future career, but now he wanted to control my dating life too? Was he trying to marry me off to this man?

Holy shit.

I wouldn't put it past him to do just that.

My father had it in his head that he was so powerful he could control his only daughter's entire adult life. It wasn't enough he controlled my childhood—he wanted the rest of my life too, as though it was just some possession to him.

Something inside me broke at that moment.

I wasn't a person to him. Not his daughter, his flesh and blood. I was an object. A pawn in his game of chess. The final piece of the puzzle needed to tick all the boxes for his accomplishments.

I couldn't do this anymore.

Thanksgiving afternoon, I would show up at four as he requested. I'd dress the part, bat my lashes at whatever man he was trying to force me on, and as soon as the whoeverthe-fucks left, my father and I'd sit down and have a nice long conversation in his home office.

Or a super short conversation.

It would all depend on if I had the lady balls to go through with it.

WARM HUES of orange filled my apartment through the open curtains as the sun went down behind the horizon. I hadn't moved from my spot on the couch, its cushions permanently indented by my ass and torso, since my legs—now both of them—were hanging over the top of the couch.

Caleb was a no-show, and I did my best to brush off the anxiety laced pain centered in my rib cage.

Honestly, I had expected this. What I hadn't expected was him completely ghosting me. I thought he'd at least tell me to my face that this wasn't what he wanted. I knew we'd be a complicated mess, but I had still remained hopeful. Maybe I shouldn't have.

My stomach growled as I mechanically scrolled through Louis Vuitton's website on my phone, lusting over the gorgeous tourterelle gray Nano Noé I could no longer afford. Retail therapy used to be my favorite way to cope with the disappointments in my life, but these days my version of retail therapy was picking out which flavors of Cup of Noodle soup I was going to add to my basket.

A fifty-five cent soup was now my retail therapy when it used to be a two thousand dollar bag.

My mind ricocheted between thoughts of Caleb ditching me and thoughts of my father selling me off like a cheap whore. Okay, maybe an exaggeration, but it's what it felt like. He was up to something. A lifetime of tip-toeing around my father had proven he was a selfish man, always out to benefit himself.

Toggling to a different page on my phone, I scrolled through the new arrivals on Chloé's website, fawning over the ankle boots I desperately wanted to give a home to. I built my cart, adding everything that caught my eye just to torture myself. As materialistic as it was, the best part of growing up in my lonely house was access to my father's black card. He never cared how much I spent, and shopping on his dime was more gratifying.

My gaze shifted to my Louis, sitting on my entryway table, and I looked longingly at the bag that still brought me so much joy. I could feel my privilege showing. And I hated myself a little for it.

I can't believe he never showed up.

I *knew* he felt it, too. Every kiss, every touch—it wasn't just physical between us, though. He saw me. The *real* me. Caleb broke through my walls and got me to open up to him in ways I hadn't expected to open up to anyone. I had never told a soul about how I came to be, or about how much contempt my father holds for me.

The face of perfection was just a mask for sorrow.

Caleb made me addicted to the way he made me feel. He never tried to silence me, or make me feel lesser than.

For once in my life, I felt special and cherished—dare I say *loved*.

Because dammit, I think I loved him. And I had a sickening feeling in my gut it was too late.

CHAPTER FIFTEEN

"Well, kid. You ain't gon' like this estimate. If I was in the auto insurance biz, I'd do you a favor and deem your car as totaled. It's a miracle you're even alive after driving this thing for so long, boy."

A low growl vibrated through my chest as I raked my hand through my hair, leaning forward on the folding chair my ass was parked on for the last five and a half hours. I was angry, hungry, and going out of my mind thinking about Isla and the cold, hard fact I had completely vanished on her. But my phone died ten minutes after I got to the garage, and no one in the facility had a phone charger they could lend me.

What I thought would be a quick thirty-minute task ruined my entire day.

"What are we looking at?" I asked, digging my thumb and pointer finger into my eyes, rubbing them roughly, trying to ease the stress that had built behind them. My head was pounding.

"Busted valves, overused piston rings, disintegrating

filters—not to mention—no friggin' oil." He stopped and scratched the top of his head, looking at the carbon paper in front of him with the mile long list of problems with my car. "Don't get me started on the state of your transmission. Kid, I don't know how you've been driving this around. Even your camshaft is startin' to break."

My eyes closed, and I took a deep breath, inhaling the scent of new tires and lingering gasoline. "Anything else I need to know about?"

"Your tires are bald."

Fuck. This situation couldn't possibly get any worse.

"Even if I give you a huge break on labor, you're still looking at upwards of sixty-five hundred."

Well, I was wrong about it not getting any worse.

Bracing my elbows on my knees, I leaned my head into my hands and took a few deep breaths, trying to figure out what the hell I was going to do. I'd been driving in a death trap for who knows how long.

I couldn't knowingly drive Isla in my car now. Not with all the repairs needing to be done. Her safety came first, and I could never jeopardize it for the sake of taking her somewhere.

"What are my options?" I asked, putting pressure on my eye sockets with the heel of my hands. As much as I hated to admit it, this made me want to fucking cry, and I hadn't cried since the first week my mom left and my dickhead dad told me to *'man up and stop being a pussy.'*

Repositioning myself to sitting upright, I extended my arm to take the paperwork Dave was handing me.

"Look, kid, I'll shoot it straight. This car isn't worth the amount of work it needs done. You're better off junkin' this and gettin' yourself a new one."

"I can't afford a new one," I stated, my eyes grazing over the notes and numbers on the paper in front of me.

"You can't afford this one either. We can fix all this crap—I can give you a hefty discount, put you on a payment plan even though we don't normally do 'em—but you'll be back in here soon enough with another list of things for us to fix. The car's old, kid, and you haven't been keepin' up on it. Regular maintenance is important. When was the last time this thing saw the inside of a shop?"

I could feel his eyes on me as he waited for me to answer the question, but I couldn't bring myself to look away from the paperwork I held, pretending to read it over as I avoided his question. My mind raced, but I couldn't focus on any one thing.

"What are my options?" I repeated my earlier question, hoping my choices would somehow change. Because as it stood, I had no choice. I was fucked, no matter the outcome.

Dave stepped toward me, turning and grabbing the chair. He sat slowly, lowering himself with a care that told me his body ached. Bringing his hand to my shoulder, he gripped it in a way I knew was meant to be reassuring. "If you were my kid, I wouldn't let you get back into that thing until it's fixed completely. Do you have any other way you can get around right now? Borrow a car? A bike?"

I heard his words, but the only thing my brain could process was that I wouldn't be driving my car out of here tonight. Maybe not ever. "The bus," I stated on an exhale, defeat pouring out of me in one big wave.

"Let me give you a ride home tonight, kid. Shop's closin' anyway. Leave the car here for a few days and let me talk to some friends, see if they can pull salvageable parts off other junkers."

"Why do you want to help me?" My tone was sour, although I hadn't meant it to be. But with the universe shitting on me, it was also hard to care.

"You remind me of my kid. I didn't do right by him, so maybe I can do right by you."

I nodded once in acknowledgement, knowing I wouldn't get a further explanation, nor did I need one. I had plenty of experience with shitty fathers. At least Dave here seemed regretful of his faults.

"Alright, thanks," was all I could manage as we both stood. He called out to the other guys who were still cleaning up the garage, letting them know he was taking off. I followed him silently to his truck, climbing into the passenger seat when he unlocked it. I was grateful for the ride home, but couldn't help feeling like a complete and utter failure.

Just when things started to look up for me, and I was actually proud of how my life was going, I got kicked down again.

And all over again, I felt like that sad little boy being told to man up and stop being a pussy.

THE STENCH of vomit permeated the air as I stepped through the threshold of my house and closed the door behind me. Light from the hallway illuminated the otherwise dark space, showing me the lump passed out on our couch again. As I stepped into the living room, I flicked the light switch and took in my surroundings. Vomit puddled on the carpet beneath him, still dripping from his mouth as he lay on his side with his arm jutted out from under him.

The last thing I wanted to deal with after the day I had was this. I rolled my eyes, my head shaking as I fought against the anger sweeping through me.

"Dad," I said from where I stood at the side of the couch. I didn't dare step closer—not when I knew how disgusting the carpet was. He never cleaned his messes up properly, and over the years, I stopped caring enough to do it for him.

"Dad," I called again, my voice louder this time. He continued to snore softly. Reaching out, I gave his shoulder several firm shakes, trying to wake him. "Dad."

With a phlegm-filled snort, he startled awake with annoyed grunts and words slurring as he came to. "What? Who—er—what is it?!" He tried to sit up, swinging his legs over the side of the couch, his foot landing in his vomit puddle as he did.

I gagged at the sight, forcing my eyes to travel to his face instead, and I watched as he rubbed his eyes, his body swaying slightly despite still being seated. "You puked all over yourself again, and on the floor. Clean it up, Dad. It's disgusting."

He groaned and rubbed his eyes, collapsing back onto the couch and ignoring me. I didn't stick around, retreating toward my small bedroom. What I wouldn't give to walk into a house that didn't smell like the bottom of a dumpster and be as germ-filled as one, too. I longed for a clean, warm, inviting space where I found joy in being.

It was coming. I knew it was. An image of Isla opening the front door to our modest, yet beautiful house, waiting for me after a long day at work, filtered into my mind. I smiled at the sight, practically smelling the warm vanilla scent I knew would linger in the air.

My feet led me to my bedside table, where I bent and picked up the phone cord that had fallen to the floor, plugging in my phone as I sat down on my unmade twin-sized bed.

I didn't bother removing my shoes as I waited for my phone to come back to life. Instead, I sat staring at the screen, wondering how I was going to explain to Isla the reason I didn't show up was because I was a broke son-of-a-bitch who quite literally couldn't even afford to keep her safe.

How was I supposed to be the man she needed—a man who she could trust would provide for her one day—when I didn't even have a car?

I had less than two months left before finishing my degree, then I would apply to the police academy, also applying for a night-shift job with them, while I went through it. I still wouldn't be able to work full-time while in the academy, but I had to assume the police department paid more than my minimum wage position at the Pack N Mail. Eventually, I could afford another car.

Or maybe I'd be the luckiest bastard in Ridgewood and old Dave would find scrap parts to use, cutting down my estimate.

Either way, I knew I needed to stay hopeful while I continued to try and better my life.

One day, things would be easier.

I let out a relieved breath when my phone restarted, rushing to the messages as soon as I could unlock the home screen. My brows pinched together when I had none waiting for me, but I typed a quick message to Isla without stopping to put much thought into why.

> I'm so sorry, Starlight. My phone died and my errand took a lot longer than expected.

Send.

Minimizing the messages, I went to my call log next to check to see if she had called. She hadn't.

I checked the time, seeing it was almost nine.

Nine and a half hours had passed, and she hadn't reached out to me either. Hadn't she wondered why I didn't show up?

Immediately, I clicked her name, and the phone began to ring. The abrasive sound echoed through the speaker, my foot tapping anxiously while I waited for her to pick up.

"Hey, you've reached Isla, sorry I—"

I hung up, not wanting to leave a voicemail. I switched back over to the messages, typing another one to her, explaining myself further.

> I needed to stop and get an estimate on getting my car worked on, and it took a while for the guy to do. I'll make it up to you. Call me, I just want to hear your voice.

Fuck.

I knew she was mad. It was too early for her to be asleep, and despite her busy course schedule, she'd never not responded to me within a few minutes. Until now.

The way I saw it, I had two options. Sit here, do nothing, and hope she'd respond at some point tonight or tomorrow, or show up at her place and demand she talk to me. Even if she was pissed off or refused. With any luck, she'd hear me out, and I'd explain why I wasn't there, even if the embarrassment killed me.

This wasn't the end of her and me.

Quickly, I typed out *'I'm coming over'*, pushed send, and tossed my phone down onto the bed. I needed to change into some fresh clothes: I could still smell the scent of tires on me. What I really wanted was a hot shower, but the idea of wasting more fucking time had me reaching for my deodorant instead. After swiping it beneath my armpits, I recapped it and shrugged on my slate gray tee shirt and black hoodie, turning to reach for my keys off my dresser, only to remember they weren't there.

I ran my hand down my face again, feeling completely exasperated. Looking around the small space of my bedroom, I took an inventory of the things in this room that were truly *mine*. A tattered copy of *Catch-22* and my phone charger sat on the nightstand. The clothes in my closet and the couple pairs of shoes sat beneath them. The shoebox I kept in the far corner of the shelf in my closet held a few baby photos of me and my mom, along with the necklace—two hearts—one for me, one for her. She'd always remind me that the necklace represented the two of us, and I remembered her wearing it every day.

Finding it under the end table in the living room after she left, laying carelessly beneath it with the clasp broken, had always been unsettling to me. There was never a time I could remember her taking it off, and I'd never been able to figure out why she would have left it behind.

A notification sounded from behind me as I continued to stare at the box, pulling my attention to the phone sitting in the middle of my bed. Picking it up, a smirk played on my lips at the name flashing across the screen. Swiping the notification, our string of messages pulled up and I read the newest one, my face falling as I scanned the words.

Don't bother

"Fuck," I roared, pocketing my phone.

Ripping my bedroom door open, I stomped out of the room, letting the door slam behind me. The lights were still on from when I had returned home earlier, and my father was in the same spot on the couch, head tilted back so far it looked painful, open-mouth snoring loud as fuck.

Ignoring him, I left the house, not slowing until I reached where the sidewalk met the street. I looked around, taking in the thick fog that'd rolled in tonight, and began walking in the direction of the bus stop. Pulling out my phone again, I found the schedule I had taken a screenshot of earlier, hoping I hadn't missed the last bus. I picked up my pace, realizing I had less than five minutes to make it to the bus stop two blocks away.

I swear, I was so fucking done with tonight. This was the last bus running, and if Isla didn't let me spend the night—or worse, not let me in at all—I'd be completely screwed.

Picking my pace up into a jog, I felt a fat raindrop hit the bridge of my nose, and then another on my cheek as the rain came out of nowhere, falling hard and fast until drops colored the sidewalk. My feet hit the pavement fast and as I rounded the corner of the street I needed, I watched as the bus veered away from the sidewalk, driving away without me on it.

I FELT like a literal fish out of water as I approached Isla's apartment door, soaking wet from the rain, my hand already hovering in the air, ready to knock. My mind was spinning, trying to rehearse exactly what I would say, but sounding like a dickhead idiot, even in my own thoughts. I knew I should just be honest and tell her my car was a piece of shit and I didn't feel comfortable putting her in the passenger seat. She'd understand I tried to do the right thing by getting an estimate to get it fixed, but I ended up fucking myself in the process because there's no way I could actually afford to fix it.

Those are the things I should tell her, but fuck if that didn't make me sound pathetic and weak.

But I wasn't. Just broke. And my mouth went dry, realizing she meant more to me than anything money could buy.

My hand fell instantly as it sank in that I was falling for this girl. I couldn't stop thinking about her; she was on my mind all the time and had been since I first saw her all those weeks ago.

Dammit.

Raking a hand through my already disheveled hair, I looked down at the ground, hesitating instead of knocking on her door like I should have. Swallowing the lump in my throat, I raised my arm again, and just did it—rapping my knuckles against the wood three times.

I took a step back, moving my hands to the pockets of my jeans as I fought the urge to bounce on the balls of my feet. My heart thundered in my chest as doubt sunk its claws further into my confidence with every passing second she didn't answer the door.

When she didn't answer, I stepped forward and knocked again. I could hear a faint shuffling sound from inside her apartment, but the door remained closed. "Isla, please open the door," I begged, pressing my forehead against it.

I flattened my palm to the door, closing my eyes as I listened for the sound of footsteps approaching, hearing nothing but an eerie silence.

"Isla—," I began. I was going to tell her the truth, but apologizing didn't feel right when I wasn't even sure she was listening. "I'm sorry. Please, just open the door so I can explain what happened. Please, Starlight. Open the door."

My forehead was still firmly against the wood and slowly I rolled it side to side, although I wasn't sure why. Exhaling a breath, I forced air between my tightened lips so it made an exasperated raspberry sound. I righted myself and took a backward step from the door when the sound of her voice stopped me in my tracks.

"Why are you here, Caleb?" she asked as she pulled her apartment door open. She looked gorgeous, albeit pissed off, in her baggy black sweatpants and white long-sleeved shirt that showed off a sliver of her stomach. Her dark hair sat piled into a bun on the top of her head, and her storm colored eyes—though narrowed at me in a glare—looked bright contrasted with the white of her shirt. She wrapped her hand around the edge of the door, holding it open just enough for her body to block my entrance and stop me from walking in.

"Because I told you I'd meet you at your apartment—"

"At twelve."

Reaching up, I massaged the back of my neck. "At twelve," I confirmed. My gaze traveled up the length of her body until I reached her eyes. "Let me explain."

She stared back at me, her lips hardening into a thin line. I took a step forward, pushing back the short baby hairs curling in front of her ear, tucking them behind and letting my finger tips linger. To my surprise, she didn't pull away from my touch.

A good sign.

"I left my anatomy class to go grab everything I needed from my house to take you to the river. When I got in my car, pretty much every single engine light was lit up. The nagging realization that I was about to put you into my deathtrap of a car and drive you forty minutes to the river wasn't sitting right with me. So I called a shop, and the guy told me to stop in for a free estimate to find out what needed to be fixed. What should have been a quick thirty-minute thing turned into almost six hours."

"So why didn't you call? Or text?" Isla asked the second I finished my sentence.

"Because my damn phone died. And look, I really like you, but I haven't memorized a phone number since I was four and my mom made me memorize hers in case of an emergency."

Isla tried to hide it, but I caught the way her lips pursed to conceal her smile at the admission. It *was* true. I barely had my own phone number memorized, but now I made a mental note to recite her phone number repeatedly in my head until I knew it from memory.

Trailing my fingers down her arm, I caught her hand and brought it to my lips to kiss the inside of her palm. "Please, Starlight. Can I come in?"

CHAPTER SIXTEEN

ISLA

The confidence I had in myself to stand my ground and not let him in wavered with one look of those puppy dog eyes, and he wasn't even trying to give me puppy dog eyes.

I knew he was trouble. I knew it from the moment I saw him, but I still couldn't stay away. And now I needed to figure out if he was lying to me or not.

His story seemed plausible, but six hours at the mechanic? For an estimate? Come on. I didn't know a thing about cars and I wouldn't pretend to, but that amount of time just seemed excessive.

But why would he lie?

Naturally, my mind spiraled into the first thought any woman would have when her boyfr—*hookup*—completely disappeared after they blew them off for a date. Was there someone else who had drawn his attention?

But as I blocked my doorway and stared at him skeptically, I could practically feel the remorse roll off of him, and I caved. Keeping my mouth shut, I pushed the door open more, releasing it and turning to walk into my living room. The door closed behind me and I heard Caleb flip the lock.

Something about it made me smile and his earlier words about not wanting me to ride in his *deathtrap of a car* echoed in my mind. It seemed like he truly cared about my safety, but could I trust him to keep my heart safe?

I still wasn't fully convinced.

Taking a seat on my couch, I crossed my legs and curled them beneath me, pulling a pillow onto my lap as though it could offer me emotional protection from this conversation. I had no idea which direction it would go and nerves had filled my body on the short walk from the door to the couch. Caleb followed me into the room and stood in front of me, not taking a seat, which only made me more unsettled.

"I'm sorry," he repeated, crouching down, so we were eye level. That's when I noticed he was soaking wet. He looked chilled to the bone, completely saturated as beads of water rolled down his cheek from his hair and his clothes clung to his body.

My eyes widened, putting together there was no way a quick walk from his car to my apartment door would have drenched him so thoroughly. "Did you walk here?"

He nodded his head, realizing too that his hair was dripping. He swiped a hand through his hair, rainwater coating his palm, and he wiped it onto his jeans, which also looked uncomfortably wet. "My car's still at the shop. The owner asked me to leave it for a few days and said he'd try to find some scrap parts that were needed to fix what he could. The estimate came back higher than the cost of buying another piece of shit car."

"So you walked here?" I asked again in disbelief that he

would walk in the rain to come over. I didn't know for sure how far apart we lived, but I knew it wasn't super close.

He shrugged as if it was no big deal. "I missed the last bus."

The last of my resolve crumbled, and I stood from the couch, pulling him up with me. He had to take a small step back to accommodate both our bodies standing in such a close space, and once he did, I reached for the hem of his sweatshirt. Curling my fingers around the bottom of it, I took the soft, wet fabric of his sweatshirt and t-shirt between my fingertips. I pulled them up his body, stretching my arms until I couldn't reach anymore. Caleb finished what I had started, pulling the clothes up and over his head. He held them in one arm, his curious gaze watching as I sank to my knees in front of him and unlaced his black Vans, lifting each foot one at a time to pull off his shoes and socks.

Once I had completed the task, I pushed further onto my knees, elevating myself, and unhooked his belt. I left it dangling from the loops before pushing the button of his jeans into its loophole and unzipping his zipper. A huge sigh left his body, and he shivered, his eyes never leaving mine as I pulled his jeans down his legs, leaving his boxer briefs in place so he wouldn't be completely naked.

His skin was frozen beneath my fingers as they grazed his skin while I removed his jeans. My heart sank knowing the lengths he had gone to get to my doorstep. I watched as a dusting of goosebumps pebbled his skin, the lack of clothes doing nothing to help with how cold he was. He needed a hot shower, a warm bed, and body heat. Though the hurt hadn't completely dissipated, I was happy to be the one to heat him back up.

Stepping out of his jeans, Caleb's fingers circled around

my arm and pulled me to stand. He moved his hand to cup the back of my neck, pulling me forward, and crashed his lips against mine. A shiver—more from the intensity of his kiss than how cold he was—racked through my body and I emitted a soft whimper as I relented some of my anger.

For the second time since I met him, it felt like there had been a shift between us somehow, though a small pang in my gut reminded me there was more than met the eye with Caleb, and I still had a lot to learn.

Wrapping my arms around his torso, my head tilted back further as I lost myself in the moment, letting all the hurt and anger seep out of my body and evaporate into thin air.

When we parted, I grabbed onto his hand and pulled him into my small bathroom, making the first move to finish getting him taken care of after being chilled to the bone. As I reached for the knob on the shower and turned it on, Caleb's arm wrapped around me from behind while the other reached up and pulled my hair aside, exposing the right side of my neck.

Warm lips brushed against my skin, kisses trailing from my shoulder up to my ear. He stopped kissing and whispered, "Will you be joining me?"

"Do you want me to?" I countered, leaning back against his chest as we waited for the water to heat up.

Caleb placed his hand on my hip and spun my body to face him. Moving his hand to my face, he cupped my cheek in his palm, using his thumb to tilt my head back so I was looking into his eyes. "More than I want my next breath."

He reached up to my hair and pulled the elastic securing my bun, tugging it gently to release the tendrils of hair so they fell in a messy cascade down my back and shoulders. He pressed his lips to mine, kissing me slowly, while placing his hands on either side of my hips. His fingertips brushed the sliver of exposed skin before tugging my shirt up, our lips parting only to remove it before they connected again.

My bra was a front closure—my most unattractive, yet most comfortable one I owned—so I unhooked it with one hand, letting my breasts spill out as it gave way. The straps slipped down my arms and I shook them gently, allowing the bra to fall completely.

As it landed on the floor with a silent thud, I wrapped my arms around his neck and lifted onto my tiptoes to deepen the kiss. My heart soared, feeling so much relief.

Caleb wound his arm around my middle, pulling me into his nearly naked body. His erection pressed into my stomach, pushing my thoughts to salacious images of us in my bed, his face between my thighs. Desire ripped through my body as I suddenly fantasized about the movements of his tongue against my throbbing clit, and a moan caught in my throat. I felt my pussy contract, desperate to feel him inside me.

Breaking the kiss, I forced myself to take a step back from him and pointed to where the water still ran.

"Go," I rasped, turning to see the hot steam floating past the shower doors. "Get in, I'll be right back." I was already straying from my plan of getting him into the shower, so much more interested in jumping his bones instead.

When did I become this sexual?

He obliged, not taking his eyes off me as he hooked his thumbs into his boxer briefs and pulled them down, stepping out of them and turning to get into the shower. As he entered, I was given the beautiful sight of his ass and couldn't help but smile at the dimple in his right cheek. Clearly he was flexing, tossing me a coy smile as he closed the shower door, and I laughed out loud before turning to exit the steamy bathroom. Swooping down, I picked up his underwear on my way out.

His clothes were where we left them, sopping wet, creating small puddles on my floor. If he didn't want to go home tomorrow in his birthday suit, he'd need dry clothes, and since I wasn't in the habit of keeping men's clothes lying around my apartment, I wanted to make sure his things ended up in the dryer before I forgot—which was inevitable considering my state of undress at the moment.

Grabbing everything he'd arrived in, I threw them into the small all-in-one washer dryer, and started it on high heat.

"Hurry your sexy ass up," Caleb called from the bathroom. I rolled my eyes, laughing as I walked to my bedroom instead.

Pulling off my sweatpants and underwear, I dropped them into the laundry basket. They weren't technically dirty, but I had this thing about not liking to re-wear clothes even if I had only worn them for a while.

Deodorant stains and dead skin cells gave me the heebie-jeebies.

Sauntering across the hall, I found Caleb standing with the shower door open, looking like a sculpture as the water hit his shoulders and back, rippling against him as it cascaded down his body. His hands covered his face briefly before he raked them through his hair, slicking it back before he turned and smiled at me.

"There you are," he said, water poured down around him like a waterfall. My mouth watered at the sight and I bit down on my lip, my gaze dropping to the ground.

I needed to compose myself if I expected to *only* shower with this man.

Stepping in, I closed the door behind me before turning to face Caleb. The small shower was *not* made for two people and our bodies filled the space, giving us just enough room to function.

Caleb's hands cradled my hips, but I swatted him away, pushing him off me while I reached around him to grab my body wash. "You ready to smell like vanilla?" I asked, quirking a brow and squeezing a generous dollop of the liquid soap into my palm. "Not just any vanilla either, sugar-spun vanilla cupcake."

"Sounds good enough to eat," he mused. "Are you going to clean your entire body with it? I could think of some places I'd like to eat."

He watched as I lathered the soap between my palms before reaching up to his neck. Smearing the soap down his shoulders, I continued to work the lather into his skin as I made my way down his torso and wrapped my hands around his back to scrub whatever I could reach.

"We're going for warmth and comfort, Caleb. No funny business."

"How am I supposed to stop resisting when you're naked, wet, and have your body pressing into mine while you rub your hands *everywhere* on me?"

I gave him a look that clearly said 'that's a you problem' and refocused on my ministrations.

Lowering myself down to my knees, I rubbed soap up and down his legs and the tops of his feet. Sinking further down until I was practically seated on my calves, I encouraged him to lift one foot at a time, focusing on the task at hand as I kneaded the soap into the soles of his feet, giving him a foot massage.

"*Fuck*, Isla," Caleb groaned from above me, his palm

pressing against the cheap tiles of my shower. Pride swelled in my chest, knowing I was making him feel good.

Looking up from my lashes, I saw his cock had grown thick, hanging heavy and erect just above me. Caleb's eyes were hooded as he looked down at me.

"Did that feel good?" I asked, a hint of innocence in my voice. His cock was a hair's breadth away from my lips, but I restrained touching him—or taking him in my mouth—like I felt desperate to do.

"Incredible."

"Good," I replied, shifting back onto my knees and grabbing onto Caleb's thigh to help myself have some momentum to stand.

Once I was firmly on my feet, he fisted my wet hair, curling the inky strands around his palm. He pulled them tight to bend my body back, giving himself access to my breasts. My nipples were already peaked from the cool air that prickled through the shower's steam, and he leaned down, sucking one into his mouth.

His tongue was hot against the sensitive skin, and I whimpered from the sensation. Caleb had me at his mercy, arching my back to the point of pain, but he quickly soothed it into pleasure with the strokes of his tongue.

Feeling like I was about to explode if he didn't touch me, I tried aligning my body to rub against his cock—which had found its way between my legs—but the angle he held me at made it difficult. "Please," I shamelessly whimpered, not really sure what else to say as the pleasure bloomed deep within and worked its way outward. My body was needy, sensitive. Begging to be touched.

He popped off my breast and reached around to lift me by my butt, coaxing my legs around him. Securing my ankles,

I clung onto him and wrapped my arms around his neck, meeting his lips as he lifted his chin. With one hand planted firmly on my ass, he opened the shower door and stepped through it with me in his arms.

"The towels," I said against his lips.

"Fuck the towels," he growled, striding across the hall to my bedroom.

Water fell from our bodies, leaving a trail on the carpet, but I didn't give it a second thought as he stopped in front of my bed and dropped me onto it. My body bounced, breasts swaying as I landed on the plush comforter.

My legs spread wide, begging for him to take me, as he stood at the edge, looking down at me predatorily.

"Look at how your legs spread for me, showing me your pretty pussy. Even your body knows you're my little slut, doesn't it?"

I squirmed against the bed, his words twisting within me, sending a shockwave through my body. "This wasn't the plan I had in mind. I was supposed to take care of you tonight."

His knee hit the bed between my legs and he lowered himself down on top of me, his hard shaft pushing against my swollen clit. Heat ignited through my body, so aroused I thought I might combust. I rolled my hips into him, chasing the pleasure.

"I don't deserve to be taken care of after letting you think I had abandoned you all day."

The sincerity of his words broke my heart. He truly thought he didn't deserve to be taken care of, and despite the disappointment I'd felt earlier today from his actions, I made it my new mission to show him he was worth *everything*.

Catching him off guard, I pushed his hips and rolled us

so I was straddling his lap. I bent back, lowering myself so I could grind my pussy against his cock, and we groaned in unison and his cock throbbed beneath my wet heat, begging to let my soft walls embrace it. Caleb's ability to let me have control in the bedroom whenever I wanted it was freeing. It *showed* me we were equals. Caleb's head tilted back into my bedding and I watched as he exhaled a deep breath, his eyes falling shut as he seemed to battle something within.

Somehow, I knew exactly what he needed—I had seen it clear as day the first night he had come to my apartment and I wrapped my fingers around his throat. He not only allowed me to have it, there were times he *needed* me to take control.

The pieces of the puzzle fell together, and I tried not to let it reflect on my face. I was well aware I was making assumptions—something I got really upset about him doing —but I couldn't help it. Something clicked, and I realized almost his entire life, Caleb had been on his own. His mother had left him, his dad was a drunk, and he essentially was left alone to... what? Grow up when he was a child and parent himself. Caleb never had guidance or structure, let alone someone to make menial decisions for him, like what was for dinner that night, or the simple comfort of knowing how he was getting to school the next day.

It made sense that there needed to be some *give* in his life, an outlet where he could relinquish control and let someone else take the reins. I let my thoughts simmer as I glided my hand up his chest, lightly trailing my touch along his collarbone. My fingers reached the soft skin around his neck, and I spread them wide, letting my palm press against his throat and curl naturally into a grasp.

Our gaze connected, and I smiled, feeling confident as I leaned down and pressed my lips against his chest. My kisses started featherlight, moving all over his torso, finding sensitive places to suck on roughly. I wanted to mark him, if only for myself to see later. My realization made me feel like I had peeled back a layer of him. It would somehow bring us closer.

Suctioning my mouth to his skin, I brought blood to the surface and left light marks all over his chest, all while keeping my hand firmly in place around his neck. My intentions were clear—*stay still*—and he did, only the sound of his steady breath turning ragged and wanton clued me in on how much he was enjoying this.

More confidence bloomed within me and I reached my free hand down to grip his cock, stroking it slowly. As firm as it felt in my hand, the motions felt hindered and I knew I could make it feel better for him than what I was doing.

Releasing his cock, I moved my hand to my face, spitting into my palm before returning it back to Caleb's shaft. It throbbed in my hand as I resumed my strokes, falling quickly into a rhythm that earned me a cluster of groans.

Heightening myself on my knees, I aligned his cock with my center and slowly lowered myself onto him until I was flush with his body. He filled me up, completely encased within me as my walls clenched around him. I moaned, every nerve ending in my body twinkling like the stars in the sky.

Releasing my hold on Caleb's neck and bringing both hands to his chest, I steadied myself as I began to ride him, slowly rising up until only the tip of him was inside me, then sliding back down until he reached the hilt. I repeated these motions, my hips slowly moving in a figure-eight, until my entire body tingled with the first signs of my orgasm building.

I was drunk on pleasure as I looked down at the

gorgeous man below me through a hooded gaze, almost too wrapped up in my own indulgence to notice he hadn't moved or said anything since I stole the show.

"Caleb," I moaned, chasing the friction as I rode him faster, reaching down to rub my clit as I continued to increase my pace. His eyes followed my touch and the moment my fingertips met my clit, it was like a switch flipped within him.

"*Mine*," he growled, pushing my hand away and replacing it with his own. He began massaging my clit, and I threw my head back, succumbing to ecstasy.

"Fuck, Isla, you look *and* feel incredible. Look at my slut riding my cock like a pro."

"*Yes*," I moaned, grabbing at my breasts as they bounced furiously. My fingers raked over my nipples and they were so sensitive to the touch, a whimper fell from my lips.

"I made a mistake today, baby," Caleb said with a hint of sadness as he slowly dragged his fingers to cover my clit. Circling the sensitive spot, he massaged it with a precision that made my toes curl. "Can you forgive me?"

Could I forgive him?

I already had.

"Yes," I moaned again. "Please—*faster*," I begged, my hand floating down to cover his own. I used my fingers to guide him, applying more pressure to my clit as he rubbed it.

Breathtakingly fast, Caleb sat up and shifted his other hand to my waist, pushing me down onto him. I took a moment to readjust my legs for the position, feeling the bite of his fingernails as they dug into the flesh of my hips. He took control, bucking beneath me, driving his cock upward.

My eyes rolled back in my head, absorbing the way my orgasm bloomed outward as I felt myself climbing, hyper-aware of every part of his body against mine. With every thrust, I forgot about the day and let go of any feeling in my body other than the pleasure.

Caleb fucked me hard and fast, thrusting his hips up as I bared down, pushing him deeper into me. His fingers moved expertly against my clit, the rush inching closer like an ocean wave, ready to crash onto the sand.

"Don't stop, Caleb. I'm so close." My hands moved to grip his arms, holding on as he cursed and clamped his teeth against my shoulder.

"*Fuck*, Isla. Come all over my cock, use it and take what you want."

He stilled within me and let me regain control, moving with an authority that pushed me further while his fingers still worked my clit, knowing how much I needed his touch in order to fall to ruin.

Using his shoulders as leverage, I guided his cock, working my body so he slid in and out of my wetness as I used him as my own personal dildo.

Though it had been simmering near the surface, my orgasm slammed into me hard enough to cause me to cry out, and I gasped his name in a long, drawn out moan. Pleasure coursed through my body with more strength than I'd ever felt before, and I quaked visibly as my forehead dropped to Caleb's shoulder. It felt like it would never end as I soared sky high. It was earth-shattering, in the best way possible.

Caleb placed both hands on my hips, flipping me onto my back, and I lifted my legs, pulling my knees up to his shoulders and locking my ankles as he slammed back into me. My thighs gripped his sides, holding on as he pounded into me with intensity.

Long strokes tempted my body again as he withdrew his smooth cock, brushing against my sensitive clit. The angle hit me perfectly as Caleb chased his release, the veins in his forearm rippling as he held his body over me.

I couldn't help but run my hand over one of his arms, my thumb brushing against the protruding vein. Why was that so damn sexy?

"I'm keeping you," he growled against my neck. I shivered from his words, and fought against the feeling battling in my chest.

Love.

I didn't dare say it, not out loud, but even to myself, I wanted to deny it. There were still so many unanswered questions. So many things I needed to learn about him before I could surrender to that admission.

We locked eyes, his gaze darkening to an expression that was hard to read. Pulling out with sudden, harsh movements, he yanked my ankles apart and my feet fell to the mattress. Watching him gaze down at my pussy with an unabashed look of desire, a flare of exhilaration spiked in me.

"Spread your legs wide, baby. I'm hungry." He licked his lips and guided my hand between my legs, placing it against my wet center. I propped myself up on one elbow to reach where he was tugging my hand. "Let me see you, Isla."

I knew instantly what he was asking for, the act making me feel so vulnerable, but at the same time I had never felt so sexy, so desired. Exhaling, I moved my fingers to spread myself for him.

The way Caleb was looking at me was indescribable. It urged me to continue, and I drew my fingers into the wetness between my thighs.

Lowering himself onto his stomach, Caleb leaned in, drawing his tongue flat against my pussy.

"Oh my god," I gasped, dropping my body onto the mattress. My hands were flailing around the bed, looking for something to grab on to while he thrust his tongue into me, only to pull it back out and run its tip along my clit. He repeated the movements, and I writhed beneath him, hardly able to catch my breath.

"Holy shit, Caleb. I can't. *I can't*," I whimpered, the stimulation so overwhelming, it felt as though I'd black out from his sweet torment.

With smoldering eyes, Caleb released my clit with a slight pop from the suction of his mouth, and firmly held my gaze. "You can, and you will. Come on my tongue, Isla. Let me drink you up."

His words and the incredible pressure he applied on my clit again were my undoing and I came instantly, moaning loudly into my darkened bedroom. My body lifted from the bed as he pulsated my clit with his mouth and plunged two fingers into me. His fingers curled, hitting my G-spot, and I thrashed beneath him, grasping at my sheets in a frenzy. "Oh my god," I whined, arching my back to push further into his face, but he refused to stop, pumping his fingers relentlessly while licking up every ounce of desire he pulled from my body.

When my back finally dropped to the bed, Caleb removed his fingers and kneeled on the bed in front of where I laid lifeless, in a bliss-filled daze. "On your knees, baby," he commanded, and despite my state of reverie, I pulled myself to a seated position and pushed onto my knees. "If it's too much, I want you to pinch me, okay? Reach up and pinch my arm, pinch my thigh. It doesn't matter what. Just make sure you tell me to stop if I start to hurt you."

"I'll be fine," I promised, reaching for his cock and guiding it to my lips. His fist wrapped around the base of his cock as I pushed forward, easing him into my mouth until he hit the back of my throat. My lips wrapped around him, creating a deep suction and I slowly pulled backward, stopping at his engorged head so I wouldn't release him fully.

"God damn, you're such a dirty fucking slut, aren't you? Look at the way your plump little lips wrap around my cock —how you suck me perfectly." He grabbed my hair and circled his wrist, wrapping the loose tendrils around his hand. Tugging it roughly, he pulled my mouth away from his cock and forced me to look up at him. "I'm going to fuck your gorgeous face now, okay? Hold on to the backs of my thighs—this shouldn't take long."

My lips barely parted before he pushed his length into my mouth, sliding in swiftly and hitting the back of my throat without warning. I gagged on reflex, the burn of my throat forcing tears to spring to my eyes. He pulsated his hips, not giving me much time to adjust before his thrusts became hurried and purposeful, using my mouth to get himself off.

I continued to fight against my gag reflex and relaxed my throat, hollowing out my cheeks. I strained to breathe through my nose, finding it hard to concentrate on breathing at all when I was so focused on Caleb's actions. After a few seconds, it became much easier to take him and I was able to reach back up and wrapped my hand around his shaft. I stroked him the best I could, keeping in time with his every thrust.

"*Fuckkkkk*," he groaned, moving the hand in my hair to

grip the hair at the back of my head instead. He used it to guide my motions, sliding my mouth along his cock exactly how he wanted against my tongue and into my throat. He became completely unhinged, the string of moans and grunts spurring me to readjust, situating back on my heels to give me mobility of my free hand. Reaching up, I cupped his balls and gently massaged them.

"I'm so close, Isla. So fucking close."

Reading the signs of his body, both of my hands moved to his butt, using my hold to thrust deeper and faster into my mouth, doing my best to swirl my tongue and hold suction. A jolt of pleasure pulsated in my clit, so turned on by the way he was using my body.

Caleb came with a roar, holding my head firm while I swallowed him down. My tongue lapped against the underside of his cock, trying to pull every last drop of pleasure from his body. His muscles flexed beneath my grasp, his chest heaving as he came down from his orgasm.

When he finished, he released the rough hold he had on me and pulled me into his arms, pulling us down to the soft linens while we continued to catch our breath together.

I turned into him, and he peppered my cheek and neck with soft kisses while pulling the blanket over both of us. A lazy smile tugged at my lips, my eyes growing heavy. Catching my mouth, Caleb slipped his tongue between my lips and kissed me with a sweet passion that made my heart flip-flop, that four letter word popping into my head again.

Stretching one arm beneath me, Caleb scooped me into his side, bending his other arm behind his head to stretch out. "Damn," he breathed. "I could taste both of us on your tongue."

"I kind of like it," I admitted, hoping the darkness hid

the blush creeping onto my cheeks at my admission. It felt dirty to say, but it was true.

"I fucking *love* it."

Love. My heart soared, and I wondered if maybe my thoughts weren't too off base after all. If he was feeling what I was feeling... It was still too early to say it out loud, but I had a feeling in my soul that saying those eight letters out loud might not be too far off for us.

With Caleb, I was exactly who I wanted to be. I wasn't the spoiled rich girl who was now pathetically broke. I wasn't the puppet my father saw me as, or the disobedient daughter my mother accused me of being.

I was just me.

Isla.

And for the first time, I was finally able to like the woman who'd been forced to hide her true self.

CHAPTER SEVENTEEN

CALEB

I smelled like her.

The sweet scent of vanilla and sex permeated the air around me as I lay in Isla's bed with my hands locked behind my head, elbows outstretched.

Isla had fussed over me, making a show of tucking me into her bed—she *actually* pushed the blankets under my body so I was secured in a cocoon of warmth—before she hurried off into the kitchen to make us something to eat. My stomach rumbled embarrassingly loud, interrupting our after-sex bliss as we laid in a heap of tangled limbs.

As she walked out of the room, it almost felt like she took my heart with her.

She was just a few feet away, but having her out of my sight and not next to me ripped a possessive gut reaction through me and I wasn't sure what to make of it. Mostly, I had been the guy in the background, the wallflower, watching everyone around me date and play the field, but I always refrained, never having the urge to bring someone else into my mess.

College had opened up doors in the beginning—I wasn't ashamed I had pushed off my metaphorical wall and gone a little crazy getting my dick wet. How could I not succumb to temptation when women suddenly flocked to me and showed me attention? For once, I wasn't being ignored.

Apparently, I had a 'bad boy' appeal that made college women a little feral.

I didn't tell them this 'bad boy' was actually a *nobody* who had zero fucks to give and was just trying to survive. They didn't care for my backstory anyway, so why wouldn't I try to find some sort of comfort, balls deep in a willing woman or two?

Point was, when I was around Isla, I felt a sense of contentment I hadn't felt in years.

Meaningless hookups never equated to anything more than plugging a phone number into my phone and empty promises to call when I wouldn't. Getting their numbers was just standard procedure. They didn't actually expect me to call, and they didn't really want me to either.

I couldn't remember the last time a woman had cared for me—*hell*, the last time anyone had cared for me—and it felt good, even if it was just a simple act of making sure I was comfortable in her bed.

Shit, she even cared enough to undress me once she realized I was soaked from the rain, and immediately led me to a hot shower to warm up.

Being cared for felt good. It felt better than good. It felt like I didn't want to take it for granted or lose it.

Isla deserved more than a guy like me, but I would do everything I could to keep her and never make her feel the doubt she had earlier today.

I was such a fucking idiot. We were still in the getting-to-know-you phase. The no-label, therefore, no reassurance phase. I should have realized insecurities would surface and doubt would set in. She didn't fully trust me yet, and honestly, for good reason.

She didn't know the things I hid from her.

The insecurities and fears I pushed down to hide deep within me.

If she knew, she'd leave.

Because with the Hart men, history seemed to repeat itself with every generation.

I've vowed to break the cycle, and never become like them, but the thought that I *could* still kept me in a chokehold.

A CRASH of thunder rattled through the apartment, jolting me awake. My eyes snapped open as a burst of light illuminated the room, feeling dangerously close as the storm raged just outside the window. Isla stirred slightly, scooting closer to me and nuzzling into my side further.

So far, sleeping next to her had been the most restful night's sleep I'd had in as long as I could remember. When she was next to me, there were no fitful bouts of tossing and turning, and the nightmares were suppressed. It felt incredible to wake—even if it was only after a short sleep—without a sheen of sweat coating my body and my heart racing. The nightmares weren't a nightly occurrence, but the number of times I'd dreamt of blood was alarming—even for someone who wanted to work on crime scenes.

As my eyes adjusted to the darkness, I craned my head to check the time. The small clock on the bedside table read four in the morning and, as I yawned, I noticed the plate sitting next to the clock. Curiosity and hunger egged me on, and without disturbing Isla, I pulled the arm I had wrapped beneath her free and turned, edging closer to see what she had made.

I was so irritated with myself. She had gone through the trouble of cooking something for me, and I had fallen asleep before she even made it back into the room. What had she even thought at that moment? Had she laughed or been upset?

Picking up the plate, I brought it to my lap as another burst of lightning illuminated the room, giving me a brightened view of the food.

Grilled cheese. She had made me a grilled cheese sandwich.

This woman was fucking *perfection*.

Picking up half, I shoved most of it into my mouth, stifling a groan at its deliciousness. It didn't matter if the sandwich was cold; the savory taste of butter and cheese exploded on my tongue. It tasted like heaven.

After practically swallowing the first half of the sandwich whole, I reached for the other and started eating it, forcing myself to savor the second half. If it tasted this good cold, I could only dream of what it tasted like straight from the pan. Isla was a grilled cheese Master Chef, and I made a mental note to beg her to make me another on a day I wasn't likely to pass out before it was ready.

Shamelessly, I licked my fingers after swallowing the last bite, wishing there was more of it, and looking around the room as though another plate would magically appear. It didn't, but now that I knew my girl was a grilled cheese wizard, I'd be begging her to make them for me all the time.

The small sandwich did little to satisfy my hunger, but it'd hold me over until morning. I wonder if she could make French toast, too?

As my mind went down the food rabbit hole, an idea popped into my head—a way to thank her. I reached over and patted the surface of the nightstand, looking for my phone before I realized I'd never brought it into the room.

Kicking my legs over the bed as carefully as I could so I didn't disturb Isla, I pushed my feet to the floor, standing. A feminine squeak caught my attention before I could take my first step and I looked back to find Isla with her arms outstretched in the air, stretching and scrunching her nose and eyes as she woke up.

"Where are you going?" she asked, her voice thick with sleep. She dropped her arms back onto the bed next to her before curling to her side and cracking open her eyes to look at me.

Her dark hair fanned out behind her as she rested her head on her hands, pressed together between her head and her pillow as though she were praying. She was so effortlessly beautiful, even when I could hardly see her through the darkness.

Pressing my palms to the bed, I leaned forward and kissed her forehead. "Just looking for my phone so I can set an alarm for the morning."

"I already plugged it in; it's next to the lamp on the nightstand. And I set an alarm on my phone. I have class in the morning, remember? So do you." She ended her sentence with a yawn, her eyes falling shut. "Come back to bed."

A feeling I wasn't ready to accept shot through my chest like a bullet, piercing my heart as it burst throughout my entire body.

Climbing beneath the covers, I pulled her close and tucked her into my side. Her smooth leg wrapped around mine and I felt the hem of the t-shirt she wore bunched around her hips. *My t-shirt.* Unable to resist, I pulled up the blankets and snuck a look at the goddess next to me, and as suspected, she looked sexy as sin in my shirt.

But... how was she wearing my t-shirt if it had been wet when I got here? It couldn't have dried out so quickly.

Staring into the darkness, I thought back through the night and tried to figure out how my shirt could have dried so fast. It didn't seem plausible... I had left it sitting on the floor. I shook my head, struggling to wrap my mind around all the minor details she seemed to think of for me.

"How—" I began to ask, but stopped, hearing soft snores coming from Isla. She had fallen asleep again. It could wait until morning.

Settling into the pillows, I listened to the orchestra of sounds surrounding me as Isla slept soundly and the thunder rumbled outside, drifting further away as I willed sleep to take me again so I could get a few hours in before I woke early to make my girl coffee and breakfast in bed.

CHAPTER EIGHTEEN

ISLA

"Shit, shit, *shit*!" I cursed under my breath, staggering out of bed and running over to my dresser. My fingers curled around the knobs as I yanked it open, pulling out clean panties and socks before slamming it shut.

Caleb yawned loudly behind me. The sound of the mattress springs whined softly as he shifted to sit up. "What's wrong?" he asked, groggy from being woken abruptly.

I fumbled through another drawer, looking for the jeans I needed for the outfit I'd planned in my head.

Dark wash jeans, cream sweater, black leather Moto jacket, black booties.

Except my dark wash jeans were nowhere to be found, and my drawer was filled with light wash denim, black denim, and leggings, instead. I was already running late as I scanned the room, looking for the jeans I *swore* I had folded and placed in my drawer. My eyes connected with Caleb's as he watched me from his spot in my bed.

"I can tell you want to say something," I commented.

"Just say it." Annoyance sat heavy on my chest. I reminded myself it wasn't Caleb's fault I didn't get up in time. I'm the one who hit the snooze button on three different alarms, four times each.

"You're cute when you're frantic," he quipped in a playful tone.

Swinging his legs over the bed, he stood, coming to stand by my side. Caging me against my dresser, he leaned down to my ear, his hot breath sending a shiver through my body. "Skip your class. Come back to bed."

"I can't skip my class! I skipped a class yesterday! Plus, there's only two days left before break. I have to go."

Caleb nuzzled his nose against my cheek, guiding the soft point over my skin. "Do you though? There's *only* two days left before break. I bet tons of people won't be in class today."

His warm breath rushed against my skin again and ignited my body like a match lighting a candle. I could feel my resolve crumbling with every passing moment, my body charged and desperate to feel his touch again.

"I have to go," I whispered, more to convince myself than him. My eyes snapped shut, and I felt my breathing grow labored as desire pooled low in my belly.

I was so attracted to Caleb even just being in close proximity to him turned me on. He had barely touched me —his touch hadn't even been sexual—yet here I was, giving him 'fuck me' eyes and panting while we stood chest to chest.

"If you have to go to class, you'll need your supplies," he drawled, swiping the pens I had on my dresser, pushing them to the floor. They scattered in disarray, two landing next to my foot, while another flew halfway across the room.

"Oops." His voice feigned innocence, but the smirk on his face was anything but.

Dropping to one knee, Caleb acted like he was reaching for the pens. He looked up at me sinfully, his tongue darting out to wet his lips. Placing my hands on my hips, I quirked a brow and turned to step away, but he caught my ankle and brought it back to the floor.

Propping one elbow on his bent knee, Caleb started dragging his fingertips slowly up the inside of my bare leg, beginning at where he held my ankle and traveling north. He looked like he had all the time in the world as he held my gaze, torturing me with the smallest of touches.

My heart was wild in my chest, beating erratically as I watched, and I found it hard to swallow. Once he finally reached my thigh, my breathing hitched completely—sweet anticipation building deep in my core.

I wore only his t-shirt I had pulled from the dryer last night, and nothing else. Once his hand slipped under the hem, I knew I was a goner. Wetness seeped out of me, dripping between my thighs—a mixture of mine and his. I shifted on my feet, fighting the urge to press my legs together.

"Everything okay, Starlight? You seem a little flushed." He removed his fingertips from my thigh, toying with the hem of my—*his*—shirt instead.

I inhaled a shaky breath, composing myself as much as possible before I answered. "Perfectly fine, thanks. You're the one who's taking a while to clean up his mess. Are *you* okay?" I did my best to make my voice sound playful with a hint of sarcasm, but it came out strained and shaky.

Caleb's eyes sparkled with mischief and he tapped two fingers against my thigh, pursing his lips like he was really thinking about my words. Slowly, he nodded his head. "You know what, Starlight? You're right. I am taking way too long to clean up my mess." On the same breath, he gripped the hem of my shirt, pulling it up to my stomach, as his mouth descended on my slick pussy, licking through my folds. Sucking in a harsh breath, I threw my head back and let out a gargled moan. His tongue swirled around my opening, lapping at my pussy before flicking his tongue against my pulsating clit.

"Caleb," I moaned, reaching down to fist his hair. "Caleb, seriously... I... don't have... time."

"You're already too late to go," he declared, still torturing my clit with the tip of his tongue.

The harsh movements did wicked things to my body and, faster than I thought possible, I could feel the tingles of my orgasm building. My hips rocked into his face, chasing the pleasure he was gifting me with his tongue.

Pulling back abruptly, he let the shirt drop from his hold, and lifted my ankle, guiding my foot to his bent knee. Through hooded eyes, I watched him trace light circles around my calf, teasing my sensitive skin. My knees practically buckled at the mental image of him, finger fucking me while his tongue was on my clit. He knew exactly the effect he had on my body, figuring out just how to tease me, and exactly what got me off.

As if he were reading my thoughts, Caleb's right hand came to rest on the back of my thigh, holding me in place, while his two fingers on his opposite hand slid into me effortlessly. I jolted at the intrusion, but mild surprise quickly morphed into elation. A wistful sigh passed through my lips as I moaned, shamelessly rocking my body against his hand.

Slowly he withdrew his fingers entirely, before pushing them back into me and curling upward, caressing my walls torturously. Reaching down, I crossed my arms to grip the hemline before tugging it over my head and tossing it to the floor. Watching him pleasure me was such a turn on, I didn't want to miss a second of it, hidden beneath clothing.

Caleb groaned, staring up at me as he tongued my clit. Completely naked before him, I cupped my breasts, massaging them as his fingers worked me, scissoring within me as I shamelessly rode his hand. The sensations made my body tingle, but still, it wasn't enough. He'd ruined me with his cock, and as good as his fingers felt, I wanted *more*.

"Add another," I commanded, feeling my body escalate.

He obliged, slipping a third finger in. I cried out, bucking against him, thankful for his grip on my thigh and the dresser behind my back or I would have fallen from the lack of stability. The rapid soar of pleasure made me lightheaded, my vision blurring as a string of unintelligible curses and moans flew out of my mouth.

I wasn't ready when my climax hit violently, much faster than I expected, and I screamed—*I actually fucking screamed.* My soul felt like it left my body, hovering above me, as Caleb finger fucked and tongued me through my free fall. He moved his hand to push against my hip, pinning me in place against the dresser, letting me ride out my orgasm for as long as possible, only relenting when he felt my body shudder. I went limp against the dresser, only held up by his hands, as my chest heaved.

A sheen of sweat layered my skin, and I felt like I had just finished running a marathon I hadn't trained for.

Was I about to have a heart attack?

What a way to go.

Caleb withdrew his fingers, unabashedly licking them clean as he stood. His cock bobbed with his movement, painfully erect and begging for its own release, but Caleb seemed unfazed as he closed the gap between us and kissed me hard.

"You're insatiable," I muttered, smiling with his lips against mine. My fingers reached between us and curled around his shaft, feeling precum leak from the tip as I grazed it with my thumb.

"Stop being so damn delicious, then." Caleb kissed me again, distracting me as he positioned his hand on top of mine, uncurling my fingers and dropping my hand away from him. He wrapped his arm around the back of my waist, pulling me with him as he took a step backward.

Spinning me toward my closet, he pushed me forward gently, slapping my ass as I took a stumbled step forward. "Go get dressed. You're late for class."

I tossed my hands in the air, groaning as I kept walking. "You're impossible," I called, louder than I needed to. He was still practically right behind me, pulling on his briefs and pants I had waiting for him on the small chair by my bedroom window.

"I'm pretty sure I warned you about that, Starlight. It's not my fault you didn't listen."

"It's not too late for me to start," I mused, thumbing through the sweaters hanging neatly in color order. Pulling the cream one from its hanger, I flipped it in my hands, about to pull it on when Caleb crowded my space from behind. His erection dug into my back as his arm wrapped around the front of my chest, his hand curling up around my throat. His fingers brushed my jawline as he tilted my head backward and pressed his lips against my ear.

"Oh, it's definitely too late. I warned you if we started something, I'd never let you go. Did you think I was lying?"

"I thought I got to decide what was best for me?" I goaded, my mind thinking back to one of our previous conversations.

Caleb turned me slowly, using the hand holding my jaw to guide me to face him. "You do."

Releasing his hold, he leaned forward and brushed his lips against mine in the softest of kisses before he pulled away and bent slightly to lift me up. With one arm placed firmly just below my ass, he tossed me over his shoulder so I was upside down, giving me the perfect view of his as he walked me across the room.

"Good," I quipped, laughing. His hands shifted up to my hips, and I knew he was about to toss me onto my bed, but before he could, I added, "Because I think I'll keep you, too."

When he stopped in front of the bed, he gripped my ass with his free hand and squeezed the plump flesh. Hard.

Asshole.

My face didn't reflect the sentiment, though, because my mouth felt like it was about to split open from how wide my smile was.

CHAPTER NINETEEN

Eight long classes, and we were finally on break. The weekend felt like it sped by, racing alarmingly fast to when I'd have to see my parents. I was dreading it, but the time spent with Caleb helped to calm my nerves.

It had only been a week since the night Caleb walked to my house in the rain, and our relationship had only become stronger. He stayed at my apartment every night and parted ways only when it was absolutely necessary to get to work. Everything was perfect between us and, for the time being, I buried the little voice in my head still insisting he was keeping something from me.

Warm sunshine engulfed my bed, making it harder to find the will to get up and start my day. I was so cozy when I cracked my eyes open, finding Caleb propped up on his elbow and watching me sleep.

"Morning," I croaked with a yawn, stretching my arms out in front of me. "Watching me sleep, like a creeper again?"

"How could I resist? You look so peaceful when you're asleep. It's a beautiful thing to watch."

"You know what's even more beautiful? Sleeping in. You should try it sometime."

He laughed and tugged at my hips, rolling me on top of him. Coming to my knees, I leaned over him and kissed the tip of his nose, my dark hair blanketing around us.

"I want to ask you something, but it's probably going to sound a little juvenile." Caleb pushed a piece of my hair behind my ear and cradled my cheek against his palm. "I know I was hesitant to start anything in the beginning, but I'm all in now and the thought of you with anyone else makes me want to slam my fist against glass and welcome the pain of it cutting my skin. I want to lock you down, Starlight. Can we agree to be exclusive?"

The cheesiest smile painted across my face and I nodded a little too eagerly, watching as his smile matched mine. "Are you asking me to be your girlfriend, Caleb?"

"Yeah, Starlight, I am." He bucked his hips upward, rocking against my core.

It was so sweet, and so unexpected. Never did I imagine I'd hear Caleb ask me to be his girlfriend; I just assumed we would continue down the path we were and our relationship status would fall into place–becoming mutually exclusive but never discussing it. My heart was already his. A new link added to the chain connecting it to him with every kiss, smile, and silent expression of his feelings he gave me. I knew I was knocking down his walls without even trying; he showed me a bigger piece of himself every day, and I could feel his hesitancy lessening. This was unfamiliar territory for both of us. But there was no one else I would rather explore it with.

As I lost myself in thought, Caleb trailed his fingers against my bare thighs, traveling upward and grazing the fabric of my panties. His knuckles stroked my center, building me up while I bit my lip and acted as though I was debating his offer.

Pushing my panties to the side, Caleb traced his finger against my pussy, finding me already wet for him. He pulled the wetness to my clit, orbiting his touch. "What's it going to be, Starlight? Will you be mine?"

The head of his cock nudged at my entrance, and I reached down, taking the base of him in my hand and lining him up perfectly.

"What if I fall?" I asked, barely above a whisper. I knew I couldn't protect my heart much further, my love for him already spiraling and burning brighter with each passing day. If I fell in love with him—*fully* fell in love with him—and he changed his mind about us and walked away, I'd be devastated. More than devastated.

Caleb pushed up, supporting himself with his palms against the bed, pulling me into a breathtakingly deep kiss. My heart flatlined. With Caleb, anytime his lips were on mine, my mind stopped working and my heart took over all thoughts, decisions, and logic.

Without breaking the kiss, I sank down, taking his cock inch by inch until I reached the hilt, fully seated around him. Wrapping my arms around his neck, I held him close as we kissed—making out with a feverish passion while we connected our bodies in every way possible.

Our lips parted, pausing only so we could catch a breath.

"You're all that matters to me, Isla. I'm already falling, so if you fall too, I'll catch you. No matter what."

PULLING up to the front of my parents' elaborate home on Thanksgiving made a lump form in my throat. Nestled in a lavish mountainside suburb on the edge of Ridgewood, the neighborhood was gated with an electric fence and around the clock security who sat in the guard stand, constantly looking bored out of their minds. Houses sat an acre or more apart, and had long, extravagant driveways serving as a paved version of a red carpet, introducing guests to the ostentatious homes at the end of them.

The term *home* loosely described my parents' house, which was emptier than a crumpled can of Coke at a barbecue, both in love and occupants. Despite the full staff that maintained the appearance of the property and the *comforts* of their lifestyle, it was the loneliest place I had ever stepped foot into. If walls could talk, they'd have some stories. The tragic tales of three people sharing a roof: the villain who hated his own child because of what was—*or wasn't, rather*—between her legs, the clueless not-so-step mother who stuck her head in the sand and pretended like everything was just perfect so she could maintain her glamorous lifestyle, and the heroine who dreamed of breaking free, determined to write her own story one day. Preferably one with a happy ending.

Parking my Mercedes next to my father's red Bugatti—because why wouldn't he have a car that screamed *giant asshole*—I killed the engine and sat for a moment to calm my nerves. I had desperately wanted to bring Caleb home for Thanksgiving just to spite my family and my father's request to 'dress to impress' a guy he intended to set me up with, no doubt for the sake of a business deal, but bringing him would have been a disaster I wasn't ready for. I already had news to break to my father, and I didn't need to add more fuel to the fire. My father wasn't exactly the type to filter his thoughts, and there was not a shred of doubt in my mind he was going to hate Caleb simply because of his socio-economic background.

The sudden rap of fingers against my window made me jump. My hand flew up to my chest, and I craned my neck to see who had made me almost pee my pants. Unsurprisingly, Bernard, my parents' eyes and ears of the property, stood by the driver's side door. His head dipped down to look at me through the window.

Bernard was in his mid-sixties and had been working for my parents since my father formed his company, acting as my father's private security detail, though it wasn't a position that was necessary. As Bernard entered his fifties, he requested a change in job location—no longer interested in following my father around like a puppy—and became stationary to the house, providing security on the property.

In short, Bernard was a glorified butler, though the grumpy ass would never admit it.

Luckily for me, grumpy ol' Bernard always had a soft spot for the ignored little girl who floated around the house like a ghost, unseen by her parents. I caught glimpses of his gooey interior when he felt obligated to act as a father figure, stepping into the role whenever necessary. Though now as an adult, I realized it was probably less out of the goodness of his heart and more because he was getting paid to be there.

Nevertheless, Bernard was the one who patched up my scraped knees when I'd fallen off my bike, which he taught me how to ride when my father was stuck in board meetings and my mother was shopping or at the spa. He also taught me how to drive a car, and the basics of self-defense. It was apparent Bernard cared about me, even if he actively tried not to show it.

Reaching for the door handle, I opened it and stepped out of the car. My cream colored Jimmy Choo patent leather classic pumps touched the pavers and Bernard reached his hand forward, offering it to me for assistance.

"Hello Miss Donohue, Happy Thanksgiving," he greeted through gritted teeth as I placed my hand in his and pulled myself from the car, grabbing my clutch from the passenger seat as I did.

Great, something was wrong already. Bernard was practically immune to my father's behavior, so him being irritated was never a good sign.

Letting go of his hand to adjust my sweater dress, I sighed dramatically, already reverting back to old habits after barely stepping foot on the property. "What do I need to know, Bernard?"

Rounding the car, he popped open my trunk, expecting to grab an overnight bag, but it was empty. His brows furrowed with confusion, and he looked at me through narrowed eyes. "Not staying, Miss Donohue?" He knew damn well I always went into a Thanksgiving food coma after dinner and would stay the night, retreating to my old bedroom where I'd fall asleep, stuffed beyond belief, to a Hallmark Christmas Movie.

Everyone knows as soon as Thanksgiving dinner is finished, it's immediately Christmas.

Slowly, I shook my head. "No," I stated simply. "There's no reason to when I live less than thirty minutes away. I'd prefer my Christmas movie at home this year."

At home, in my own bed, naked, with Caleb by my side.

I didn't tell Bernard that though, but as he eyed me skeptically, I could tell he had something he wanted to say but was holding his tongue.

My phone vibrated inside my clutch as I sauntered to the front doors of the eight bedroom, two-story mansion. Unzipping the clutch as I walked, I pulled my phone out, my eyes bouncing over the message I received.

> Happy Thanksgiving, Starlight. I hope all
> the fancy food you eat today is as delicious
> as you are.

My mother's shrill screech cut through my inner voice as I read the message, my dopey smile quickly fading as I shoved my phone back in my clutch.

"Isla!" she gushed, sashaying as she walked over to me with her arms open like she gave a shit. "How are you, darling?"

"Fine," I replied mildly, extending my arms to embrace her in a hug. My mother patted my back the same way someone would pat a dog on the head before pulling away. "How are you, mother?"

"Doing just fine, keeping busy with my garden club and our HOA. Did you hear they appointed me as HOA president now?"

I hadn't, but it didn't surprise me one bit. Samantha Donohue took on as many extracurriculars as she could to elevate her social standing.

She always pulled her platinum-dyed hair in a perfect twisted chignon, not a flyaway or frizz in sight, and her makeup was the epitome of flawless—worn day and night. There wasn't a time I could remember my mother fresh-faced and makeup free. And in true, wealthy housewife fashion, there wasn't a board or society she didn't work toward becoming a high-ranking member of, nor a brunch she didn't attend.

Now, ask me how many important events for *me* she'd attended over the years.

"Nope, I hadn't. How exciting for you." My tone was bland, but she didn't notice as she turned on her heel and began telling me every detail about her "stressful journey" to becoming HOA president. I followed her, stepping over the threshold to my childhood house. I inhaled a sharp breath, instantly being transported back in time.

"What good is she, Samantha? I needed a male to carry on my company's legacy. A son. But instead, we have a daughter."

"Why can't she? This isn't the 1950s, Andrew. There is absolutely no reason why Isla can't receive the same training—"

"You honestly expect a female to be taken seriously in a board-room full of men?"

"By the time she's old enough to take over Skyline, there may very well be a woman or two on the board. Won't that help her? To be taken more seriously?"

The room fell silent, and I pressed my ear against the wall harder, straining to hear the rest of the conversation, but my father had stopped talking. Tears pricked my eyes, my fourteen-year-old heart racing. It didn't matter how many times they had the same fight, or how many times I had overheard it, it still pierced like a knife through the heart every time my father expressed his disdain. It was bad enough he barely gave me the time of day, but for him to be so open about it...

"And if there isn't a woman or two on the board?" My father's voice echoed through the wall, questioning my mother's suggestion.

"Then you appoint a few women and accept the fact that you

have a daughter, not a son. She's a bright girl, Andrew. Beautiful, smart. You can train her just as you would have trained a son."

Pushing off the wall, I stumbled back in the dark, before falling onto the plush down comforter on my bed. I didn't want to hear anymore. I couldn't. His hate for me spewed like venom and I hated him for it. I would never take over his stupid company. I would rather die.

Slithering under the covers, I laid on my back, tucking my arms beneath my pillow, and fell asleep crying.

Nausea encircled my stomach and I could feel bile rise in my esophagus, the memory throwing me back into a time where I felt helpless and insecure. My father was never cruel enough to belittle me to my face, but I was confident he knew the walls were thin enough for his voice to carry. He was a smart man.

It had been nearly nine months since I had stepped foot in this house.

Nine months wasn't nearly long enough.

"Sweetheart, did you hear me?" my mother questioned as her pointed toe Valentino flats tapped lightly against the marbled floors. Her manicured hand rested against her hip, popped slightly as she looked at me with annoyance. "I asked you if you were excited to meet Blake Bradley. Your father and I just adore him. He'd be a wonderful candidate for you."

Not friend.

Not boyfriend.

Not lover.

Candidate.

As though my life was a transaction, or a job position that had an opening.

Fire licked my insides, rage rearing its ugly head. "Candidate for what, mother?" I asked, with innocence. We were still standing in the foyer, already facing off before I had even set my clutch down.

She waved her hand dismissively. "For marriage, of course! You're twenty-two now, Isla. It's time to think about these things. You have your entire life ahead of you but without a clear path... Well, what's the point? A young woman needs to have a plan."

"Yikes," I muttered under my breath as I plastered on the fakest smile I could. "It's not like you and father don't already have a plan for me," I rebutted, trying to keep my hands from forming into fists at my sides. "If it's all the same to you, mother, I'd like to go set my purse down and grab a glass of water. Could we chat later?"

"Of course, darling. Go rest, the Bradleys will be here in about an hour and a half. Our waitstaff will serve dinner at six o'clock sharp."

I nodded curtly and placed my hand on the banister, readying myself to go upstairs. Mid step, my mother's voice called to me again.

"Oh, and Isla? Your father is in his office. He's not to be disturbed."

Um, okay. Speaking to him was the last thing I wanted to do right now, anyway.

With a curt nod, I wordlessly made my way upstairs, letting my feet guide me to my old bedroom. As I turned the doorknob, I expelled a shaky breath and entered, relieved to be amongst things that once brought me joy. My room was exactly how I left it, except for the items I deemed important enough to take with me.

CHAPTER TWENTY

ISLA

I don't think I'll survive the next few hours.

Not only do I think you'll survive, I'm
counting on it. I'm ready to be back at your
place.

I told you to just stay there while I was
gone.

You could be searching through my
underwear drawer right now. What a
missed opportunity.

You're right, that was stupid on my part.
Rookie mistake.

I had to go home, though. Check on my
pops. It is Thanksgiving, after all.

I guess you're right. That's why I'm here, at
hell on earth.

It can't be that bad. Plush furniture, fancy
waitstaff, all the Thanksgiving fixings you
could want.

Turkey... mashed potatoes... pie...
mmmmmm.

> I'm looking forward to my tryptophan coma
> later on tonight. You'll watch a Hallmark
> Christmas movie with me, right?

Count me in for the Christmas movie, but
out for the Hallmark. Can't we just watch
Elf or something? It's a classic.

> A classic is White Christmas. Not Will
> Farrell dressed in an elf costume.

But the narwhal...

> Okay, fine. The narwal is the best part of
> the whole movie.

Oh, COME ON. The whole movie is the
best part of the whole movie.

> Eh.

Next you're going to tell me Die Hard isn't a
Christmas movie, aren't you?

> Well...

No.

Absolutely not.

Abort mission. Rewind. Delete, delete,
delete.

> I've actually never seen Die Hard, so it
> could persuade me.

Thank fuck for that.

> Gotta run. Time to pretend to be something
> I'm not. I'll message you when I'm
> leaving. X

"Ah! There she is," my father's voice boomed as I walked into the dining room ten minutes before six. Despite my early arrival, it appeared I was late. A table filled with food was the first thing I noticed; piping hot entrées and side dishes were placed perfectly across the span of the table, while each of the chairs was occupied, aside from mine. Faces I hadn't met stared at me with wonder, the men at the table sliding their chairs back and standing as I made my way further into the room. "This is my lovely daughter, Isla. Isla, the Bradleys."

"Hello," I said sweetly, tipping my head in greeting. Though my parents had been inattentive, they still found the time to drill me with manners and made sure I was the perfect daughter. Couldn't let me ruin their pristine reputations. Faking my life came so naturally while in these four walls, I had no trouble melting right back into the role they had molded me for.

"Isla, this is Steven, Claire, Levi, Willow, and next to you is Blake." My mother's hand fluttered toward each person as she spoke their name, giving me the rundown on who was who of the Bradley family. They were all gorgeous, and frankly, it was a little intimidating. They looked like the perfect family from the outside. Too good to be true.

They probably were.

Blake pulled my chair out for me and I sat, lifting myself slightly as he pushed me in. I smiled tightly and reached to pull my linen napkin into my lap.

The men took their seats again once I had settled. My father was in his normal seat at the head of the table, naturally, while my mother sat on his left, and Mrs. Bradley—Claire—sat next to her. The Bradley's daughter, Willow, sat between her mother and father—Steven—who sat at the opposite end of the table as my father. Rounding the table was Levi, their youngest son, Blake, and then me. Much to my dismay—but not surprise—I was also next to my father.

As if on cue, the waitstaff moved forward and removed the silver cloche covering the turkeys, serving small portions of each dish to our waiting plates.

"So, I'm thinking this is a setup," Blake whispered, leaning into me once the waitperson between us finished serving and walked away. His eyes were crystal blue, his light brown hair styled with a thin layer of product to keep from falling in his face. He wore navy blue smart pants paired with a white button-down shirt that had two buttons at the top popped open. No tie, no suit jacket. I liked that he went against the grain of what surely his parents expected of him, judging by his father and brother's attire. Still, he was no Caleb, and as stunning as his bright eyes and million-dollar smile were, I set my heart on a set of sinfully gorgeous chocolate brown eyes and a panty melting smirk.

There *was* a difference. Caleb had a whole vibe to him that made me weak in the knees.

"I think you may be right." My father caught my eye, watching mine and Blake's exchange.

When the servers retreated, my father clapped his palms together and stood again. "Steven, thank you and your beautiful family for joining us for Thanksgiving this year. We hope this is the first of many." My father looked at me as he ended his sentence, silently daring me to defy his words. He knew I wouldn't, but it still made me physically sick to know he was enjoying this. "Join me in a quick toast and then we can let the feast begin!"

He raised his glass of scotch. "To family, new friendships, and lasting partnerships."

"Here, here!" Steven replied animatedly, raising his own glass and tipping it in my father's direction.

All around the table, glasses clinked and sips were taken.

I downed my champagne, gulping it in one breath before setting the flute down on the table. I felt Blake's eyes on me, but he said nothing as he opted for his water glass instead.

A server rushed over and refilled my champagne flute. I smiled up at her as I picked it up. "Thank you. This will be my last. I'm driving."

"Of course, Miss."

"Please, begin," my father commanded, gesturing to the surrounding feast.

The kids wasted no time scooping up their forks and digging in, as the adults followed suit. Everything tasted delicious. Savory flavors from the turkey had me swallowing a groan as I dipped another bite into my cranberry sauce. My eyes fluttered closed as the tangy taste of cranberry with a hint of orange crossed with the salt that stood out from the turkey's seasonings.

Quiet chatter filled the air, everyone made small talk

amongst the table, talking about mundane things such as the weather and plans for the remaining holidays. At one point, Blake leaned toward me and asked if I'd like to take a walk with him between dinner and dessert. Against my better judgment, I agreed before shoving a large bite of stuffing into my mouth.

"So! Isla. Your father tells me you opted for Ridgewood U instead of an Ivy. That's awfully humble of you. What are you studying?" Steven asked with glee. His question seemed genuine, and for some reason, it unnerved me.

Looking down at my plate, I pushed food around with my fork, mixing the mashed potatoes with the green bean casserole. "I did," I replied, lifting my head in his direction and offering him a small smile. "Going to an Ivy didn't feel like it was the right path for me. Ridgewood University has been wonderful. I'm almost finished with my degree in business."

Steven patted the corners of his mouth with his napkin before placing it back in his lap. "Blake here is working on his degree in business communications at Yale. Aren't you, son?" A smile spread wide against Steven's face, pride radiating out of him.

Blake gave me a tight-lipped smile, embarrassment pouring out of him in waves. It was obvious what was happening here: Steven was serving his eldest son on a silver platter, hoping the next thing I would consume would be him.

See, my father thought I was a complete moron, but I had thought ahead and done my research the moment he uttered the name *Blake Bradley*.

Blake Bradley, the eldest son of Steven Bradley, founder and CEO of Interface Technologies, Inc., which, not so coincidentally, was Skyline Tech's biggest competitor. Twenty-two years old and about to graduate Yale University with a degree in Business Commutation and enough volunteer time at the local animal shelter he could have made a career out of it. Blake was the first in line to take over his father's company once his father stepped down from his position.

At least he was an animal lover.

The writing was on the wall for what our fathers were planning, and I just couldn't help but wonder if Blake knew of their scheming.

"Blake," I sing-songed, touching his forearm. I felt eyes drilling into me from both heads of the table, encouraging me to widen my fake smile. "I'm incredibly full and could use some movement. Are you ready for that walk?"

Setting his napkin down next to his plate, he stood, stepping away from his place at the table. "Absolutely," he said, pulling my chair out for me. I tossed my napkin on top of my plate, watching my mother cringe from my periphery. Blake offered me his arm, covering my hand with his as he pulled me away from the table and out of the dining room.

Once we were out of earshot, I expelled a huge breath, tugging at the neckline of my sweater dress.

"That room was stifling," he groaned as we walked to the French doors leading out to the back porch and down to the gardens. There was a bench where we could sit and talk. I had questions.

"It always is around the Donohues." Once we reached the bottom of the stairs, I removed my hand from his arm, sidestepping to put some distance between us. Keeping a close-proximity wasn't necessary.

"So Ridgewood U, huh?" he asked. "How'd you talk your father into that one?"

His tone was curious, but I knew better than to trust a rich boy right off the bat. I wouldn't be divulging any more information than was absolutely necessary to him. "It took a lot of persuading, but eventually it was a battle he chose not to fight. At the end of the day, a degree is just a piece of paper, right? Doesn't really matter where it came from."

"Doesn't it though?"

"Not when your path is already laid out."

He laughed, the deep chuckle floating into the night air. "Touché."

Taking a seat on the stone bench nestled between my mother's rose bushes, I decided to cut right to the chase. I'd already been here longer than I wanted and the pie hadn't even been served yet. If I had any shot of getting out of here and getting back to Caleb anytime soon, I needed to be the one to speed things up. And that started with finding out if my assumptions about this Thanksgiving dinner were correct. "Why are you here, Blake? Why is your family here? I have my theories, but I'd love to hear the truth. I'm assuming you know?"

He nodded, confirming they had filled him in on the matter.

So I was the only one left in the dark. Per usual.

"Skyline Tech and Interface Technologies are merging next summer. Our fathers are golfing buddies, despite their deep-rooted competitiveness toward each other. They came to the conclusion two heads are better than one and decided to merge. They plan on making a lot of changes together in an effort to catapult the company further."

"And you and I come into this how exactly?"

His eyes met mine. "Like I said, two heads are better than one. I could have sworn this was the twenty-first century but evidently being wealthy kicks you back a century or two. The short answer to your question, Isla, is our parents are trying to force us into marriage. My mother has already set aside my grandmother's wedding ring, all polished and ready to be slipped onto your finger."

A frustrated laugh bubbled out of me at the conclusion of his words. I knew it. I freaking *knew* it.

The final nail in the coffin of my father dictating every aspect of my life. So full of himself, he was trying to dictate who I *marry* too.

"This is the twenty-first century, Blake. While I'm sure you're a stand-up guy, I'm not interested in being someone's trophy wife or being told who I can or can't—wait a second. Why are you so calm about this? I get that you've had more time to digest it, but you can't possibly be interested in this arrangement? You don't even know me!"

Again, he laughed loudly. "Despite you being absolutely stunning—like, drop-dead gorgeous, honestly—I won't be marrying you. Truly, if I was interested in an arranged marriage, I wouldn't be disappointed about you crawling into my bed every night. But, as it is, I'm more of the 'never going to get married and will happily just stick his dick into whomever I please' type of guy. That, and I have no interest in being my father's puppet. What I am interested in, however, is taking over I.T., and unfortunately it means I have to act like I'm willing to do whatever it takes. At this time, whatever it takes—by my father's standards—is getting you to fall in love with me. Or at *least* agree to marry me."

"I don't agree to marry you."

"Excellent, because I don't want to marry you either, beautiful. But I wouldn't be opposed to taking the consummation part for a test drive." Blake waggled his eyebrows, but I didn't laugh. Too annoyed by this whole notion of my father forcing me into marriage. "Tough crowd," Blake muttered to himself.

"Sorry, I just learned my father's trying to sabotage my life even more than he already has over the last twenty-two years of my existence." Standing, I pulled up the sleeve of my dress to check the time on my diamond encrusted Rolex. It had been a Christmas gift from my parents when I was seventeen—an ostentatious substitution for actually spending time with me. "We should get back inside so we can eat our pie and I can get the hell out of here."

As I went to step away, Blake caught my elbow, turning me to face him. "I know you don't know me, but you can trust me when I say I won't be pursuing you. Whatever ideas our families have for us are just that. Ideas."

"Good, because I have a boyfriend and I have no plans on breaking things off with him for the sake of a company merger."

"Wouldn't dream of asking you to."

"I'm not going to ruin my relationship just because my father expects me to."

He looked down at his own timepiece before shoving his hands into his front pockets. Looking at me pointedly, Blake said, "And I'm not going to ruin the constant stream of pussy I have lined up at my beck and call. So don't stress, Isla. I want absolutely *nothing* from you."

"Good," I barked, crossing my hands over my chest. "Can we go inside now?"

Blake closed the distance between us, standing beside me with his arm bent, waiting for me to take it. "Let's get this night over with."

CHAPTER TWENTY-ONE

ISLA

The moment the Bradleys said goodnight, escorted out the door by Bernard, I slumped against the white leather couch of my parents' formal sitting room. Exhaustion settled deep within my bones and I dreaded the half an hour drive I had back to my apartment. All I wanted to do was kick off my shoes, change into comfortable pants, and sink into my soft bedding.

"What a wonderful evening!" my mother cooed to no one in particular, passing by the room I was in as she meandered up the staircase to the second floor.

My father poured himself another scotch, swirling the amber liquid gently in his glass, addressing me as he did. "I understand you're not staying in your old room tonight?" he asked, taking a sip.

"No, I'm going home tonight."

"This is your home," he stated blandly.

"This hasn't been my home for a long time," I muttered, more to myself than in answer to him. My voice wasn't quiet enough, and from across the dimly lit space I could see my father's eyes blaze with annoyance.

"You're telling me you feel more at home in a run-down, eight hundred square foot box than you do in the home you were raised in?" My father prowled across the room and came to stand directly in front of me. Instinctually, I sat up in my seat. "Why don't we go talk in my office, Isla?" His voice was commanding, unwavering. Normally I would have scurried to my feet to obey my father's orders, but the betrayal of his arranged marriage plan still burned brightly in my veins.

"No, father. I need to get on the road. If you have something you'd like to talk about, we can right here, before I leave, but I am really quite tired and have a thirty-minute drive." My heart beat wildly, my nerves racing. I couldn't believe I had just spoken to my father like that, and by the look on his face, he was surprised as well. He quickly morphed it into a look of impassiveness though, and continued.

"Very well. Your degree is almost finished, which means it's time to get serious about your training at Skyline. I trust that once you finish, you'll be moving out of your shack you call a home, and back in here? Because you do realize, Isla, once your degree is out of the way, my obligation to pay for your pathetic little apartment is over and without my monthly payments, you won't be able to afford the rent."

Heartache slammed into me, his words sinking in. Of course, I knew time was looming, but hearing them felt so much more real. I didn't want to leave my apartment, and I certainly wouldn't be moving back in here, but he was right. He committed to giving me just enough to get by on my own throughout the duration of my degree, but once I graduated, all bets were off.

Now, more than ever, I had to find a job. And quickly. One that could afford me to continue to live on my own, away from the rule of my tyrant father.

"Oh for God's sake, Andrew, just give her access to her trust fund and stop making her suffer," my mother chastised, rounding the banister and sashaying her way into the formal sitting room as though my father and I were having the most pleasant of conversations. She had changed out of the formal dress she had worn for the guests, and into a silk pajama set and matching robe—her hair and makeup still perfect.

"I don't want my trust fund," I snapped immediately. "What I want is to make my own choices. I want to live my life and pave my own way. I... I want to be a veterinarian."

Way to word vomit, Isla.

My palms turned clammy, and the already quiet room fell so silent you could hear a pin drop. *Real* vomit threatened to materialize.

Laughing with malice, my father shook his head slowly. With his arms crossed over his chest, he lifted one hand to rub his chin as he stared at me with scrutiny in his eyes. "A veterinarian? What makes you think you'd have any success with being a veterinarian? Stop being ridiculous, Isla. You're set up to run Skyline. And now, you'll be doing so with Blake Bradley by your side. You should be *thanking* me for the success and wealth I'm handing you on a silver platter. It goes so well with the silver spoon already in your mouth."

"Andrew!" my mother shrieked. Her hand flew up to clutch her necklace. She was sitting in the armchair across from me, her head bouncing between my father and I like she didn't know where to look, or whose side to take. I already suspected it wouldn't be mine. "Isla, your father is right. Your life is set up so beautifully now. You'll have it all, sweetheart. An established, successful company, a dashing husband if you marry Blake—"

"*When* she marries Blake," my father interjected. His eyes pinned me, narrowing into a glare. "Surprise, by the way. You're engaged."

"The hell I am," I spat back, rising to my feet. "You can't force me into marriage, father."

"It's already a done deal, Isla. The merge. The marriage. Everything is already in motion. You and Blake Bradley will run Skyline-Interface together—"

A gurgled gasp lurched from my throat, the puzzle pieces rapidly clicking together as I realized what this was all about. It had nothing to do with the companies merging or the Bradley family at all, but it had everything to do with my father's lack of confidence in me. "That's what this is all about. *Together.* You're setting everything up so there is a male as the face of your company after you step down. You don't want your daughter to run your company, so you're appointing yourself a son."

Sinking back down on the edge of the couch, I brought my hands to my face, covering my nose and mouth as I sat staring down at the intricate pattern of the area rug. My mind was reeling, trying to process everything I had learned tonight—everything my father had planned.

After several tense, soundless minutes, my mother spoke. At some point, she had moved to sit beside me on the couch, but I hadn't realized until she placed her hand on my knee. "Darling, this is good news. Running a company—it's a lot of work. With Blake in the picture, the stress won't just fall on your shoulders. You can make a difference together, as a team. Share the workload. And Blake comes from a great family. He's smart, driven, and is setting himself and his future family up for success too."

I snorted a laugh and stood, my feet moving me in the direction of where my clutch sat on a decorated credenza in the foyer. I had stashed it behind a large vase of roses from my mother's garden.

Bernard stood awkwardly by the front door, unknowing that when he walked back in after escorting the Bradley's to their car, he was walking into World War III.

I couldn't bring myself to say anything else, and instead wedged my clutch under my arm and gestured to the door. Bernard pulled it open for me and let me pass.

My parents didn't try to stop me.

Bernard, on the other hand, followed me out, trailing me to my car. He opened the driver's side door, pulling it wide so I could slip into the seat. Immediately, I pressed my foot on the brake, and my finger on the ignition button, and the engine came to life.

"Drive carefully, kiddo," Bernard said, using the term of endearment he reserved for when I really needed someone who cared.

Tears pricked my eyes as I clicked my seat belt into place and switched the car into reverse. "Thanks."

Bernard shut my door, the light from the car cloaking me in darkness seconds later. I wasted no more time in reversing my car and angling it back down the obnoxiously long driveway and out of this suburban hellscape.

Before pulling onto the main road, I reached over and

grabbed my phone out of my purse, sending off a quick message to Caleb. Because at the end of this awful, draining day, the only person I wanted to be around was him.

I'm on my way. See you in thirty.

CHAPTER TWENTY-TWO

CALEB

"Where the fuck have you been these last few days?" my dad demanded when I opened our front door for the first time in over a week and a half. The only reason I came back was because Isla had to head to her parents' house and it didn't feel right to stay at her apartment when she wasn't there.

My father's coherent abilities shocked me, and I did a double take. I couldn't remember the last time he spoke without slurring his words. Dropping my backpack by the door, I assessed him through narrow eyes. "Didn't think you'd notice."

"Course I did. This place is disgusting."

Ah, so there it was. I hadn't been around to clean up his messes, and he had noticed the lack of maid service. I stomped into the small kitchen and yanked open the fridge, looking inside at the few contents it housed. A six-pack of cheap beer, expired condiments, and some bread was all that was left. It'd been a couple weeks since I went to the store, and since I hadn't been home to stock it, it sat empty. I had to wonder what the old man ate while I wasn't around, but part of me didn't care. "It's not my job to clean up after you."

"Fuckin' lazy, just like your bitch mom was," he spat under his breath from his spot on the couch.

My spine went ramrod straight, anger filtering through my blood. Turning slowly, my nostrils flared and my hands curled into tight fists by my side. "What did you just say?" I grit out.

Ten-thousand emotions flooded my system. It'd been months, possibly years, since he had uttered a word to me that wasn't mid-intoxication, and here he sat, taking a lazy pull on his beer, a cruel smile enveloping his face as he talked down to me, and talked badly about my mother.

"I said," he drawled, gripping his beer around the neck of the bottle and bringing it to his lips. He chugged half of it before lowering it and continuing. "You're fuckin' lazy, just like your bitch mom was."

All I saw was red.

"Keep her name out of your mouth. You're the reason why she left us. Why she left *me*," I seethed, restraining myself more than I thought capable. I wanted to deck him. Knock him to the ground, climb on top of him, and not stop punching until his face was marred and bloody beneath my knuckles.

Every time he opened his mouth and said something about my mom, it felt like a switch flipped inside my mind. It was his fault she left, and without me—I was sure. It was also his fault I could never look for her. He had no information on anything of her past. Couldn't—or wouldn't—tell me where she came from, or any family names. He wouldn't help at all, and because we were broke as shit, I couldn't afford to hire someone to help me find her. I'd always just waited, and hoped, she'd finally come back for me. But she never did.

Once again, my dad tipped the beer bottle back, polishing off the rest of the contents before tossing it to the floor. I watched as a bit of foam spilled from the rim onto the already disgusting carpet. He laughed sinisterly, scooting down on the couch, and angled his legs wide. He looked incredibly relaxed with his hands cupping the back of his head, as I stood in front of him diffusing nothing but hatred.

"I regret nothing. She deserved everything she got," he told me cruelly, his voice reflecting his words. "You'll see, son. All women are the same. Good for nothing except when they're on their knees. Betcha your woman will prove herself to only be a useful hole."

It was unsurprising he had figured out I was with someone, but bile rose in my throat regardless. The last thing I wanted was for him to ever meet her. This interaction with him further solidified it.

Our hatred for each other ran so deep, my blood boiled and my entire body shook with rage. My only two options were to walk away or kill him. As appealing as the second choice was, I didn't think a felony murder charge would help secure me a position on the police force.

When I finally turned away from my father, I went back and grabbed the backpack I had dropped by the door, picking it up and slinging it over my shoulder. As I passed by him, I shot a brief glance in his direction, just long enough to see him grab onto the handle of his half empty vodka bottle, forfeiting the uncapped beer on the table next to him. He smiled mockingly at me again and took a swig.

Stepping into the solitude of my room, I slammed the door, shutting the bastard out completely. He made me physically sick. The power he'd had over me since I was a child was a constant reminder of how broken I truly was.

A stronger man would have killed him on the spot. But instead, he had the power to reduce me to feeling like a small child who hid in his bedroom.

Enough was enough. I had to get out of this house, away from *him*. Which was a little impossible when I didn't even have a car right now.

Thankfully, Dave and his crew were scouring junkyards for the parts needed to fix my car, and they were working on it. I was warned it would take time, though. It'd been less than two weeks but felt like an eternity of relying on Isla for rides to school and the bus for all other transportation.

Still, I was carrying on. I knew what needed to be done in order to leave this life, this house, and my father behind.

The guilt I carried about leaving him alone to drink himself stupid had practically evaporated into thin air and I suddenly gave zero fucks. For years, a darkness gnawed at the pit of my stomach every time I was in his presence and I couldn't figure out why. I'd always thought it was just the alcohol, but the way he just spoke about my mom left me wondering if resentment had buried itself deep within me.

If he drank himself to death, at this point, he'd be doing me a favor. Plus, it'd serve him right for all the stress and heartache he'd caused my entire life.

Dropping onto my creaky twin bed, I pulled my phone out of my pocket to text Isla. I missed her, and she hadn't even been gone for an hour. My stomach grumbled as I typed out the message and hit send and tossed the phone onto the bed next to me.

It was barely after four in the afternoon, which meant I

had at least another four miserable, hours stuck in this house.

Staring up at the yellowed ceiling, I thought about earlier when Isla agreed to be mine, exclusively, and the sounds she made when I had her coming all over my cock right after.

She was my complete undoing, and I was still utterly terrified I'd ruin her life.

Not only could I not give her a life like what she had grown up with, I knew one day—maybe not any time soon, but one day—she'd be packing her bags and fleeing, just like my mother had. The Hart men had a knack for hurting their women. My grandpa had been abusive. My father was an insufferable drunk.

The difference between the two men was my grandma never left my grandpa. Instead, she made the choice to hide the bruises he left with layers of makeup and a pretty excuse.

She was the only reason I hadn't turned into an empty shell of a human after my mother left. But unfortunately, I still lost my grandma shortly thereafter when she passed away from cancer. My grandparents were about as well off as we were and couldn't afford treatment. She declined rapidly, leaving this earth, and me, behind within a few months.

The memories I had of my mother were happy ones. She used to hold me in her arms and sing to me at bedtime, and read me *Goodnight Moon* as many times as I asked her to. I remember she always had a smile on her face when I was around, and an even bigger one when *he* wasn't. My memories faded, but I distinctly remember her holding me one night in particular. She was shaking like a leaf, holding me close as we sat on my bed and my dad pounded on my bedroom door. I was so young, crying because I was afraid of how loud he was being. I didn't understand why. My mom was rocking me, whispering promises of *we'd* get out of there soon, and *we'd* go somewhere safe and away from him. My chubby hand reached up and touched the necklace she wore every day, two hearts on a thin, delicate chain.

"This represents us, Caleb. The two of us, baby boy. Two hearts, always together."

And then one day, a couple years later, she was gone.

Leaving me behind, along with the necklace she never took off until then.

Driven away by the man who had promised to love and protect her, but had instead hurt her.

Like father, like son.

And that's what I was afraid of.

I COULDN'T TAKE it in this room anymore. The walls felt like they were closing in on me and I needed to get as far away from this house as possible. My stomach roiled, my hunger turning painful.

Still laying on the bed, I thrust my hips into the air and removed my wallet from my back pocket, flipping it open and pulling out the cash.

I had fifty-six dollars left to last me until I got paid again. I could easily spend some now and stretch the rest over the next week. Nothing sounded better right now than Chinese food, and since it was Thanksgiving, I deserved a proper meal. I had something to be thankful for this year, so I figured why not celebrate?

Hopping off my bed, I unzipped my dusty old backpack and shoved some fresh clothes into it. Isla had a washing machine at her place she let me use, but I was growing tired of re-wearing the same two shirts, pants, and boxer briefs.

Zipping the backpack again, I flung it over my shoulder and glanced around the room, debating on if I wanted to take anything else.

I didn't.

The house was silent when I stepped out of my bedroom, the space dark and only illuminated by the light in the kitchen.

My father stood in front of the open, empty fridge, his back to me as he rifled through the contents, likely trying to find something to eat. He didn't deserve the respect of a valediction, so I kept my mouth shut as I walked to the front door, twisting the knob to leave.

Unfortunately, my presence wasn't undetected, and his voice stopped me in my tracks halfway through the door. His speech was unintelligible. Over the years, I had become pretty well-versed in decoding whatever bullshit he spewed when piss-drunk, but this time I didn't have it in me to even try.

Slamming the refrigerator door, he spun to face me, ramming straight into the small two-seater table sitting in the middle of the kitchen. He doubled over, his stomach hitting the center before he righted himself, only to stumble and sway on his feet.

My moral compass ticked within me, trying to sway me to stay and help my father. I was so close to releasing the knob I was holding, my knuckles turning white from how hard I grasped it, but then his voice filtered into my mind, repeating his words from earlier and turning my blood into lava again.

"I regret nothing. She deserved everything she got. Betcha your woman will prove herself to only be a useful hole."

Fucking bastard deserved to fall and crack his head open on the tile.

Sending the door flying behind me, I walked down the porch steps and away from *him*, not caring that the door had bounced back and was swaying on its hinges. I was only two blocks and a bus ride away from feasting on Chinese cuisine and until Isla was done at her parents' house, I'd be spending the rest of my Thanksgiving alone.

CHAPTER TWENTY-THREE

Caleb texted me back, asking me to pick him up at Lucky Palace, a Chinese restaurant near Ridgewood University's campus. It was almost nine o'clock, but Lucky Palace stayed open late since it had a constant stream of college students coming in at all hours.

As I pulled into the parking lot, I looked around and noticed it was completely empty and the building was dark. Not a soul was in sight, including Caleb.

Worry prickled the back of my neck: the feeling of being alone was a deep-rooted fear, especially when I was alone in a normally busy place. My fingers patted against the passenger seat, searching for my phone while my eyes scanned the empty parking lot. Once secured in my grasp, I glanced down and touched Caleb's name on my call-log and hit speaker.

"Hey," he answered on the first ring. Relief rushed through me when I heard his voice and I instantly calmed.

"Hey, where are you? I'm in the parking lot at Lucky Palace, but it's empty."

"Cool, I'm around the back of the building. Be right there."

Caleb ended the call and my phone went back to the call-log screen.

That's weird, right?

Looking up, my eyes landed on Caleb as he jogged over to my car from behind the building. He pulled open the passenger door and climbed inside, leaning over to kiss me on the cheek before settling in and putting on his seat belt.

"Hey, beautiful," he greeted me warmly. "How was your Thanksgiving?"

"Why were you behind the building?" My tone was unintentionally sharp, and I winced a little, hearing my simple question come out as more of an accusation.

Caleb searched my eyes, likely wondering why I had an attitude.

He reached over and grabbed my hand, lacing his fingers through mine. "They closed an hour ago and there's a bench next to their back door where employees take their breaks. The owner told me I could hang out there until my ride came."

"Why didn't you just go back to your house? I could have picked you up from there. Or you could have met me at mine?"

"Did I do something to upset you, Isla?"

"I just don't understand why you were hanging out behind a closed restaurant."

With every question, his eyes darkened, narrowing further. "Going back to my house wasn't an option."

"Then why didn't you just go to mine?" I pressed.

"Go back to your place and do what exactly?" he snapped. "Sit in the hallway next to your door? Pace in front of the building? I don't have a fucking key, Isla. What do you expect me to do?"

I looked down at my lap, feeling foolish. "I'm sorry, it's been a really shitty night," I admitted quietly, glancing over at where our hands sat on top of the stick-shift.

"Yeah, mine too."

Releasing his hand from mine, I switched the car from park to drive and placed my foot on the gas. "Let's go home."

Throughout the drive, Caleb stared at the window. His beautiful features were coated with exhaustion and he looked like he had close to no fight left in him. I wondered what had happened in the hours we had been apart. I wondered if he'd tell me.

But now wasn't the time to ask him to talk about his day —not when his body language was so clearly telling me he was at his breaking point. This was a conversation for another day, and I needed to shelve it.

Later that night, after we had showered and washed the day away, Caleb pulled me in close, settling me into his side. In my bed, beneath the covers, Caleb and I created a happy place. A safe space where we could be together and all of our problems melted away.

Flipping through the Netflix carousel, he groaned deeply and gently tossed the remote onto the cloud of duvet covering my body. "There's never anything on," he complained.

"You're too picky," I quipped, pulling my arm out of the blankets and reaching for the remote. Clicking through the options, I found the Christmas movies and scrolled through them.

"It's still Thanksgiving. Tell me again, why you are turning on a Christmas movie?"

"It's my tradition. Once Thanksgiving leftovers are put away, it's officially Christmas. And what better way to kick off the holiday season than with a cheesy Christmas movie?"

"It's still November."

"Christmas," I sing-songed, shrugging my shoulder into his side a little.

"So what's this one about?" he asked as the opening credits rolled, spanning back to set the scene of a woman running late to a singing audition.

"This woman, Holly, has been dying to get a spot in a singing group her mom started when she was a child, but there hasn't been an opening since—"

Caleb cut my sentence off with an obnoxious groan and lifted the covers overhead before bringing them down over us, encasing us inside. "You are *not* making me watch a Christmas musical on Thanksgiving, Starlight."

I laughed, moving my hands wildly above me, attempting to rip the covers back down. "I am, and you're going to like it. She ends up falling for her grumpy boss in the end. We love a good HEA."

He rolled his eyes, shaking his head as he settled the blankets back down across our chests. He snatched the remote from where it sat on the blankets. "I'm going to hate this movie," he grumbled, though I could see the smile pulling at the corner of his mouth.

"No, you're not. You're going to love it. I'll have you singing along to the songs in no time."

"Wonderful," Caleb grunted.

Snuggling down into the blankets further, I leaned my head against Caleb's shoulder and watched my favorite Christmas movie, letting all the hostility I was holding onto melt away.

"Hey, Starlight?" Caleb whispered, his lips pressing against the top of my head.

"Yeah?"

"Merry Christmas."

MY PLAN TO stay in bed and do nothing with Caleb for the rest of the break crumbled the next morning, when he jumped out of bed and tugged his clothes on faster than I could even open my eyes. Late for work and about to miss his bus, Caleb hopped around my bedroom trying to do everything all at once, making it even harder on himself.

"Why don't you just let me drive you?" I offered, climbing out of bed to get myself dressed. The only place he ever agreed to let me take him was to campus, when I was already heading there. I respected his independence, but there was a time and a place for it. Now didn't seem like the appropriate time to pick a fight over transportation.

When your girlfriend had a perfectly working car, you let her drive you.

But, evidently, that wasn't the case for men named Caleb.

Rounding the corner of my bed, he gently pushed me so I fell back onto the mattress. "Nope. Stay in bed. I'll see you tonight." He gave me a chaste kiss on the lips and tugged his sweatshirt on, grabbing his phone and wallet off my dresser before pocketing them.

"But—"

"But nothing," he called, surprisingly cheerful as he walked down my hallway toward the front door. "Bye! Love you."

Every last breath of air whooshed from my lungs with those last two words.

Caleb's footsteps stopped, and the apartment became ghostly quiet. I didn't dare say anything, but my mind raced. Did he mean that? Did he love me?

It was on the tip of my tongue to tell him I loved him too, but I wasn't sure he fully meant the words that came out of his mouth. It was probably just a natural response. A closing saying goodbye. Something he had likely said a thousand times.

Bye. Love you!

See. It just comes out so naturally.

If it came out so naturally, why hadn't he slipped and said it before?

Standing, I lunged through my bedroom door to go to him, wanting to look him in the eyes and find out if he meant it, but as my feet touched the carpet, the door's lock clicked into place as it shut behind him.

Dropping back onto my bed, I climbed back under my covers, my heart racing. I was trying to fight against the smile tugging on my lips, not wanting to get my hopes up, but the butterflies in my stomach wouldn't settle. I felt like a giddy little girl, so hopeful of what could be.

FOR THE SECOND time that morning, I denied my mother's call.

The only time she ever called me was when she knew I was upset, and this time, upset *barely* covered what I was feeling. Having no interest in hearing what she had to say, I couldn't see the point in wasting time with a one-sided conversation where my mother made excuses and down-played what had happened. The bottom line was my father treated me about as well as he treated the dirt on the bottom of his shoe—like it was merely a necessity to get to where he was going. That's how it had always been with him. The concept of 'daddy's little girl' was something I had never experienced, because where most fathers fell madly in love with their daughters once they were born, mine took one look at me at birth, confirmed I was in fact a female, and tossed me aside like yesterday's newspaper in the driveway.

I wasn't still angry—sure I had a lot of pent-up rage and internal trauma associated with the role of being Isla Dono-hue, daughter of tech-titan Andrew Donohue—it's that I had lost all interest in keeping up the charade of being their perfect, moldable daughter. It was like the last thread connecting the part of me harboring the need to please them had completely snapped.

Being forced into a career path I didn't want and taking over a company I had no interest in was one thing, but being forced into an arranged marriage? Ha! Absolutely not.

The last several days had given me time to think and plan. I was still applying for jobs, sending out follow up emails, and had even resorted to cold-calling businesses to ask if they were hiring. So far all I had heard was a bunch of no's, and a few 'the hiring manager is out of the office but let me take your name and number...'. It was exasperating, and even though I was trying my darnedest to not let it, the feeling of rejection was taking a toll on my confidence.

I began to dread December as it approached, even though it was my favorite month of the year. Only a few weeks remained until I finished my business degree and graduated—an exciting time I should have been looking forward to celebrating was proving to be more of a death sentence for my short-lived independence. The clock was ticking, but I did everything I could to hold on to my freedom—my saving grace being my apartment lease not ending until March.

That gave me three additional months to get my act together and find a job. Then I'd either have to follow my father's path for me or cut ties completely.

As nauseating as the thought of losing absolutely *everything* was, it was my only option. Not the slightest part of me wanted to run a tech company or be even more connected to my father. And I certainly wouldn't marry someone for the sake of business.

I wasn't a transaction. I was a person.

And I was done being a pawn in my father's game.

CHAPTER TWENTY-FOUR

CALEB

Something wasn't sitting right.

It was four o'clock—my final hour at work—and I was the last one here for the day, sorting packages into their respective bins for carriers to pick up tomorrow morning. The task was mundane—hell, the whole job was mundane—but it was necessary for my paycheck.

Unfortunately, with mundane came less focusing on my job and more time to let my thoughts linger on every other aspect of my life.

It had been a week since I'd been back to my house and had last seen my dad, and I couldn't get his words out of my head. The hostility in his tone was haunting me, and the way he had said *'she deserved everything she got'*.

The longer I mulled over his words, the more nauseous I felt. Missing pieces and discrepancies from my childhood had me questioning everything about my mother leaving us. Why, after so many years, had she never come back? Was she so fearful of being face to face with my dad again, keeping her from even trying? And if she was fearful of my father, why would she leave me with him? She swore we'd be together, but then she left me behind. I was her son. Was I really so insignificant to her she wouldn't even wonder about me after so much time had passed?

The entire interaction with my dad and my spiraling questions left a pit in my stomach I couldn't shake no matter what I tried.

And then there was Isla. My starlight. The girl I didn't deserve yet still had agreed to be mine.

Telling Isla I loved her as I was on my way out the door the morning after Thanksgiving had been a complete fuck up on my part. It wasn't that the statement wasn't true, it's that it should have never fallen out of my mouth like it had. The slip up had been so natural, I almost hadn't realized I said it. But Isla had heard it, I was sure of it. The way the apartment fell silent and neither of us said anything before I finally turned and bolted out of the front door. Not so fast that I hadn't locked the bottom lock, securing her safely inside, but either way, I ran away fast as hell, like a dog with its tail between its legs.

It had been almost a week since I uttered the words I wasn't ready for her to hear yet, but ironically, it was like I had never said them at all. I had expected Isla to ask questions the moment I got back to her place that night, but she hadn't, and like the coward I apparently was, I never brought it up.

So all week long, my mind had been a battlefield, hyper fixating on one explosion to another.

Despite the chaos in my head, Isla and I fell into an easy routine full of sex, studying for finals, and work. Well, I had work.

Unfortunately, Isla hadn't had any luck with nailing down an interview. She was determined—I'd give her that. The fire inside of her to make it on her own and get away from her father was inspiring. She made me want to be a better man, and I was working on it every single day. Watching her apply to so many... It killed me to watch the hope filter out of her eyes every time I asked if she had heard back from anyone yet, and she had to say no. By the fourth day, I stopped asking.

When the Pack N Mail was closed up for the night, I walked toward the bus stop nearby, ready to see my girl, eat something, and chill. I was off tomorrow and they canceled my first class thanks to the professor getting hit with the flu, which meant I could sleep in and enjoy a morning in bed with Isla. Preferably naked.

The sun had nearly set, and the streetlights had come to life, basking me in their dim glow as I approached the empty bus stop and took a seat on the bench. The cold bite from the stone seeped through my jeans, sending a small shiver through my body. I tucked my hands into the pocket of my sweatshirt, but within seconds, my phone vibrated in my pocket.

A number flashed on the screen that seemed vaguely familiar. "Hello?" I answered, hoping it wasn't a spam call. They were getting more resourceful lately and calling from numbers with the same area code. It was annoying.

"Kid, it's Dave. Got a minute?"

"Sure," I told him coolly, even though an unprecedented excitement ran through me, hoping my car was repairable and I could pick it up soon.

"I've got good news, bad news, and a proposition," Dave

grunted through the speaker. "The good news is, I've collected most of the parts we need to fix your junker."

Relief washed over me. I licked my lips, suppressing a smile. "The bad?" I prompted.

"Gettin' there. The bad news is, still lookin' for a transmission. Haven't found a single one that's worth a damn. And now, before you interrupt me again, the proposition. I'm lookin' for someone to run the desk. Stephen quit on me last week and I don't got time to do everything myself. Pay is decent, but I thought you might be interested in workin' out a deal to pay off what ya owe for your car. Was thinkin' two-thirds of your hourly earnings could go to a paycheck and a third of it'll be put toward your debt. Whatcha' think, kid?"

My eyes widened at his offer—I was so caught off guard, it rendered me speechless. Running a shaky hand through my messy hair, the word 'yes' sat on the tip of my tongue while my mind honed in on the only—but arguably most important—question lighting up in my brain like a neon sign.

"I'm hoping to start the police academy in the spring, and it doesn't leave me with much of a schedule to work with. It's full-time, Monday through Friday, eight to five. Are you willing to work with my schedule once I'm enrolled in the academy?"

"You sure you're going in the spring?"

"Well, no. I still need to apply. If they take me, I might not get a spot until summer, or even fall."

"Then you work a normal schedule until ya know when you're goin' in. Once they take ya, we'll renegotiate a shift. I can always use help after hours cleanin' the place and catchin' up on paperwork."

The city bus rounded the corner, its gears whining as it

slowed to a rolling stop. A loud, groaning air release expelled as the doors opened, and the driver, Larry, greeted me with a friendly smile, tipping his chin.

I lifted my hand in a short wave, cradling the phone between my face and shoulder as I reached behind in my pocket and pulled out my TAP card to scan. "What's the starting wage, sir?"

"Seventeen an hour. Need ya eight hours a day."

Seventeen an hour? That was nearly two-fifty an hour more than I made at Pack N Mail.

Tossing my backpack onto an empty seat, I slid in next to it with a huge grin on my face. "You've got yourself a new desk guy," I told Dave happily. "I'm in my final few weeks of college though and can't start an eight-hour shift until I finish up my finals at the end of the month. Is starting off as part-time going to be an issue?"

The bus groaned as it accelerated down the road, heading to the heart of the city. Four stops stood between me and the stop closest to Isla's apartment, and for once I was grateful for the time it would take to get there. This conversation wasn't done—details surrounding my car still needed to be worked out.

"Nah, kid, that works for me. You gotta 'nother job you gotta quit first?"

Shit. Giving notice hadn't even crossed my mind. Pack N Mail had been a relatively good employer. It didn't feel right to leave them high and dry. As much as I hated the idea of putting *seventeen dollars* on hold for another two weeks, I also wanted to keep them as a good reference.

"I do." I tried to keep the disappointment out of my voice. "I don't go in tomorrow, but I will give them my letter of resignation on Saturday. I'd like to give them two weeks, out of respect. So realistically I wouldn't be able to start at the shop for another two weeks."

"Damn right you need to be respectful," Dave laughed. The sound felt unnatural coming from him. Based on our brief interactions, Dave struck me as a very serious man. A little rough around the edges—someone who took no shit, had a very dry, practically nonexistent sense of humor, and who had seen some things in his lifetime. "Your first day will be December 20th, then. Sound good?"

My head was nodding even though he couldn't see it. "Yes, yes, sir, sounds great. Thank you for this opportunity."

"Alright, kid."

"Oh, another couple of questions before we hang up."

Dave's grunt echoed into my ear, and I took it as my sign to continue.

"You said it was hard to find a transmission. What are my options with that? And—this one's a long shot—does the garage have any spare vehicles I can borrow or rent in the meantime? This bus shit is eating up so much time."

The line was silent for a moment, and if it hadn't been for the sound of tools muffled in the background on Dave's end, I would have wondered if he hung up. My knee bounced, the heel of my shoe tapping against the rubber flooring of the bus while I waited nervously for his response. I knew it was bold to ask him about borrowing a car—he didn't owe me shit. But I had to ask. I hated this fucking bus and the reliance I had on it.

"Your options with the transmission are we keep lookin', or you choose to buy one new. Either way, that's the last thing on my list. We're workin' on your car between actual payin' clients, so it'll be awhile. You can make that decision later." The phone went quiet again before Dave's voice boomed in my ear. "No! Tony, that ain't Mr. Mitchell's car. Wait—*dammit*. Sorry, kid. Lemme get back to you on borrowin' a car. I gotta deal with these fuckheads here. Come by next week and we'll work it out."

The line went dead, and I clutched my phone, a shit-eating grin plastered across my face. I couldn't believe the opportunity that'd just fallen into my lap: a higher paying job and a practical way to afford my car getting fixed. Things were finally feeling like they were falling into place. My girlfriend was amazing and gorgeous as fuck. I was about to get my degree and apply to the police academy—something I had dreamed of my entire life. And now, *this*.

With me leaving Pack N Mail, maybe I could even convince my boss to give Isla an interview to take my spot. Sure, it wasn't ideal for her being since she had her heart set on working with animals, but a job was a job. At the end of the day, her biggest ambition was to get out from under her father's thumb, and in order to do that, she needed to have some cash flow of her own.

Maybe Dave's offer was beneficial to both me and her, and the Pack N Mail would take a chance on her.

An unfamiliar feeling gnawed in my chest, and for the first time in forever.

Hope.

And I welcomed it. Because I finally felt like maybe things were looking up for me.

ROUNDING the corner to Isla's apartment, voices amplified down the hallway as an argument transpired in one of the apartments. I ignored it as I strode further down toward

Isla's; there was a pep in my step the closer I made it to her door, so excited to tell her about my conversation with Dave and my hopes of getting her a job at Pack N Mail, but as I approached and reached for the doorknob to let myself in, as I always did after work, the yelling carried out from her apartment.

"There's a reason why I've been avoiding her calls. I'm not interested in hearing whatever excuse she's come up with to try and make me forgive you."

"Honestly, your forgiveness, or lack thereof, is none of my concern. I'm here because your mother insisted I make contact with you. She thinks by sending me, you'll answer her calls. I'm also here because I spoke with the Dean and she informed me you've been absent from numerous classes in the past months. Care to tell me why you've been skipping your classes?"

Isla sounded exasperated, and the male voice was condescending and spiteful. I had no doubt in my mind who the man attached to the voice was. My hand stayed frozen on the knob, readying myself to go in while still listening to their conversation.

"I haven't been skipping that many classes, Father. Why are you talking to the Dean, anyway? How do you even know her?"

Footsteps moved around the apartment in slow, calculated steps. I couldn't see Isla's father, but I pictured him moving around her apartment, scrutinizing everything she owned through pompous, judgmental eyes.

"You have three weeks left in your business degree, Isla, and once you've graduated, you'll move out of this vile little box you call an apartment and back home."

"You know damn well that was never a home for me. I won't move back there."

"You will, you have training to complete for Skyline. It's non-negotiable."

"Father, I'm an adult. I can make my own decisions, my own choices."

"No need. Your path is already paved, Isla."

My gut told me I needed to turn around and leave, give her time to have this conversation with her father without my interference. As I told myself it was the right decision, my heart had a mind of its own and the desire to protect her ran deep through my bones.

Turning the knob to her apartment, I pushed the door open and stepped over the threshold, met with two pairs of eyes who had opposite reactions to my arrival.

The gorgeous stormy gray-blue I'd fallen in love with looked at me, softening as they searched my face and a soft smile dusted her face.

But next to her, her father stared at me with such hatred in his eyes, my heart rate accelerated.

"Who the hell are you?" he snarled, taking a step toward me and asserting his dominance.

Isla scampered across the room to stand beside me. Reaching down, she grabbed my hand in solidarity, lacing our fingers together. "This is Caleb," she told her father with her chin held high. "My boyfriend."

A fake smile instantly spread across his face, and he crossed his arms over his chest. "And does your boyfriend know you are an engaged woman?"

The feeling of being sucker punched exploded in my abdomen.

Engaged?

I ripped my gaze from Isla's father, turning my attention

to her, noting the way her eyes widened and she shook her head furiously.

"I'm not engaged!" she raged, fury taking over her body so deeply she was trembling. She pointed at her father. "He's trying to force me into a marriage to a man I *just met* on Thanksgiving, all for the sake of his company."

Turning to me, she brought her hands to my face, and I could see the fear in her eyes. "Caleb, I'm not engaged, I swear to you. I swear." Tears welled up in her eyes and began streaming silently down her face as she trembled against me.

Wrapping my arms around her shoulders protectively, I turned us both so I was facing her father again. "Why are you here?" I questioned as I held Isla close. Her face was buried in my chest, and although I was the one who appeared to be comforting her, she unknowingly was keeping me grounded.

"I should ask you the same question. Or rather, I should ask my daughter. Isla, why is this lowlife in the apartment I pay for? Have you truly been keeping company with someone like him?"

"Someone like what exactly?" I prodded. "You don't know me, and with all due respect, you have no right to make assumptions about who you think I am."

"I don't need to make assumptions, boy. I know exactly what type of person you are, and that's all I need to know."

"The type of person I am? Based on what, exactly? The way I look?"

"Exactly. You can tell everything you need to know based on how they carry themselves, and you are exactly the type of person I do not want my daughter around."

I went to open my mouth to speak again, but the bastard cut me off by holding up his hand like he could command me with just a gesture. And unfortunately, because his actions surprised me, he did just that.

"You come from nothing and probably have some sort of parental issues. You go to Ridgewood University on a scholarship awarded to you because of your unfortunate home situation, and you work a terrible job—if you even have a job, making less money than necessary to take care of yourself, let alone take care of my daughter."

"Father! Stop. You have no idea the type of man Caleb is, he—"

"No car. Still lives at home, unless you count freeloading off my daughter and subsequently, off me. But it ends now. You are the type of boy who will ruin my daughter's life by bleeding her dry."

Rage boiled within my body, my hands curling into tight fists by my side. This man—Isla's father—I've never wanted to bury somebody so badly. "You think you have me pegged—"

"I do," he cut me off, reaching into the inside pocket of his suit jacket, producing his cell phone. "You have sixty seconds to get out of this apartment and out of my daughter's life. If you won't leave, I'll be calling my contact at Ridgewood Police Department and having you arrested for trespassing on private property."

"You can't do that!" Isla shouted, pulling away from me to turn toward her father.

"I can. My name is on this apartment, Isla. If I say he's not welcome, he's trespassing." He glanced down at the silver watch on his wrist. "Thirty seconds," he said with boredom.

Fuck.

My world came crashing down around me. I knew something like this would happen. Being with her was like playing with fire. But I was a pyro, so fully addicted to this woman I'd play with fire until the world burned down around me. Hell, I'd burn it down for her.

Isla crashed into me, wrapping her arms around my waist as I brought my hands to her face, rubbing my thumb against her cheek.

"Don't leave, Caleb. He won't actually call them. He's bluffing." We both knew he wasn't, and it killed me to know I had to leave. I couldn't risk getting arrested when my dream was to join the police force and become their forensic analyst.

"I have to leave, Starlight. I can't get arrested." Tilting her head back, I brought my lips down on hers and kissed her deeply—audience be damned. My eyes shut as I let myself imagine I had just gotten home from work, was able to say hello to my girl and deliver the good news I had to share with her, and pretend we weren't dealing with a tyrant right now.

"Thomas! How are you?" Isla's father spoke, presumably into his phone, as I continued to kiss his daughter as though he wasn't in the room. "Hey listen, I need you to send an officer to my daughter's apartment. Yes, she's fine, but unfortunately we have a young man trespassing..."

As he kept spewing lies to whoever he had on the phone, I leaned down to Isla's ear so only she could hear me. "I'm going to leave, but as soon as he leaves, call me. We'll give this a few days to blow over and move forward. Everything will be okay. I promise."

She nodded her head as I wiped her tears away with my thumbs and leaned forward one last time to kiss her on the forehead. Releasing her, I ignored the feeling of her father's eyes on me and left the apartment, closing the door behind me as I went.

He may have won the battle, but I planned on winning the war.

I loved his daughter, and his disdain only fueled my fire more. She was mine, and no man, especially not her piece of shit father, was ever going to keep me away from her.

CHAPTER TWENTY-FIVE

ISLA

"How could you?" I seethed, turning back to my father, my cheeks still wet from the tears Caleb had attempted to wipe away. The anger I felt coursing through my body was unsettling. I had never been so upset in my life, and I had no idea how to control the rage within me that was beginning to feel like physical pain. Every morsel of my body wanted to collapse onto the floor, but I refused to let my father see the weakness I felt.

Rolling his eyes, my father gave me his back and walked over to pull a chair out from my small table. Sinking into it, he frowned when the chair creaked under his weight, and brought his leg up to cross his left foot over his right knee, relaxing back into it with finesse. His body language told me he was readying for this fight like a boxer entering the ring: full of confidence and ready to go for the jugular. "Relax, Isla. I ended my call with Chief Collier. He's not sending officers over."

"That's not the point!"

He scrolled through his phone, not bothering to look at

me as he spoke. "Contrary to what you may believe, Isla, I have your best interests in mind. I'm working on setting you up for instant success, so you won't have to run my company. You can stay at home like your mother—enjoy shopping and spa days, brunch with other incredibly dull housewives. You'll have money, and a husband to take care of the company. I don't see why you would fight me on all I'm giving you."

"I don't want the life you're trying to force me into, father. I've already told you what I want from my life, and that's being a veterinarian, not running your company. I have no interest in living in a mansion or marrying *Blake Bradley* and becoming a trophy wife. I want to have a career I love, a husband I love, and go on adventures with the family I've created. Even doing everyday things like grocery shopping and laundry would be preferable to being miserable in a life that isn't mine. Living life as a mirror image of you and mother is not one I imagine ever having for myself. *You* made sure I would never want that."

He stopped scrolling and snapped his eyes up on mine. "What is that supposed to mean?"

"You think growing up I couldn't hear you through the paper-thin walls? Eight bedrooms in your multi-million dollar mansion, and the contractor couldn't even build soundproof walls. Year after year, night after night, I had to sit in my bedroom, right next to yours, and listen to you and mother fight. Your resentment for me has never been a secret—at least not a very well-kept one to anyone inside the four walls of the Donohue mansion."

"Who said I was trying to keep it a secret?"

I whimpered, closing my eyes to keep from losing it completely. My heart was shattering into a million pieces.

Deep down, I loved him. Of course I did—he was my father. I had always held onto the small sliver of belief that he did love me, he just had a really terrible way of showing it. But now... Now I see I was completely wrong. "How can you hate your own daughter so much?"

"I don't hate you, Isla. There's a lot you don't understand."

But you sure as hell don't love me.

"Try me," I pushed. Shifting from one foot to another, I swallowed thickly and swiped at a tear that had escaped.

My father shook his head, glancing down at his watch to check the time. "I have no interest in rehashing the past with my *ungrateful* daughter. The past is in the past for a reason. There's nothing we can do to change anything that transpired."

"You have no interest in rehashing the past, and that's fine. But hear me when I say there is no room for your plans in my future."

Standing from his chair, my father buttoned the top button on his blazer. "You say that, Isla, but are you really ready to give up everything? I am tired of fighting you on this—you have never been the person I have wanted to take over my company. I wanted a son, someone I could pass my legacy onto, and instead, I ended up with a daughter. If you do not want to step into this role, I will not force you. But the moment you make your choice, there will be no going back.

"I am not a man who offers second chances, nor am I a man who negotiates. Your two options are as follows—you let go of your little fantasy of becoming a veterinarian and having a normal life, and become the head of a one billion dollar industry where you're set up to thrive. Or you walk away from everything. If you walk away, you will no longer be a daughter of mine. You can say goodbye to your trust fund, everything you own with my signature on it—such as this apartment, and your car—and you say goodbye to your *family*. What your mother does outside of our home is up to her, but you will no longer be welcome there, and I will no longer be acknowledging you as my kin. So choose wisely, daughter. Like I said, I am not a man who offers second chances."

"All because I want to create my own life and not have you force me into one?" I choked back a sob. It felt as though I was floating above my body, watching this play out. Never had I felt so shattered, so utterly alone.

"No," he replied, his voice void of all emotion. "Because you are a letdown. A mistake. And I knew you would be from the moment you were conceived in a Petri dish."

"Get out," I croaked, my voice cracking as I produced the sentence.

My father's lips turned up in a sardonic smile. "Ah, so you've made your choice, then?"

"Get out, father."

"I told you if you chose wrong, you lose everything. Myself included. Are you sure you're willing to live with your consequences?"

"GET OUT OF MY APARTMENT, ANDREW," I screamed so shrilly my vocal cords were instantly sharp with pain. I couldn't breathe, the air expelled from me in ragged, choppy exhales.

My father rubbed his chin, his head nodding in acceptance of my decision. Taking the time to push in the chair he had occupied, he then moved toward my front door, twisting the knob and pulling it open. His back was to me as he held the doorframe in his hand, twisting his neck to deliver his final blow. "You have until the end of the month to move out. I will be calling the property manager and canceling your lease effective immediately. Don't bother coming to the mansion for Christmas. Bernard will know not to let you on the property."

His words ricocheted around me as he stepped out of the door and let the door slam shut behind him.

For several long seconds, I stood unmoving aside from the tremors that pulsated through me, my eyes pinned to the door my father had walked out of. Internally I crumbled, wailing and screaming, cursing my father, while externally, I stayed silent, too exhausted to make a sound.

All I wanted at this moment was to curl up in Caleb's arms, knowing he'd let me shatter completely before helping me to rebuild. I so desperately wanted his comfort. But he wasn't here, because my father threatened him and sent him away.

So instead, I forced myself to place one foot in front of the other until I made it to my bed. I pulled back my duvet, removed the jeans from my body, and climbed beneath the covers. Later tonight, I'd call Caleb and apologize for how my father treated him. I'd ask him to come over, and he would. But for now, I'd decided I needed to break on my own before I picked myself back up again.

CHAPTER TWENTY-SIX

CALEB

I knew this would happen. From the moment I saw her, I *knew* if I let myself grow close to her, it'd blow up in my face.

Her father took one look at me and decided he knew everything he needed to know in order to make his snap judgment. And I couldn't exactly fault him for it. They came from money. I came from nothing. It was written all over my exterior. Walking into Isla's apartment in my worn-down clothing, childhood backpack slung over my shoulder...

Hell, I'd judge me, too.

What was really bothering me, though, was that he threatened to fuck me over simply if I did not leave her apartment. He'd used his connections with the police department to threaten to call and have me arrested for trespassing, when we both know damn well I was more welcome there than he was.

But with his simple threat, he had my hands zip-tied behind my back, forced to submit to his demands, otherwise I'd pay the price. I couldn't afford to get arrested, or even have the cops called on me for that matter—not when I was trying to become one of them.

Not that he knew, or cared. Anyone who didn't have a pristine pedigree and an overflowing bank account was beneath him. Period.

Walking out of the apartment and away from Isla when I knew she needed me was the hardest thing I'd ever done. But as I rode yet another bus to the stop closest to my house, I began to question everything again. All of my prior fears and hesitations were rising to the surface, even though I thought they had been dead and buried.

The last thing I wanted to do was hold her back or bring her down to my level, struggling and fighting an uphill battle every single day when the universe continuously made things hard. I wanted her to thrive and be happy. She was too astounding to be weighed down by me, yet I had no interest in saying goodbye to her. If anything, I wanted to make sure the bastard who was nothing more than a mentally abusive sperm donor didn't hurt her again.

The way he spoke to her—about her—made me want to wrap my bare hands around his neck and watch the light go out of his eyes. But I couldn't resort to physical violence if I hoped to fulfill my own dreams. One of which included her by my side.

If anything, this just lit an even bigger fire beneath me to get my shit together. To become the man who empowered her independence but still provided her with safety and comfort. I needed to be someone she could rely on when shit got tough, and that started with having the finances to keep us afloat, or at least keep a roof over our heads.

Was it too soon to ask her to move in with me? It'd only been a couple of months, but it wasn't like I wasn't practically living with her already. Maybe once I started working for Dave, we could get a studio somewhere. Something modest we could split the rent and afford.

I fucking *loved* that plan.

As the bus whined to a stop in front of a crowded bench, I hopped out of my seat, ready to jump out as soon as the doors opened. The thought of stepping foot back into my house made my stomach churn, but it was late enough in the evening where I could shower and retreat to my bedroom for the rest of the night and he wouldn't even realize I was there.

Tonight, I would wait for Isla to call and make a list of studios available for rent to call this weekend—see if I could get ahead of the game. Tomorrow, I'd give notice at Pack N Mail, then go to the library and use their computer to apply to the police academy. And if all went according to plan, maybe I'd be able to see some rentals by Sunday.

I was excited, and as I stepped through the door of my house and found my father passed out on the couch once again, I didn't let the anger take over. Instead, I shut the door behind me, and went into my room, feeling exhilaration spike and hope bloom. This weekend would be full of preliminary steps to jump-start mine and Isla's life together, and I was going to make sure everything went off without a hitch.

CHAPTER TWENTY-SEVEN

The night my father stomped on the last sliver of my heart that was loyal to my family, I cried myself to sleep and hadn't woken until late the next morning. My eyes were heavy and swollen from crying. The sun streaming in from the open curtains stung to where I snapped them shut again.

Tapping my fingertips against my nightstand, I felt for my phone, gripping it in my hand and pulling it toward me. I peeked through one eye to check the notifications, only mildly surprised to see I had none.

My heart sank at not seeing Caleb's name lit up on my screen, and a deep-rooted fear gnawed in the pit of my stomach. What if he was giving up on me? On us? Was the altercation with my father the wakeup call he needed to realize his initial hesitations were justified?

I wouldn't accept him just walking away. I couldn't. Not now. I refused to give him up after I'd already walked away from everything else in my life. Which I did willingly, and so far, without regrets. But Caleb mattered to me in a way nothing else did. I would *not* say goodbye to him.

Pressing his contact, I brought the phone to my ear and listened to it ring while I waited for him to answer. Rings switched to his generic voicemail, and I hung up, not wanting to leave him a message. It was late morning, so he was probably at work.

Not wanting to lie around and sulk, I forced myself out of bed and went to get ready. I had one week left of classes before finals hit and I needed to put myself in the headspace to study, even though it was the last thing I wanted to do. Regardless of what the degree was in, it was one step closer to getting me into veterinary school. And that was the mindset I needed to push me through these last two weeks.

Grabbing my laptop, I shoved it into my oversized purse and adjusted the straps comfortably on my shoulders before grabbing my car keys. While I locked up, the sound of heels against the linoleum clicked up the hallway, catching my attention. Facing the sound, I smiled at my property manager as she approached me. Liliana, was in her late forties and took a lot of pride in managing the apartment building. Every time I crossed paths with her, she was always dressed to the nines, with a huge smile plastered beneath her cherry red lips.

I lifted my hand, giving her a small wave before pulling the key from the lock. "Hi, Liliana."

"Isla! How are you, sweetheart? I'm so disappointed to hear you'll be leaving us at the end of the month."

My heart seized up, and I felt my face fall. He had already made the call to the leasing office. It hadn't even been twenty-four hours. Suddenly I felt desperate for information, but I knew I needed to save face if I had any hope of getting it from her. I may live in the building, but it was my father's name on the lease, and that meant Liliana could be as tight-lipped as she wanted to be with what she told me.

"I know!" I faked enthusiasm. "I told my father I really wasn't comfortable breaking the lease, but he tends to go a bit rogue, and do what he wants. I'm so sorry for any inconvenience it may cause."

She waved her hand, her wrist bending with a dramatic swipe. "Oh, honey, it's no big deal. Your dad is a sweetheart and paid out the last three months of rent. I'm just sorry now the apartment has to sit empty until March! It's such a beautiful place, and we have a waiting list a mile long."

He paid the remaining months instead of breaking the lease? But why? The better question was why was I questioning it? Of course, he had done it for his benefit. How embarrassing it would be for Andrew Donohue to break a lease.

Just like in the cartoons, an idea formed in my mind and I could practically see the light bulb appear over my head. "So the lease is still in effect? He just prepaid for the last three months?"

"Yep! He was so funny. I told him it'd be cheaper for him to break the lease and lose the deposit, but he wouldn't even entertain it."

"So..." I started, feigning innocence. "The apartment is fully paid for, and you can't allow another tenant to move in since it's still under contract. Correct?"

Liliana sighed dramatically, flipping through the pages on her clipboard. "Correct. And just look at how long this interest list is!" She flipped the clipboard around and flicked through the pages, showing me the numerous pages of names and phone numbers.

None of that mattered to me though, because at that moment I realized I could solve one of my problems and was about to have three months of no rent payment. "Liliana, since my father already paid through the end of March and I currently am living in the apartment, I can just stay through the end of the lease, correct?"

"Well, yes, of course. But your father said you had to—"

"It's fine!" I burst, relief and excitement rushing my body in a heavy wave. "It seems so wasteful to let this beautiful apartment sit for months. I'll speak to my father this afternoon and let him know I'm just going to see the lease to the end, especially since he's paid for it. Consider this conversation an official retraction of leaving early, and instead a little more than a ninety-day notice."

"Oh! Well, that's wonderful then. I'm so happy you're staying, Isla."

"Me too, Liliana." I smiled warmly, shifting the keys in my hand, subtly signaling I was about to leave. She returned the smile. "I'm so glad I ran into you this morning. Have a beautiful day!"

"You too, Isla. And if I don't see you before the holiday, please enjoy it and tell your father I said Merry Christmas."

"I will. Absolutely." Spinning on my heel, I moved down the hallway with tears of joy prickling my eyes and a smile that made my cheeks ache. I *had* to tell Caleb.

Not wanting to call again and seem like a crazy girlfriend by blowing up his phone, I pulled my cell out of my purse as I walked and typed out a quick message.

I have the best news. Call me when you can?

Approaching my car, I clicked the lock twice to unlock it before pulling open the door and sliding into the driver's seat. Sitting in my car, my excitement quickly morphed into fear. My father had threatened to take back anything with his name on it. I knew for a fact his name was on my car. Thankfully, he had paid cash for it when I turned sixteen, but if the title was in his name, I had no doubts he would rip it from my grasp just to spite me.

I blew a steadying breath from my mouth and yanked open the glove compartment, rifling around through the contents to find the title. Quickly, I realized the title wouldn't be in the car. I did, however, come across the registration and the insurance, both of which were in my name. I took it as a good sign, and with a quick search online I learned that while the car can be registered to someone other than who's listed on the title, it felt like it was safe to assume having my name on the registration would make it more challenging for him to just up and take the car away from me.

My phone danced on the passenger seat, vibrating to alert of an incoming message. Caleb's name popped up on the screen, and I quickly swiped at his message. As I read the first, a second immediately came through.

> I'm at work today and it's slammed. I also
> have good news to share.

> I'm off at 6. Are you willing to grab me from
> my house around 8?

Caleb had never asked me to pick him up from his house before, and I felt myself get giddy at his request. Would I meet his father? Does he want me to meet his father? Either way, picking him up from his house felt like a step in the right direction. My fingers flew across the touch-screen keyboard to respond to him.

> Of course, send me the address.

127 Logan Grand Blvd.

Text me when you get there and I'll come out.

> Perfect! Have a great day at work.

Tossing my phone back onto the passenger seat, I checked my mirrors before reversing out of my parking spot. I couldn't believe how quickly my day had turned around, and now I got to spend the day in one of my favorite places. It was a shame I had to spend it studying and not getting lost in a smutty book, but at least I would be at the library.

If you had told me when I was younger my happy place as an adult would be a public library, I would have laughed in your face. Back then, my comfort was more Burberry than Brontë. Now—well, it had been too long since I paid the library a visit, and I was excited to immerse myself between the shelves again.

CHAPTER TWENTY-EIGHT

ISLA

The headlights on my car illuminated the dark street as I idled outside Caleb's house, waiting for him to come out. The street was lined with lights, but most of them were dark, giving an eerie feeling. He lived in a not-so-great part of town, but the street seemed relatively kept up on, aside from the lights. Still, I couldn't help but double check my doors were locked a couple of times since I'd been sitting here.

I texted him almost ten minutes ago, letting him know I was outside, but he had yet to respond or come out. Shadows danced around me, my eyes playing tricks, and I debated on knocking on the door, but he had asked me to wait outside. If he wasn't ready to introduce me to his father, I had to respect that, right? What we had was still relatively new—only a few months.

After another almost ten minutes of idling, I turned off the engine and headlights, and made a snap decision to knock on his front door. He had told me eight, and even these last few weeks of having to rely on bus schedules and walking, he had never been late.

As I approached, I curled my fingers into a fist and rapped them against the door. The frigid December wind whipped around me, causing me to pull my jacket closer against my body as I tried not to shiver. Several long seconds passed before I knocked again, this time hearing a drawn-out groan directly after.

"Caleb?" I called, my heart rate accelerating, plagued with nerves.

A resounding boom came from the other side of the door, the crash sounding like a large piece of furniture colliding with the floor. The noise took me by surprise, and before I could stop myself I was twisting the doorknob of Caleb's home and pushing the door open.

Taking in my surroundings, my panic turned to confusion as I watched who I could only assume was Caleb's father, right himself from where he hung awkwardly over the end table he had tripped over. His leg was still twisted with the table's leg as he stood, stumbling again but catching himself.

The man grunted with his movements, adjusting himself to standing upright, though he swayed on his feet. Caleb's father—and I realized then I didn't even know his name—blinked slowly, as though his eyes were still adjusting to his whereabouts.

He scrubbed his hand over his hair before pulling it down to rub against his beard that desperately needed to be groomed, wearing a pair of pajama bottoms and a grungy, white t-shirt. In his hand was a half-full bottle of what looked to be vodka, which he held loosely by the neck. When his glassy gaze finally landed on me, confusion took over his face. I felt awkward under his stare, and with every passing moment he watched me, the confusion disappeared, and instead, a look I was familiar with from my own father blazed across his features.

Hatred.

"You," he seethed as he continued to sway on his feet. He lifted his empty hand, pointing his finger directly at me.

I was so taken aback, I couldn't figure out what to say as I stood in the doorframe of this man's home, but I knew I needed to figure it out quickly.

"Um, hi," I began, finding a cord of bravery within me. I took another step into the house, reaching behind me to push the door, closing it. "I'm—"

"How are you here?" Caleb's father demanded, his finger still hanging in the air. "How is this possible?"

Hesitating, I fought against uncertainty and attempted to steer the conversation. Clearly this man was in no condition to be having a fluid dialogue, but I was also in no position to wander further into the house to go find out where Caleb was.

"Is Caleb home?" I asked, leaning forward on my toes to peer into the dark kitchen. A small part of me had been hopeful he was hiding in the dark, maybe grabbing a snack with his headphones on and hadn't heard us.

"How are you here, Lucy?" His voice was low, predator-like.

Prickles of awareness instantly skated up my spine, and I tried to remain calm despite the fear rising in my system.

My eyes darted around the room, desperately trying to figure out what to do in this situation. Part of me wanted to call out to Caleb, while the other part wanted to dart out the door and flee to the safety of my car. Instead, I did nothing. Frozen like a deer in headlights as my heart threatened to jump straight out of my chest from the terror making it beat so rapidly.

He took a step toward me, his jaw clenched tightly. "How the fuck are you here?"

Opening my mouth to speak, I fumbled with my words, unable to form a sentence. I wiped my sweaty palms against my jeans, wondering if I should call out for Caleb.

"ANSWER ME," he boomed, taking two quick steps forward and stumbling. He caught himself midair, looking at me with such malevolence it nearly reduced me to tears.

Taking a step back, I bumped against the wall. "I... My name is Isla... I'm... I'm Caleb's..."

"HOW THE FUCK ARE YOU HERE, LUCY?"

"My... My name is... Isla."

An unsettling stillness surrounded us, and with three more steps, he was in my space, his large body engulfing mine as I was caged between him and the wall. He looked down at me, the smell of stale vodka wafting around me as his warm breath hit my forehead and cheek.

Years of self-defense lessons with Bernard completely evaporated from my brain the moment I could use them the most. The man in front of me had become completely unhinged, the alcohol impairing him so drastically he confused me with someone else entirely.

"This isn't fucking possible," he thundered, and droplets of spittle hit my cheek. I turned my head away from his face, closing my eyes in hopes I'd wake up from this nightmare. His empty hand slammed against the wall above my head, causing me to jump.

I should have stayed in the car. I should have listened to Caleb and waited outside or called him again, or *something*.

"This isn't fucking possible, Lucy. I killed you. I fucking *buried* you."

A deafening explosion rang out as glass and liquid shattered against the wall above me. The bottle Caleb's father had been holding now smashed into shards rained down onto my hair and clothes. I screamed on impact, my fight-or-flight kicking in from the direct attack, and I threw my hands against his chest, pushing him backward to escape his proximity.

Caleb's father stumbled back from my shove, falling to his butt on the floor. He bellowed at me, "I killed you! I fucking killed you, you bitch!"

"You *what*?!" Caleb bellowed, appearing from the hallway, confused, but angry. A sob erupted from my chest in relief. He was bare chested with a pair of gray sweatpants hung low on his hips, his wet hair dripping down in his eyes. A towel still hung in his hand, but the moment our eyes connected, he dropped it.

"Isla? What the fuck is going on in here?" he screamed as he ran across the room, pulling me into his arms the second I was in reach. "Starlight, tell me what happened. You're bleeding."

His presence made me lose control completely, tears flowing from my eyes as though a river dam had broken, and I felt myself begin to shake. Swiping his thumb against my cheek, I winced, my heart sinking at the sight of blood on his thumb when he pulled it away from my face. "He... He thinks I'm someone else."

Shifting our bodies so he faced the room, I felt his body stiffen against me as he took in what had happened.

Without a word, he pulled me out of his living room and into the cool night air, guiding me back to my car. My keys still dangled from my hand—though I'm not sure how I held onto them that whole time—and he reached down, taking them and unlocking the car before depositing me into the passenger seat. "Stay here, lock the door," he instructed, shutting the door behind him and jogging back into the house.

I sat shaking, likely from a combination of adrenaline, fear, and the cold, and leaned my head back against the headrest. I prayed Caleb wouldn't be long, desperately wanting to get away from this house and into the safety of my own.

Closing my eyes, I hoped when I opened them again, I'd wake up from this nightmare.

CHAPTER TWENTY-NINE

CALEB

I stalked back inside with a rage filling me, threatening to shoot off like a cannon. The image of me stepping into the living room and seeing Isla standing against the wall, trembling, while blood trickled down her face and my father held the neck of a shattered bottle, was one I would likely never scrub from my brain. This was my fault. If I had only kept a better eye on the clock instead of getting lost in thought while in the shower, this never would have happened.

Today had been a good fucking day, too. Giving my notice at Pack N Mail had been nerve-racking, but as I sat down with the owner, Mal, I relaxed and we had a great conversation. I left her office, passing her my official letter I had typed out on the company's computer on my break, and she wished me the best of luck. She even told me to send Isla in to fill out an application and promised she'd be at the top of her list of interviews to replace me.

I practically skipped to the bus stop like a little fucking

girl. I was so excited to tell Isla that our luck may be turning around.

Don't worry, I didn't actually skip, but the way my heart flailed around my chest cavity with elation, I might as well have.

Not bothering to look inside the empty fridge when I got home, still full from splurging on a foot-long deli sandwich for lunch, I went straight to giving a few property managers a call and managed to set up three appointments for tomorrow to see some studios. Their rent cost was still out of reach for just my income, but if Isla was able to get a job and help with about a third of the rent, we would be able to make it. At that moment, things couldn't have fallen into a better place, and I couldn't wait to tell my girlfriend the good news.

Deciding to spend my last thirty minutes before she arrived doing something for me, I locked myself in the bathroom and gave myself a shave—even though I didn't really need it—and took a hot shower. Somewhere in there, I lost all track of time, and because of my carelessness, Isla got hurt.

My dad still sat in the middle of the living room, on the disgusting, threadbare carpet, looking disoriented. He rubbed his hand across his face, watching me walk over to him through glossy, half-closed eyes.

Crouching down in front of him, I curled my fingers around the chest of his t-shirt and pulled him to me by the fabric. "What the fuck is wrong with you?" I barked, my voice so laced with venom I hardly recognized it myself. I was doing everything I could to stay level-headed, knowing I *needed* answers from this sorry excuse of a man.

My dad said nothing and grabbed my hand that held his

shirt, clawing at it in an attempt to pull it off him. I refused to release him, ignoring the bite of his fingernails against my skin.

"Did you *kill* her? You killed mom?" my voice cracked on the last word, feeling an ache so deep in my heart I thought it was about to rip in two. So many questions swirled around my mind, so many memories of my mother and everything surrounding her leaving I'd buried deep inside. A rush of anger slammed into me, and I shook my bastard father with as much strength as I could. "TELL ME."

My father grumbled incoherently, and despite the urgency I felt to get the answers, I knew tonight I would get none—he was too intoxicated, probably blacked out, at this point. Shoving him backward, I stood and stepped over his body as he faded out of consciousness on the floor. Curling my hands into fists at my side, I forced myself to leave him and get what I needed from my bedroom, not wanting to leave Isla outside for any longer than necessary. She was shaken up badly, and while I hated having to put her in the car and come back inside this house for a few minutes, it was the only option I had. Leading her to my bedroom wasn't a choice for me: I didn't feel like she was safe in my house.

I began throwing as much clothing as I could into my backpack, not caring if I wasn't going to be able to zip it shut. The bag overflowed with clothes—everything I would need and want. I was never coming back to this house. Whatever fit, came with me, and whatever didn't, I no longer considered mine.

Shoving my feet into my favorite pair of shoes, I reached into my nightstand and collected my phone and the charger, shoving them both into the front pocket of my backpack. Next was my wallet and house-keys, which I pushed into the pockets of my sweatpants before turning to the top of my dresser, picking up my textbooks and notebooks and tucking them beneath my arm. As best I could, I scooped up the stuffed backpack and cradled it under my other arm.

As I turned to leave, I stopped myself, remembering one of my most prized possessions. I couldn't leave it behind. It was the last thing—the only thing—I had from my childhood.

Turning back toward my closet, I dropped everything I held onto the bed and moved to retrieve the shoebox sitting on the top shelf, housing trinkets from my childhood, and things that reminded me of my mom. Pulling it down, I picked everything back up and awkwardly carried everything through my bedroom door.

My father was, unsurprisingly, passed out on the floor when I exited my room. His mouth wide open, expelling small huffs of air as he slept soundly, as though he hadn't just shattered a bottle above my girlfriend's head and then passed out.

And his words. A large part of me desperately wanted to believe what he said was just a drunken rant. A slurring of words that meant nothing—maybe he had been watching a horror movie earlier, and it lingered on his mind. My dad was a lot of things—a drunk, a jackass, neglectful—but was he really a murderer too? I couldn't believe that.

I didn't want to believe that. Because if it was true, then my dad took away the one person who had loved me unconditionally.

Glancing at him over my shoulder, I walked out of the house for the last time.

My eyes stayed glued to the front door of the house as I opened the door to the back seat of Isla's car, tossing everything I owned into it. Shutting the door, I then opened the driver's door and sank into the soft leather seat, closing it once I was situated inside, and started the ignition. The overhead light immediately turned off, casting us in darkness.

Reaching over, I took her icy hand in mine. "Are you okay?" I asked, knowing she wasn't, but not knowing how else to break the silence. She stared out her window at the house and slowly nodded her head.

"Yeah," she said, her voice small. I pulled her hand to my mouth and kissed the back of it before placing it back on her lap.

Turning to face forward, I flicked the headlights on before placing both hands on the steering wheel, grabbing it so hard I could see my knuckles turn white through the darkness. "I'm never fucking coming back to this house. He's dead to me," I growled angrily, more to myself than to her. The catastrophic gravity of the situation sat on my chest, making my head spin with questions and regrets.

Slamming my foot against the gas, the car shot forward and I drove to Isla's apartment complex, away from the home I hoped to never see again.

WHEN WE PULLED into the parking lot of Isla's apartment, I killed the engine before hopping out of the car and rounding it to the passenger side. Isla was still in shock. She had been quiet as a mouse the entire car ride—not like I was feeling very chatty myself. Pulling open her door, I leaned in and unlatched her seat belt, pulling her out of the seat to stand, before lifting her into my arms.

Instinctually, Isla's arms and legs wound around me as I firmly held her and she buried her head against the crook of my neck. Ignoring the elevator, I ambled up the two flights of stairs with her in my arms, moving as quickly as I could to get her inside.

"I can walk," she said against my neck, her warm breath tickling the sensitive spot.

"No." Continuing up the last flight of stairs, the soles of my shoes stomped against the flooring and echoed in the stairwell. Once I made it to her floor, I rounded the corner and repositioned the keys in my right hand, feeling for the simple key to unlock her door.

I wasn't willing to let her go just yet, so I pinned her against the door, pressing my body firmly against hers so I could wrestle with the lock. Moving us inside, I kicked the door shut behind me and moved through the dark, bringing her into the bathroom, where I flicked on the light and sat her down on the closed lid of the toilet seat.

She looked up at me and I dropped to my knees, cupping her face in my hands as I inspected her. Tilting her head from left to right, I let out a shaky breath, relieved to see no shards of glass in any of her cuts. Thankfully, they weren't deep, and with a thorough cleaning, I was confident she'd heal quickly.

I pulled open the drawer where I knew her washcloths were and ran one under warm water, squeezing the excess out before bringing it to her face, lightly cleaning away the dried blood and mascara that had made its way down her cheeks. She winced slightly as I rubbed the washcloth against the wound.

"I'm sorry," I whispered, easing up on the pressure as I continued to clean her face. Once satisfied, I moved to the medicine cabinet for antibiotic ointment, uncapping it and applying some on a cotton swab to layer onto the cuts. "I don't see any glass, and the cuts are very superficial. They won't scar."

She nodded and offered me a small smile that didn't meet her eyes. Her fear had turned into sadness, and it wreaked havoc on my heart.

I swallowed thickly, afraid to ask my next question, but knew I needed to. "Are you hurt anywhere else? Did he lay a hand on you, Isla?"

Isla shook her head no and croaked, "Where were you, Caleb?"

My heart completely disintegrated in my chest. My gaze dropped to the floor before I mustered the courage to look at her again. "I'm so sorry. I completely lost track of the time. After shaving, I took a shower. When I finally got out, dressed, and turned off the bathroom fan, I heard the glass shatter. I had no idea you were inside the house, or even there yet," I explained, feeling like a complete asshole. "My phone was in my room, and when I went into the bathroom, I still had a half an hour..." my voice trailed off.

I was completely at fault, and I knew it. If I had paid better attention to the time, or brought my phone into the bathroom with me, I would have known it was past eight, or seen her text message. I would have known she was there and I could have gone outside and this would have all been avoided. "Isla, I'm so sorry."

She looked broken.

Shattered.

All the light was gone from her eyes.

"It's not your fault," she stated, though her voice was small and void of emotions.

I jumped to my feet, desperately wanting to fix this in any way I could. Leaning over, I started the shower, pushing the handle all the way to hot. Water rained down from the shower head and within seconds a thick steam wafted up from the shower's tile floor. I watched, transfixed on the steam, my own shock starting to sink in.

"Caleb," she said quietly, and my gaze immediately connected back to hers. "I don't want to shower. Can we please just go to bed?"

Nodding, I turned the faucet off, watching the water cease immediately. I blew out a shaky breath, forcing my own emotions down as I reached for her hand, pulling her to stand. We walked across the hall to her bedroom hand in hand, mine cupping hers as I led her into the dark space.

I didn't bother turning on the lights.

Isla stripped out of her clothes, toeing off her shoes before tugging her jeans down her legs. She was careful not to let her shirt touch her face as she pulled it over her head and tossed it into her laundry basket. Opening her dresser drawer, I watched as she removed one of my t-shirts and shrugged it on, letting it fall to the tops of her thighs.

Once she was done, I pulled back her duvet, welcoming her comfortable bed to her, and she climbed inside, curling up on her side and bringing her knees up toward her chest as I covered her with the blanket. "I'm going to run back down to the car and grab my stuff, Starlight."

I didn't want to leave her, but I wanted to grab my things and crawl in bed beside her and just let the world fade away.

"Okay," she said, staring across the room at the wall. I watched her for a few quiet moments before I left the room, grabbing her keys from where I had tossed them on her entryway table, and locked her apartment up behind me.

ISLA'S soft breathing as she slept safely beside me did nothing to ease the chaos inside my head. One sentence haunted my every thought, replaying and keeping me from falling asleep.

"I killed you! I fucking killed you, you bitch!"

The crimson sight of blood spatter illuminated behind my closed eyes. I squeezed them shut, wishing the vision away, but I couldn't push my dad's voice from my head, wondering if I should take it at face value.

It was a possibility—a slim one, but still a possibility—he had been spewing nonsense, some left over thoughts or dialogue from something he watched on TV I knew I was reaching, but I couldn't fathom the idea of him killing anyone, let alone his wife. My *mother*.

But it was plausible, and the thought killed me.

Sleep refused to come, and I tossed and turned, trying to get comfortable, but I couldn't get the feeling of my skin crawling to dissipate.

I pulled Isla's body close to me, cradling her against me in a little spoon position, and laid my hand against the top of her breasts, feeling the rhythmic rise and fall of her chest as she slept. It calmed me, and between the warmth of her body and the soft sounds of her breaths, I was able to sleep eventually, though it didn't last long.

Nightmares plagued my sleep—feminine screams, a child crying, and the metallic glint of blood—drifting through my consciousness and snapping me awake despite the heaviness of my eyes. I was exhausted in every sense of the word, both mind and body, but around five in the morning I finally gave up on sleep and peeled myself out of bed, closing her bedroom door behind me as I moved in the direction of her small galley-style kitchen. Shadows filtered around the room as the moon shone through the windows, disappearing when I flipped on the light.

Isla had one of those single-cup coffee machines that took a few minutes to warm up before you could put your pod in. While I waited, I pulled out a coffee mug and placed it on the drip tray, before opening her refrigerator, pulling out the half gallon of milk I had bought for her last week. When the gurgling noises of the coffee machine had ceased, I placed a pod of coffee into it and clicked the brew button, zoning out on the flow of the liquid as it poured from the machine.

After throwing a splash of milk into my coffee, I put it away and gripped my mug by the handle and took a large sip. The coffee burned my mouth, the singe of heat coursing down my throat as I swallowed it down. I welcomed the discomfort, happy to feel pain in another area of my body instead of it being radiated solely in my chest.

"Couldn't sleep?" Isla asked, leaning against the wall of the hallway opening up into her kitchen and living room. She had wrapped a pink plush blanket around her body, wearing part of it over her head like a hood.

I smiled at her, setting my coffee down on her counter. "Come here," I beckoned, stretching my hand out in front of me, reaching for her even though she was across the room. She did as I asked, and when she was within reach, I tugged her close by the blanket draped around her, and caught her lips with mine. When I pulled back, I saw the woman I had fallen in love with staring back at me without a glimmer of hesitation in her eyes, despite everything that had happened.

Still, I couldn't push aside the regret I felt for what I had unknowingly let happen. Because of my carelessness, Isla was placed in harm's way, and I hadn't protected her. I was petrified I would do something to end up hurting her even more. As scary as the thought was, I was even more afraid she'd look at me differently because of what happened, or she'd even begin to fear *me*.

"I'll never be like him, Isla," I whispered. I needed to say the words out loud—to reassure myself, as well as her.

"I know," she stated simply, looking at me with conviction.

"But I'm still afraid I'll—"

"I love you, Caleb. And I trust you," she cut me off, reaching up and cupping my face in her hands. "But you need to trust yourself. Not once have I ever felt like you had any rage in you, or I was or would ever be in any danger. The actions of other men in your family have nothing to do with you and the man you are." She wouldn't let me respond. Instead, she reached around and settled her hands on my neck, pulling my head down until our foreheads touched.

I let my eyes close, feeling her presence and letting it calm me down. She was right. She could trust me, and I would spend every waking moment for the rest of my life proving it to her.

Our lips found each other, and we kissed slowly, building the pieces back together from what felt so broken. Isla sighed against my mouth and let her body melt against mine. Our tongues pressed together in small strokes, exploring lazily as I held her close.

When we broke apart, I grabbed her chin between my finger and thumb, tilting her face to look at me. "I love you," I told her, unafraid of saying it out loud. I was ready to shout it from the rooftops and let this woman know how much she meant to me. I just wished it hadn't taken such a scare to make me realize I *wanted* her to know how I felt.

"I love you too," she whispered back, once again giving me reassurance I wasn't sure I deserved. Her eyes filled with tears, and she added, "I'm so sorry I didn't just wait in the car. This could have all been avoided if I—"

"Don't do that. Don't sit here and blame yourself for something my dad did to you. For what *I* did to you. If I had just paid attention to the time—"

"You're not to blame, Caleb. Really, neither of us are."

I rubbed my face with my hands, pressing my pointer and thumb into my eye sockets, using pressure to ease the pain building behind them.

"C'mon, let's go sit," Isla suggested, tugging on my hand as she pulled me toward the couch. We both took a seat, facing each other. Our knees touched, and I positioned her legs up onto my lap just to get her closer.

It felt like if I wasn't touching her at all times, something bad may happen again.

"Are we going to talk about it?" she asked. I knew the question was on the tip of her tongue, and was the one that caused me the most panic, because I knew if she had heard him say it too, then I hadn't made it up.

"Who is Lucy?"

CHAPTER THIRTY

ISLA

The color drained from Caleb's face at the mention of the name Lucy. His gaze drifted down to where my legs hung over his lap, and he picked at the fibers on my blanket. Whoever she was, she had meant a lot to him. The mere mention of her name caused him a sadness I had never known.

And then it dawned on me.

"She's your mother, isn't she?"

Caleb continued to pick at my blanket, keeping his idle hands busy. "Yeah."

I poked my hand out of the blanket and covered his. "Tell me what happened, Caleb. Why would your father say he... Why would he say he killed her?"

"Because he was belligerently drunk and talking out his ass."

"Caleb," I drawled, my heart breaking all over again for him. I needed to tread lightly on this topic—I knew he wouldn't want to hear it. But I had seen the look in his father's eyes when he thought I was her. I *felt* the hatred rolling off him in waves and slamming into me.

I would never forget it.

"Caleb... I think there's some truth to what your dad admitted. The way he looked at me... he thought I was her. When I first came into the room, it's like he had seen a ghost. Once his shock wore off, his expression turned to pure hatred and then the situation escalated quickly from there."

He looked away from me, and the way the light from the kitchen illuminated my living room, I could see the shine from tears filling his eyes. Without hesitation, I scrambled onto his lap, straddling him and wrapping my arms tightly around his neck.

Letting his head fall forward to rest on my shoulder, he asked despondently, "What do I do?" His voice cracked as he said it.

It was so early in the morning, and we were both still so exhausted. The conversation weighed heavily on both of us, but it was one we needed to deal with quickly. Caleb's father had confessed to murdering his mother, and even though Caleb still seemed skeptical of its truth, this was bigger than either of us could handle on our own. We needed to get the police involved so they could do a proper investigation.

If Caleb's dad truly had killed his mother, she deserved justice. And Caleb deserved closure.

"We contact the Ridgewood Police Department. Immediately. Chief Collier has known me since I was a baby and will take our statements seriously. They'll look into it, Caleb, and if it's true, your mom will be served justice." He remained silent, processing my words. Hesitantly, I asked the question that'd been on my mind since last night. "Caleb, did you ever have any suspicions your mom hadn't actually left and your father did something to her?"

He thought for a moment before lifting me and placing me onto the couch, standing and running over to his pile of things from his house. Picking up an old shoe box, he carried it back over to the couch and sat it on the coffee table in front of him. He glanced at me before lifting the lid and rifling through the contents.

I wanted to respect his boundaries, but I also was so curious about what was inside I craned my neck slightly to see. The box was nearly empty—only a few photos and small keepsakes inside.

Finally, Caleb pulled out a necklace from the very bottom and held it between his fingers. It was a delicate silver chain with two small hearts dangling from it. It was beautiful and simple.

"I can't remember a time growing up where my mother didn't have this necklace on. She said the hearts were me and her." I watched as he reached up and swiped at his cheek, trying to hide a tear that fell. "The morning she left, I remember coming into the living room and my dad telling me she was gone and she was never coming back. I refused to believe him, screaming at him that she would never leave without me. I didn't believe him until he grabbed me by the collar of my shirt and pulled me to his face and told me to stop being a little bitch. I ran to the couch and buried my head beneath a pillow and cried until I couldn't produce tears anymore. When I finally got off the couch was when I saw it—my mother's necklace. It was on the floor under the end table." Caleb turned to me, the wheels turning as he tried to piece everything together.

I had my theories, but it didn't feel right to voice them.

Caleb needed to talk to the police and let them investigate. Returning the necklace to the box, Caleb placed the lid onto it and scooted back, drawing my hand into his lap.

"We'll go down to the station later this morning and speak with Chief Collier. Tell him everything that happened, and you can tell him what you just told me about the morning you found out your mom left. They *will* get to the bottom of this, Caleb."

He nodded his head, swallowing thickly as he stared across the room. It had been less than twelve hours and there was so much to process, so much to think about and piece together. I couldn't imagine everything he must have been feeling, because everything I felt was so intense and confusing. I wanted to go back in time and erase everything. Start fresh.

I desperately wished I could do that for him.

Caleb and I sat in comfortable silence, enough time passing to watch the sunrise through the window in my living room. The room was cold, but I could feel the heat of the sun on my legs as I stretched them across the carpet.

"I'm never going back there, Isla. I can't," Caleb stressed. "I packed as much as I could in my bag, and the rest I don't give a damn about. I had a lot of news to share with you last night. I called around and scheduled a few appointments to go see some studio apartments." He turned his body, bending one leg as it draped off the side of the couch. "I know it's only been a few months, but we both deserve a fresh start. I figured a fresh start in a place together wouldn't be such a bad thing."

Even with everything Caleb now had to think about and process, he still managed to look at me shyly, giving me a small smirk as he waited for me to say something about his offer. Little did he know, I had news of my own that would sweeten the deal.

Biting my lower lip, I smiled at him. True happiness flickered inside me even though everything else seemed so dreary. "So... About that. I have a lot to catch you up on, but the short story is that my father has officially disowned me, and in doing so he decided he'd no longer be responsible for my rent and told me I had until the end of the month to move out." Caleb opened his mouth to speak, but I shook my head and smiled again, holding up my pointer finger to have him wait for what else I had to say.

"Yesterday morning I ran into the property manager and she told me my father had informed her of my early departure, but instead of breaking the lease, he paid upfront for the remaining months. Legally they can't release the apartment and get a new tenant until the end of the lease since he's paid. So while my father refused to break the lease in fear of someone finding out and it looking bad, he unknowingly paid in full for the next three months of rent on an apartment I am going to keep living in. He thought he'd give me an eviction notice of his own, but his plan backfired on him."

"So you get to stay?" he asked, clearly still trying to catch up with the ramble that just fell out of my mouth.

"No, *we* get to stay. And we have three months of no rent to stress about. This will give me time to graduate, find a job. You can apply to the police academy. We have three months to figure out our next steps, Caleb. Together."

For the first time in several days, Caleb cracked a real, genuine smile, and my heart soared at the sight.

"I have more good news," he blurted, pulling me back

onto his lap. Just like earlier, my legs straddled him and my arms wrapped around my neck.

"Tell me," I urged, kissing him lightly on the corner of the mouth.

"Dave, the mechanic, has been collecting parts for my car, and when he called to tell me they've almost got everything they need, he offered me a job. I gave notice to Pack N Mail yesterday."

"Caleb! That's amazing!"

"When I gave my notice, my boss told me to have you submit your application to her. She's going to put you first on her interview list. I know it's not ideal, but—"

My heart felt heavy, in such disbelief this man had found his way to me and was doing everything he could to help me pave my own way and encourage me to follow my dreams. I leaned forward, kissing him gently. "It's perfect, Caleb, thank you."

"And I already applied to the police academy, so all that's left on the checklist is for you to apply to veterinary school."

Veterinary school. My dream that still felt so out of reach.

The rope holding me back from chasing my dreams had been severed, and I was free to make my own decisions. The realization hadn't dawned on me until just now. My father had disowned me. Truly, fully, cut me off.

"Yeah," I said quietly, lost in thought about how I would be able to afford to pay for veterinary school and have a roof over my head at the same time.

But as I looked over at the man who couldn't quite seem to take his eyes off me, who filled me with such joy, love, and empowerment, I couldn't help but to feel excited for the beginning stages of our future. We had a lot of storms to weather together before we'd finally see sunny skies, but I knew without a shadow of a doubt we'd get through everything by simply being there for each other through it all.

What started as a sordid hookup in the back of the library had somehow turned into a love story I never could have imagined. It was messy, heart-wrenching, and at times it was overly dramatic, but it was *our* story.

"So where do we go from here, Isla?" Caleb asked, pulling me from my thoughts.

We were two broken, poor, almost college graduates who'd hit rock bottom, yet somehow found each other through the rubble. Things wouldn't be easy for us for a while. I had no doubts we'd have to fight every day for our relationship and for the life we dreamed of having, but I also knew that once you hit the bottom, there was only one way you could go from there. My mind floated back to a similar conversation we had what seemed like a lifetime ago, and a smile touched my lips.

"Up, Caleb. We go up."

Lacing his fingers through mine, he added, "Together."

CHAPTER THIRTY-ONE

CALEB

Ten Months Later

My foot bounced rapidly as I sat listening to the Chief of Police as he gave a congratulatory speech, telling friends and family how proud he was of this round of graduating officers. Small, but mighty, he had called us with a deep chuckle, drawing out laughter from the rest of the room.

What started as a class of sixteen ended as a class of twelve, but only four were starting at Ridgewood Police Department. The rest had accepted positions in neighboring cities, and would start their positions as soon as they were sworn in.

It had been an excruciatingly long ten months, but I had made it. I was finally going to start my career and had already had a promising conversation with the Chief about eventually working with forensics.

Wearing my uniform, I sat in the row of folding chairs with my hands placed on my lap. There was a buzz surrounding me and the rest of the graduating officers as we waited for our signal to stand. Next to me, an officer named Noah, who I had become friends with throughout our time at the academy, had a scowl on his face, per usual. He was a few years younger than me and had applied to the academy after being given an ultimatum by his parents to either enlist in the military or apply to a trade school. This seemed like the best of both worlds and seemed to suit him. Noah was a good dude, but you could tell he was going through some shit.

I knew a thing or two about going through some shit.

For the last six months, I'd been working with a therapist once a week to work through some of the nightmares that continued to haunt me. Isla had encouraged me to go this route and I fought her on it for several weeks before finally giving into her requests. Through the help of my therapist, I finally realized why forensics had always appealed to me.

The death of my mother.

My brain had repressed most of my memories of her leaving, but flashbacks still snuck through from time to time. With my therapist's guidance, we determined I had likely formed a fascination with forensics because of what happened to my mom. My therapist gave me the option of trying to retrieve the memories and explained the various methods on how we would do that, but I chose not to. The memories I have of my mom were few, but happy memories. Tainting them as an effort to get more answers I didn't really need seemed like it'd do more harm than good. I had learned enough about her death through my dad's confession.

With Isla by my side, I spoke with Ridgewood P.D. extensively, recounting what little details I knew about the day my mom had left, and giving them my statements from the night my dad smashed a bottle over Isla's head. She gave her statement as well, and because of her explicit detailing of my dad's confession to her and the way he reacted to her, thinking she was my mom, they immediately went to speak to him.

I was told when the police arrived at my old house a couple hours later, my father was sitting in a puddle of his own piss exactly where I had left him, crying and repeating the same sentence over and over—*'she was dead'.*

Chief Collier called me as soon as my dad was brought down to the station and placed in an interrogation room, offering me the chance to be there as they questioned him. I showed up fifteen minutes later.

Isla offered to come into the station with me, but I knew this was something I needed to do on my own. I'll admit, I also couldn't stand the thought of her being in such close proximity to him, even if he had no idea we were there. Kissing her goodbye, I promised to call her when I was ready to leave the station, agreeing for her to come get me instead of catching the bus.

Once inside, Chief Collier greeted me and walked me back to where they were holding him. We entered the room next to the one he was in, so I could sit and observe through the one-way glass.

"State your name for the video," *an older looking officer demanded as he walked into the room, closing the door roughly behind him. He stared at my dad as though he was dog shit on the bottom of his shoe while he awaited his response.*

"Seth Maxwell Hart," my dad grumbled, leaning his head into his hands, his fingertips pushing into his messy hair. He was sitting in one of four metal chairs surrounding a basic wooden table. The fluorescent lights bounced off his skin, which was sheeted with a layer of

sweat. There were pit stains on his white t-shirt. He looked disgusting—dark circles lined his eyes, his skin pale.

"You've already been read your rights, one of which is the right to an attorney. Would you like to call one or have one of ours appointed to you at this time?"

"No."

"Do you know why you're here, Mr. Hart?"

"I don't. Well, I think I do, but you're wrong," he stammered, fumbling over his words.

A lump formed in my throat. My eyes narrowed, focused on my dad and his words. His reactions.

"We have a police report from a young woman whom you assaulted last night. She claims you attacked her by smashing a bottle of liquor above her head, screaming—and I quote—'How the fuck are you here, Lucy? I killed you. I fucking buried you.' Is there any truth to her allegations, Mr. Hart?"

"No."

"So you're denying that you smashed a bottle of liquor above a young woman's head? Or did you not say 'How the fuck are you here, Lucy? I killed you. I fucking buried you.'?"

My dad said nothing, swallowing thickly as his eyes pulled down to the table. Every fiber of my being wanted to slam my hands against the one-way glass and scream for him to just talk to the officer and admit what he had, or hadn't done.

The officer walked slowly to the other side of the room so my dad's back was to him. He flipped through the paperwork attached to the clipboard he held.

"Who's Lucy, Mr. Hart?"

I watched as my father's jaw locked and his nostrils flared.

"My estranged wife." His hands curled into tight fists.

"Estranged wife, or deceased?"

Again, my dad said nothing. He stared straight ahead at the beige windowless wall, as the officer pursed his lips behind him as though he were settling into a long debate.

"When did she leave you, Mr. Hart?"

"Sixteen years ago."

"Have you spoken to her since?"

"No."

"What about your son? Has he spoken with your wife since she left?"

"No."

"Hmm," the officer mused, circling back around to face my dad.

For three hours, I stood just inches away from the window and watched, completely on edge, as the officer and my dad went back and forth with their questions and answers. My stomach churned the entire time, hating not knowing whether the officers would be able to extract any concrete information from him. All I wanted to know is if he actually killed my mom.

By hour four, I could recognize the signs of my dad readying to explode. As the officer continued to ask him the same questions in different formats, my dad's skin began to redden—a telltale sign he was about to completely lose his shit.

In the end, it was the simplest question that tipped him over the edge, setting him off like a firework.

"What happened to your wife, Seth?"

"I fucking killed her, okay?!"

Using the momentum from my dad's explosion, the officer leaned in, prepared to pick out every bit of his confession. "Why, Seth? Why would you kill your own wife? The mother of your child."

"Because she was a stupid fucking bitch who was about to leave me. I couldn't fucking handle that, okay?"

"Why did she want to leave you?"

My dad glared daggers at the officer, shaking visibly in his chair. "She didn't like my drinking."

"Did you ever physically harm her?"

"I might have tossed her around a little from time to time, but it's nothing the bitch didn't like."

"Why kill her? Why not just let her leave?" the officer prodded, looking at the one-way glass and giving a slight nod.

I looked over to my right and saw another officer taking notes, and to my left, Chief Collier stood with his arms crossed, one hand bracing against his mouth as he listened intently.

"What kind of man would I be if I let her fuckin' go? She was going to take all the money we had—which wasn't much—and bleed me dry. She was going to take our kid too."

"So it was easier to take her life, instead of watching her take everything of yours?"

"I hadn't planned it, alright? I meant to smack her around— maybe knock her out. When I smashed the bottle to her head, I thought it'd knock her out. I didn't think she'd hit the side table. I tried to catch her—I almost had the collar of her shirt, but it ended up being her necklace—and she fell fast. There was so much fuckin' blood. I didn't even know she was dead right away."

"Tell me what happened next, Mr. Hart." The officer pulled out the metal chair across from my dad and sat, placing the clipboard in his lap before folding his hands together on the table.

My dad rubbed his hands against his face again and inhaled a deep breath. "I called my pops. I panicked. I didn't know what to do."

The officer sat quietly, waiting for my dad to continue.

"He showed up and assured me he'd take care of everything. I was still drunk from earlier, so he didn't want me taking care of her... Her body."

"Where did he bury her?"

"I don't know."

My heart sank further with his admission. The police didn't know this yet, but if my dad didn't know where she was buried, they'd never find her remains. My grandpa died from a heart attack six years ago.

"If your father was the one who buried your wife, Mr. Hart, then why was one of the things you were yelling at the young woman you attacked, 'I fucking buried you'?"

I bit the corner of my nail, watching for any signs my dad might actually know where my mom's remains would be.

Silence stretched in the interrogation room as a few minutes passed with no response from my dad. The officer took note of his silence, and continued to ask questions that made me lean into the glass, soaking up all the details I could.

"Mr. Hart, why did no one report your wife as a missing person?" The officer titled his head in question.

My dad slowly looked up at the officer. Through gritted teeth, he told him, "She had no family. Parents died when she was seventeen and she was on her own until she met me. I saved her. Gave her a home and a child. Then the bitch wanted to leave me."

"Surely she had friends who would have reported her missing?" the officer pushed. Everything he said was in such a conversational way. It was no wonder my dad was suddenly singing like a canary.

"Nope. Just me and our kid."

"Speaking of your son—Caleb, is it?"

My dad nodded in confirmation.

"Where was Caleb while everything happened with your wife? Was he in the house?"

He sighed dramatically, leaning back in his chair and cracked his neck.

"He was supposed to be in bed, but the little shit woke up and walked into the living room right after Lucy hit the floor. He looked around, then immediately ran back into his room and I didn't see him again until the next morning. I told him his mom left us."

I couldn't handle hearing more. My chest already felt like an elephant was sitting on top of me and I had tears burning the backs of my eyes. A complete breakdown was emerging, and I couldn't be here when it happened. Officer Collier nodded in understanding as I blew past him, throwing open the door and sprinting down the hall. I barely made it to a stall before I emptied everything that was in my stomach into the toilet.

Remembering that day still made the bile rise in my throat, but his confession gave me some semblance of closure. Knowing the reason my mother never came back for me wasn't because she didn't care about me, gave me a small feeling of peace. Unfortunately, I was still waiting for justice to be served in memory of her, but it looked like my old man would serve a long sentence in prison once his case went to trial. I dreamt of the day I'd sit in the back of the courtroom with a big ass smile on my face as the judge convicted him and they finally hauled him off for good. Until that day came, I slept better knowing he was behind bars, denied bail.

Police Chief Collier flipped his cue card, giving my row of officers the signal to stand from our seats in preparation of the pinning ceremony beginning. I couldn't wait to receive my badge and *officially* be Officer Caleb Hart. Keeping formation, the other officers and I marched out of the aisle and up to where the Chief was, coming to stand behind him in a perfect, straight line.

I waited as patiently as possible while officers were called one by one to receive their pins, my heart hammering in my chest the closer he got to reading my name.

"Caleb Hart," Chief Collier called through the micro-phone, echoing through the room. As I moved forward, I heard Isla's voice whooping with cheers, while I made my way to the front of the line. Saluting and shaking the hands of three different superiors, I accepted a large envelope from the third one holding my certificate.

Chief Collier clapped my shoulder as I stopped in front of him, giving me a warm smile and a nod. When Isla and I first went to the police station, I was terrified Chief Collier would be a complete dick to us because of who Isla's father was and his connection to them. But it turned out it was exactly the opposite. He was a stern, but kind man, and took me under his wing with both my father's case and the police academy.

As he pinned my badge to the front of my uniform, he dropped his voice, speaking to just me. "Officer Hart, I wanted to let you know that while we know you are anxiously awaiting justice to be served on behalf of your mother, the Ridgewood Police Department felt we needed to do something to honor her memory on your behalf. Next week, we'll be installing a new bench in the town square in memory of your mom."

My eyes widened, and I stood speechless in front of the man who had just given me a priceless gift on one of the most important days of my life. Thankfully, he didn't expect a response and instead clapped my shoulder again, giving it a small squeeze. "Congratulations, Officer Hart."

"Thank you, sir," I managed to say before walking back to where the rest of the officers stood waiting in front of our folding chairs.

Once the final graduating officer joined the line, taking his place in front of his chair, we all sat in unison and, with our hands pressed firmly to our laps, as we listened to the Chief's closing speech.

The audience clapped and stood in ovation once Chief Collier stepped away from the podium, signaling to us officers we could now break formation. I barely had the chance to stand from my seat before Isla lunged into my arms. She cupped my cheeks with her hands and peppered kisses all over my face, congratulating me repeatedly while I held her close.

Life with Isla was everything I had hoped it would be, and even though we had our struggles navigating down our individual paths, we were persevering, boosting each other along the way. In March we re-signed the lease on her—*our* —apartment. After a couple months of working for Dave and having some paychecks rolling in, I was confident I could handle half the rent. I put in as many hours as I could at the garage until I started the police academy, and even then I'd work some nights. Dave fixed my car and tried to get me to stay on at the garage by offering me a permanent position with higher pay. I declined, because regardless of how much I loved working there, my dream was to be a forensic analyst. As grim as it was, if I could study crime scenes and help the detectives figure out what happened to the victims, maybe I could give another kid the closure they needed earlier than I got mine.

Isla took over my job at Pack N Mail, becoming fast friends with Mal despite their twenty-year age difference. Mal became a maternal figure to Isla, which is exactly what she needed at that point in her life. Her own mother took almost two months to reach out to her, and after dodging her calls for weeks, I finally convinced her to hear her mom out. She agreed to meeting her in a public place and listening to what she wanted to say. The coffee date ended with my girl coming home in tears, but ultimately she and her mom agreed to keep in contact with each other.

Shortly after the coffee date that left her in shambles for

a few days, Isla received the news she'd been waiting for—she'd be starting veterinary school in the spring.

Isla's father has still never reached out to her, but that was a loss she had no problem letting go of.

And for me, their loss was my gain. The navy blue velvet box in my pocket was lighting my skin on fire—so eager to pull it out and drop to one knee, the thought practically consumed my entire graduation ceremony. But with that eagerness also came a ball of nerves I had trouble swallowing down. We were still pretty broke, and I couldn't afford a real engagement ring—at least not like what she deserved.

Instead, I was proposing tonight with my mother's necklace. She knew what the necklace meant to me, and what it symbolized for my mother and me when I was a child.

It was a promise we'd always be together. Me and her. The same promise I was giving to Isla.

My person.

My guide through the dark.

My Starlight.

EPILOGUE
ISLA

"Are you hungry?" I asked Caleb as we walked hand-in-hand up to our apartment. Watching him graduate from the police academy brought tears to my eyes—I was so proud of him for following his dream and working tirelessly through his training and work schedule. Not once did he complain or doubt his abilities to achieve success. He was truly awe-inspiring, and I hoped to have his positive attitude and confidence once my own schooling started.

Moving in together was the best decision we could have made, not only for our relationship, but for our financial situation as well. With Caleb's help, I replaced him at Pack N Mail and started working full-time once he moved on to work at Dave's. Having dual incomes made things less stressful for both of us, and I loved waking up beside Caleb every single day.

The last ten months had been taxing—a rollercoaster of emotions for both of us—but also some of the best months of my entire life.

Being with Caleb was as natural as breathing. The love I

felt for him was one I thought only existed in the romance books I read. I could envision my entire life with this man and I knew we'd overcome anything so long as we did it together.

"Uh, yeah," Caleb replied absentmindedly a few moments later. His hand was clammy in mine, and I noticed he'd been a little quiet since we left his graduation. I figured he was just processing his accomplishment—it wasn't abnormal to have the feeling of 'what now' after a life-changing event. I'd felt the same once it sank in that I no longer had a connection to my parents and their plans for me.

Caleb removed his keys from his jacket and unlocked our front door, flipping on the light as he stepped into the entryway.

"Should we order in? Or go out? It's your night, you tell me what sounds best, Officer Hart." Shrugging my jacket off, he took it from me and hung it on the hook behind the door.

When he turned his attention back to me, his eyes blazed as he pulled me to him and kissed me. I melted into him, no longer sensing the uncertainty he held on our way up here.

Breaking the kiss, he smirked at me and he produced a satin blindfold from his pocket. He said nothing as he placed it over my eyes. "What are you—"

"Shh," he whispered. He finished securing it, and his right hand floated down the length of my arm, catching my wrist. Gently, he tugged me further into the apartment and over to what intuition told me was the living room.

"Sit down, Starlight." He held onto both of my arms as I slowly lowered myself to the floor and got comfortable.

Tucking my legs beneath me, I sat cross-legged and touched the floor with my palms, feeling that I was sitting on a plush blanket. That hadn't been there when I left this morning...

Caleb moved around the room and I could hear the faint flicks of a lighter, and a few moments later the refrigerator door closed. When he finally joined me on the blanket, I couldn't help but smile. I had a feeling what he might be doing, but I also didn't want to get my hopes up and be disappointed if I was wrong. Still, my heart raced as I sat without my sight, letting my imagination get the best of me.

"Can I take this off?" I asked, my fingers brushing against the smooth satin covering my eyes.

"Not yet."

Caleb expelled a shaky breath. The sound of clothing rustling told me he was likely removing his jacket. Was it wrong that I hoped he'd be naked when my blindfold finally came off? Images of me and Caleb celebrating his graduation in filthy ways flooded my brain.

"Okay," he murmured as he reached behind my head to undo the knot holding the blindfold in place.

As my eyes readjusted, I inhaled a sharp breath and took in my surroundings. Cream-colored candles lined the coffee table that was now pushed up against the couch, allowing us room to spread out on the blanket he had placed on the floor. Next to us was a basket filled with wrapped up deli sandwiches, chips, and cookies, and the most gorgeous bouquet of hydrangeas sat next to me, tied together with a black lace bow.

But the most breathtaking sight was the man in front of me, bent on one knee, still dressed in his new police uniform. He held a closed velvet box in his hand and my heart exploded within my chest as he stared at me with love and adoration shining through his eyes.

"Caleb..." I managed to whisper before a tear spilled over and slid down my cheek.

He reached out and wiped it away with his thumb. "We never did get to go on that picnic, Starlight. I thought I'd finally bring the picnic to you."

I choked out a laugh, thinking back to the day we had planned to skip class, but instead had our first sort-of fight. That night changed so much for me—it was the night I realized I was falling in love.

"Today was one of the most important days in my life, Isla. Arguably one of the best days of my life, too. Having you by my side has made me a better man in so many ways—a man I never thought I'd actually become. Honestly, I'm not sure I would have made it this far if you hadn't been. When we met, I was hanging on by a thread, living day by day. I knew what I needed to do to make my life better, but wasn't sure how to execute it fully. Then I saw you in the library and it was like you were there to guide me. There's a reason why I've always called you Starlight, and I hope you know how much you mean to me. I'm just eternally grateful you didn't listen when I told you no strings attached."

"I love you," I whispered, batting away another tear that fell.

"I love you more than I could ever fully express. Throughout graduation today, the only thing I could focus on was the box in my pocket and taking you home so I could propose to you. Isla Marie Donohue, will you make me the happiest man on the planet and marry me?"

As Caleb opened the box, my eyes connected with what

was inside and it was like a dam broke—tears began streaming down my face in rapid succession.

"One day, I'll take you to the jeweler and you can pick out any wedding ring you want, but until we are in a place where we can do that, I wanted to offer you a piece of jewelry that means just as much to me as the one I'll be able to place on your finger in the future. I had the clasp repaired on my mother's necklace, and I want you to have it. Two hearts, Isla. Yours and mine. Forever."

His mother's necklace glittered from the velvet box, the small crystals encrusted in the hearts sparkling. This small piece of jewelry meant so much to Caleb—it was the only thing he had belonging to his mother. A symbol of the relationship they had that'd meant so much to her. Every time I thought about Caleb's childhood, my heart broke for the woman who I'd never meet—taken away from her child too young.

When I looked back up at Caleb, he had tears in his eyes, and I realized I hadn't given him my answer.

Lifting myself up to kneel, I cupped Caleb's face between my hands and placed a soft kiss on his lips. "Yes," I said against them. "Yes, I'll marry you."

Of course I'd marry him. There was no doubt in my mind, no hesitancy or question. Caleb was my other half. The man I was destined to collide with—my beacon of hope when I thought all hope of having a normal life was lost.

He'd told me since the beginning I was his starlight—the one who helped guide him through his darkness—but I didn't think he realized just how much light he brought into *my* life. So much so, he had lit up my whole world.

Need more Caleb & Isla?
Download their bonus epilogue!

Curious about Caleb's police academy friend, Noah?

His story begins in

between the
FLAMES

**Continue reading at the end of this book for a look
into the first book of the Ridgewood Series, or grab
your copy today!**

*Pre-warning though, Between the Flames is not Noah's
full story, it is merely the beginning and his happy ever
after happens in the second Ridgewood book, Wicked
Games We Play.*

RESOURCES

If you or someone you know is a victim of domestic violence and could use assistance with leaving a dangerous situation, please call the National Domestic Violence Hotline at 800-799-7233 or visit www.thehotline.org

The hotline is available 24/7 and is available in English, Spanish, and 200+ other languages through an interpretation service.

You can also text START to 88788.

ACKNOWLEDGMENTS

Thank you for reading Wreck Me! This book hit me out of nowhere and was completely driven by the characters. What I thought was going to happen throughout the story kept being pulled in different directions as the characters dictated how their lives played out. What a rollercoaster ride Caleb and Isla took me on!

A very special thank you to my amazing editor, Virginia, and to my proofreaders: Nicole, Kaitlin, and Amanda. I also want to thank my alpha/beta readers, Amanda, Delynda, Tawny, and Kerri—you ladies helped me shape Wreck Me into the book that it is, and I am so appreciative.

To my husband, parents, and my besties Amanda, April, and Rana for always having my back, being there for me throughout my writing journey, and for being the best cheerleaders I could ever ask for. And to my PA, Cassie, who literally talks me off the edge of panic attacks and is my right hand, my backbone, and my sanity.

An extra special thank you to the amazing people on my Promo Squad and ARC team—you guys are the real MVPs!

Last, but certainly not least, thank you to the amazing readers who have taken a chance on my book(s). Without you, writing would still just be a dream I was too scared to chase. Your support and willingness to read my words means the world to me.

A.R. Rose is a wife, mom, reader, and writer, who lives in sunny California with her family and doggo. She loves to hang out at home, drink copious amounts of coffee, and eat yummy food

90% of the time you will find her with a book or her Kindle in hand, reading a spicy romance novel, which not so coincidentally is what she has fallen in love with writing.

CONNECT WITH A.R. ROSE

Join A.R. Rose's newsletter for info & updates
♥https://www.authorarrose.com/email-subscribe

Website
♥www.authorarrose.com

Reading Group
♥https://www.facebook.com/groups/authorarrose

Facebook
♥https://www.facebook.com/authorarrose

TikTok
♥https://www.tiktok.com/@authorarrose

Instagram
♥ https://www.instagram.com/authorarrose

PROLOGUE

"Eloise! Sweetheart! Noah is here!" my mom screams over the re-run of *The Price is Right* which is on the highest possible volume setting in our living room. I hardly hear her over the sound of the Plinko chips bouncing down the board and the excited shriek of the woman on TV. This is my every day. My mother always leaves the TV on loud so that she can hear it from wherever she is in the house while she obsessively cleans. The cleaning has become an obsession for her, one that she adopted shortly after she and my father finalized their divorce. A coping mechanism, her therapist called it, but what the therapist didn't know was that it completely took over her life. If my mother wasn't cleaning, she was at work, but the moment she stepped through the threshold of our modest little house tucked in the middle of Shadow Hills suburbia, the cleaning began.

Our house is probably the cleanest house I've ever been in. Like clockwork, she'd arrive home from work, push play on the DVR'd *The Price is Right,* and I'd have to listen to Drew Carey yell "Come on down!" to the next contestant. I miss the days when it was Bob on the TV. He was always my favorite.

As the blood rushes to my head from my oh-so-comfortable upside-down position of hanging off my bed, I hear the telltale sound of Noah rushing up the stairs as he stomps into my room. A fit of laughter bubbles out of him as he throws open my bedroom door, takes aim with a Nerf gun right at my forehead, and pulls the bright orange trigger. The rubber end of the foam bullet pings me right between the eyes and bounces off, landing on the ground. With a smooth somersault off the back of the bed, I land perfectly at his feet.

Okay, I actually fell into a heap after rolling sideways and falling onto my side, but whatever. Noah is laughing at me so hard I can witness a single tear escape his right eye, and I use his blurred vision to my advantage by shooting my legs out and swinging them hard to sweep him off of his feet. Victory is mine when he comes crashing to the floor in a pile alongside of me.

"You turd," he chuckles. "I totally got you, though!" My eyes roll in defiance as I use my index finger to push my glasses back up the bridge of my nose.

"Yeah, yeah," I drawl, "what do you want to do today?"

It's our last day of summer vacation before we start our freshman year at Shadow Hills High. I'm so nervous that I've felt perpetually nauseated for the last two weeks, and I think I am developing a problem with overactive armpit sweat. That's a thing, right?

"I don't know. My Ma says I have to be home early tonight though. She wants me home for dinner and says I need to get ready for tomorrow. Not sure what I need to get ready for; my backpack is ready to go, and it's not like we have homework already."

I can hear the irritation in his voice. He's tired of his mom treating him like he's still a little kid. I've tried to reason with him, but he doesn't want to hear it. He wants his freedom.

"That's cool." I keep my tone light, not letting my indifference show. I wish he would be less hard on his mom. She's absolutely amazing. "Why don't we walk down to get some ice cream and go hang out at the park? I feel nauseated again and could use the air."

The word *ice cream* barely left my lips before Noah hopped to his feet and was pulling me to mine, dragging me through my house.

"Mom! We're leaving!" I yell just before the door slams shut behind us. I doubt she heard me over the insufferably loud TV, but it's not uncommon for Noah and I to leave and go walk around the neighborhood.

Our departure wouldn't worry her, so long as we're back before dark. I'm not even sure Mom notices our coming and going most of the time, not when she's so busy scrubbing the already pristine surfaces.

Looping my arm through Noah's, we walk the eight blocks to our favorite ice cream spot and order our usual.

After buying our ice cream, we double back toward my house, stopping at the park. It was still early in the day, but we had it all to ourselves—just the way we liked it. I let my feet drag in the wood chips as I sat on the swing, drifting back and forth, basking in the warmth of the late afternoon sun. I used my spoon to poke at my half melted ice cream, not really interested in finishing it.

Neither of us was saying much, and the sound of the

swing's rusty creaking chains filled the air as we lazily glided back and forth. My shoe scuffed on the ground as I slowed to a stop, suddenly feeling uneasy. There was a tension in the air, and my skin prickled, heightening my senses. I glanced over at Noah, and my eyes met his.

"What's up, No?" I ask hesitantly. The look he was giving me sent alarm bells ringing through my brain. He'd never looked at me like this before—something was on his mind.

Without saying a word, he slid off his swing and walked over to the trash can, tossing the rest of his cone inside. I studied him as he approached me with a conflicted look on his face, opening and closing his mouth twice. Running his long fingers through his sandy brown hair, he stared at the ground and toed at a rock. Everything felt awkward. The urge to do something with my hands compelled me to pick at a piece of lint on my jeans while I waited for the moment to pass.

"Okay. This is going to sound stupid, but I'm just going to spit it out," he finally said, and I felt my heart pick up its pace. I looked up from my lap, meeting his gaze.

"Look Elle, you and I have been friends for, like, what, thirty years now?"

I snorted. Typical Noah, always trying to lighten every situation with a joke.

"It's just that we're about to start high school and neither of us has had our first kiss yet."

My eyes widen, suddenly *terrified* of where he was going with this.

"I don't want to start school without being able to say I've kissed someone. It's stupid, and you don't have to say yes, but I kinda wanted to know if I could kiss you so we can both just say we've been kissed and we don't have to risk kissing the nasty band geek with a face full of zits and spinach in their teeth." Noah had rushed through that so fast, he needed to take a second to breathe, his chest rising and falling in uneven pants. I was frozen in place, unable to respond.

"What do you say, Elle? Can I kiss you?"

I was confident what I was experiencing was an out-of-body experience. I could see Noah standing in front of me, see the pleading look in his eyes and the embarrassment coating his cheeks, but what really took me by surprise is that I could *hear* myself responding, "Yes."

I had just agreed to kiss my best friend.

I.

Just.

Agreed.

To.

Kiss.

My.

Best.

Friend.

Dear brain, next time think things through longer before you agree, okay!? Thanks. Love, Elle.

Noah didn't give me the chance to change my mind before he pulled me up by my arms. He made sure I was stable on my feet before moving his hand to cup the back of my neck. I watched his eyes close, and I inhaled sharply before letting mine flutter shut, waiting with bated breath. My heart beat wildly in my chest as I tried to focus on the erratic thump, rather than what was coming next. I wiped my sweaty palms on the sides of my jeans, fighting to keep my eyes closed as the anticipation threatened to send a wave of anxiousness through my body. Suddenly, I could feel the hotness of Noah's breath, his lips so close to mine that they were practically touching. We both stood still for several seconds and my eyes peeked open, when suddenly he crashed his mouth into mine.

Warmth flooded my body as his tongue traced the seam of my lips. I opened my mouth to let him in, our tongues dancing wildly and our teeth clanging against each other. Instinctually, my head tilted to the side, just as he tilted the same direction, making us lose our already awkward momentum and break apart.

We both instantly used our sleeves to wipe our mouths and looked around everywhere but at each other.

My fingertips floated up to my lips; they felt fuzzy from our kiss and my entire body hummed. Noah had stepped back, but I was positive he could hear my wildly beating heart from where he stood.

My judgment was clouded, full of confusion. I could still feel him everywhere, but my first kiss wasn't at all how I expected it to be.

For starters, I had never imagined my first kiss being with my best friend. I had also never pictured it being so... weird. In the movies, the first kiss is always so romantic, but in real life, in *my* life, it was wet, messy, and over as quickly as it started, lasting no more than three seconds.

I turned my head back to meet his gaze and we both instantly started laughing. Yep, that had just happened. I sat back down on the swing, my hands wrapping around the chains.

"Well, now that we got that over with, let's go get ready to start high school!" Noah said, still laughing. He pulled one of my hands free from the hold on the chain and used it to high five himself. I ripped my hand out of his grasp and stood back up, letting him slip his arm around my shoulders as we walked. Wrapping my arm around his waist, I leaned my head against his side as we fell in step and headed out of the park, back toward my house.

"Elle, what if you meet your high school sweetheart this week and I just stole your first kiss from him?"

I snort at that because we both know how unlikely that is. I'm super shy and sort of an ugly duckling. A nerd in the making. Having my first kiss wasn't in the cards for me for a very, *very* long time. At least it hadn't been until tonight. I punch him lightly in the stomach as I look up at him and roll my eyes.

"C'mon loser, let's race!" I take off running, forcing him to follow or be left in the dust.

CHAPTER THIRTY-TWO

I was hypnotized by his green eyes, full lips, and dirty blond hair. By the formfitting tee shirts he wore, showcasing his muscles that strained against the fabric and begged to be set free. His smile turned my insides into Jell-O. He radiated confidence, oozed sex, and caught the eye of literally every single female in this godforsaken school.

He wasn't an ordinary crush, but we were definitely a classic cliche.

Ryder Thompson.

Quarterback of the football team. The star of campus. Everyone either wanted to be him, be friends with him, or sleep with him. Unfortunately, I was no exception to that rule. I couldn't stop the reaction my body had every time I saw him. Hell, even when I thought of him. I wanted him so badly and I have wanted him for *years*. Almost four agonizing years, in fact. I vividly remember the first time I saw him, just moments after setting foot on campus the first day of freshman year. Noah had teased me about him possibly stealing a kiss from my high school sweetheart and I scoffed at that, but seeing Ryder had me wondering if maybe such a thing could happen.

Wrong.

I was so wrong.

Ryder never noticed me. How could he? I was the nobody nerd. I would *maybe* be remembered as the editor and photographer for the school newspaper. That's if I'm remembered at all. Most people don't even know me as that. I spend my time either in the computer lab working on articles, or in the darkroom developing photos.

I had yet to catch the attention of many guys, but when it came to Ryder, I was invisible. I might as well have stolen Harry Potter's invisibility cloak and worn it daily, for as little as he noticed me. In fact, the only guy who I knew had taken an interest in me, much to my dismay, was the school's resident playboy and walking talking STD, Tommy.

Tommy also happened to be Ryder's best friend, but so far, that didn't seem to do me any favors. Catching Tommy's attention wasn't something to be proud of either, considering he drooled after any and all females in our high school, including the cafeteria lady. Lucky for me, he was more of a "let her come to me" kind of dude, and as harmless as a fly.

I was pulled abruptly out of my thoughts when Noah tapped me lightly on the back. He pulled the chair out next to me, sinking into it. Clicking to minimize the photo of Ryder that I had pulled up on the screen, my cheeks burned with heat at the feeling of being caught staring. Although I technically had nothing to hide, since it was a photo for the newspaper, I probably shouldn't have been staring at it for as long as I had been. Once the photo was minimized, I pretended to look busy by picking up my pen and staring at my notebook. Noah watched my every move, cocking an eyebrow with a silent question, but thankfully said nothing about my guilty behavior.

"How are you?" he asked, slouching down in his chair. He removed a Reese's out of his backpack and unwrapped it, tossing me his famous sideways grin—the one that made all the girls, except for me, swoon. Noah had been my best friend since we were three and a half when our moms forced us to play together at the park. What they really wanted was a friend for themselves, someone they could drink coffee and gossip with, but they ended up forging a ride or die friendship between the two of us.

"Oh, you know, just trying to think of an angle for this article." I enlarged the webpage again, peering back at Ryder's concentrated face on the screen, admiring his features. Frozen in time, he glanced over his shoulder, smiling at who knows what.

How could I get him to notice me?

My thoughts were running away with me again. Suddenly, I felt a cold and clammy finger brush against my chin before it moved upward toward my bottom lip. I flinched and pulled my body back as he burst out laughing.

"What the hell was that for, Noah?" I scowled, crossing my arms over my chest.

"Just checking to see if the drool had escaped your mouth yet," he said, a knowing look in his eye. "Isn't that article supposed to be in tomorrow's newspaper? Cutting it a little close, huh?"

I rolled my eyes and didn't answer him, silently stewing. As I turned back to the computer in front of me, I heard the door to the computer lab slam, followed by a slur of giggles and the sound of wet kisses enter the room. I whipped my head around, ready to yell at the offenders and remind them that this was a computer lab and not a make-out spot, but before I could, my heart dropped into my stomach. Ryder and Lily, the newspaper's lead photographer, were walking through the lab, mouths connected. Neither of them bothered to see if anyone else was in the room as Ryder fell into a chair in the corner and pulled Lily onto his lap.

Lily was a friend of mine, but I never told her about my devastatingly lame crush on Ryder. There was no way that I could. Not only were they dating, they were *perfect* together. Their relationship was the whole high school quarterback dates the head cheerleader type of romance, except for Lily wasn't a cheerleader. Instead, she was the popular photographer for both the newspaper and the yearbook committee. Gorgeous in a totally understated way, with a curvy body, loose blonde curls, and big blue eyes. She wore stylish, form-fitting clothes that showed off her assets. She was friends with everyone, and kind to all the teachers and staff. Everyone adored her—the school's girl-next-door. No one was exactly shocked when she and Ryder became an item.

It had been a few months since that had happened and I still seethed with jealousy, even though I hid it from her.

No one ever suspected that I, Eloise Peters, secretly pined for the love of a boy who I didn't stand a chance with. As far as everyone was concerned, my head was shoved so far into a book, or a computer, that my teenage hormones didn't exist, and that was the way I was going to keep it. At least for these last few months of high school. I'd rather keep people at a distance than let them in. As soon as graduation happened, I was out of this town. The one person I ever let in was Noah. He had been my rock throughout my entire life and the only one to know the real me.

"C'mon, let's get out of here," Noah said under his breath, pulling me out of my chair by my elbow. My heart sank into the pit of my stomach as Lily's giggles filled the air. I quickly gathered my notebook and the various pictures I had sitting in front of me for the article and shoved them into my folder. Noah's tone of voice was sharp, and I was ready to get out of there, too. Pushing the folder into my bag without trying to organize it, I reached to grab the long strap and lifted it over my head to fit across my body. As I turned to leave, my eyes flicked to the corner of the room inadvertently. Jealousy and despair overtook my body, taking in Ryder and Lily's bodies melted together, his mouth fused to hers. As my eyes traveled further up their faces, I gasped as my eyes met Ryder's piercing green ones. His eyes bore straight into me with a heat that made my skin warm.

He's staring at me as he's kissing her. I was frozen, heart thumping wildly in my chest as my mind raced with a thousand thoughts and questions. He was staring at me with a look that I longed to have the ability to read and it made my chest heavy. A smirk pulled at his lips as his kiss continued to devour Lily, yet his eyes refused to unlock from mine. I lifted my chin slightly, not backing down from his gaze.

"Elle." A familiar voice floated into my head and snapped me out of my train of thought, causing me to blink.

"Eloise." The sound of my name being called again came through clearer this time. I turned in the direction the voice came from, finding Noah waiting with one arm firmly placed against the door, while his other arm held the strap of his backpack that was thrown over one shoulder. I could see the anger in his eyes.

"Let's go, *now*," he ordered, his tone sharp as he turned his attention to Ryder, staring him down. Following Noah's line of sight, my eyes reconnected with Ryder's. My stomach dipped as I walked backward, unable to pull my gaze away from him. Lily had come up for air and curled into him, oblivious that his concentration was elsewhere.

I bumped into Noah and he snaked his arm across my shoulders, turning my body with a nudge so that I was walking out of the door ahead of him. I ran my hand down my face in frustration. Sensing Noah following closely behind me, I quickened my pace to get us away.

"Dude's scum," he muttered under his breath, his icy tone making me shiver. I looked up at him, studying his face as we walked, noting how irritated the situation had made him.

Noah had grown quite gorgeous over the years. His light brown hair had turned dark like mine, but it had flecks of gold from the sun. His milk chocolate eyes and that sideways grin of his made for a deadly combination, one that made all the girls at our school swoon. While the thought of Noah as something other than my best friend may have crossed my mind a time or two over the years, his good looks didn't make me want to drop my panties and ruin the only friendship I've ever known.

We had friend zoned each other years ago and were both perfectly content with that. I wasn't his type, anyway. Sure, I was pretty, but I wore modest clothes and nerdy glasses that were obviously too big for my face—my mom refused to even think about getting me a new pair until it was absolutely necessary. I wasn't the type of girl who had boys lining up at her door, but I also wasn't a complete dud. At least I didn't think I was. I was comfortable in my skin and didn't feel like I was missing anything by not having boyfriends throughout my high school years.

Noah, on the other hand, wasn't your typical guy, and that's what made him so appealing to literally everyone. Despite his looks, Noah wasn't cocky or an asshole; he didn't chase every girl who looked his direction, and he really wasn't a huge partier. Add that all together and it equaled him being a total god to the girls at Shadow Hills High. The best part? He had no idea! He was so content in being in this little bubble with me, completely oblivious to everyone else, that he didn't try to change himself into one of the jocks to "fit in". Noah was a social butterfly who could hang with every group in this school, and he did. The nerds, the goths, the jocks, me. Lucky for me, he preferred the latter. I could always count on him to find me in a crowded room.

Choosing to ignore his comment about Ryder, I removed my arm from his waist and instead looped my arm through his as we continued to move through campus. My mind drifted back to a memory of us as children as I let his body guide mine toward the cafeteria.

Trotting down the white aisle littered with scattered rose petals, he wore a tuxedo, and they had dressed me in a fluffy white tutu dress. He carried a pillow that held two shiny rings on top, secured with a dainty silk ribbon. Throwing crimson rose petals in front of me with a forced smile plastered on my face, the sounds of 'oh how cute' and 'aww' urged me to keep going. Everything had to be perfect. I couldn't trip, couldn't let the smile falter. Noah's older brother was finally getting married, and they had forced us to participate. Ring bearer and flower girl. I should have loved it; being girly, wearing a pretty dress, and having people admire me, but all I really wanted to do was go run around in the field next to it and tumble through the grass. A game of cops and robbers was calling me, and I was itching to take this giant dress off. I was a tomboy through and through, and this was just plain torture. After the ceremony and what seemed like a hundred million pictures, Noah and I were finally dismissed, free to go run and play. I wasted no time tackling Noah to the ground and shoved my pointer finger into his ribs, pretending it was a gun.

"All right buddy, you're going to jail," I said, between a fit of laughter. "Give me your wrists. I'm going to put your handcuffs on."

Noah shoved his hands behind his back so I could cuff him, but his smile didn't reach his eyes.

I faltered, dropping his hands. "What, do you not want to play?" I questioned. He was really making this game not fun.

He looked down at the ground, a hint of sadness in his tone as he asked me, "Elle, do you wanna get married someday?"

My brows furrowed and my lips pursed as I thought about his question. "Uh...like married, married?!" We were only eleven.

"Yeah, like Tucker and Molly just did. I want to get married. Do you want to marry me, Elle?"

"I mean, I guess so, but not right now. I just want to play and pretend to take you to jail." Why was he asking me these things? Gross.

"Well, not right now, but when we're older like Tucker. Let's make a plan to get married when we're like 26 or something, I dunno."

I considered his words for half a second, then agreed. Anything to get him playing again. "Okay," I said, "but what if we married someone else already?"

"I guess if we married someone else, then we can't marry each other, but if we don't marry someone else, then we will. Deal?" he said, almost so quietly that I had to strain to hear him.

Why was he acting like this? Why did he seem so sad?

"Okay," I chuckled. "Deal, but only if I get to take you to jail now."

With his sideways grin that always made me laugh, he smiled and said, "Okay policeman" before handing me his wrists to pretend to handcuff him.

Loud voices lifted me from the memory as Noah held open one of the double doors for me to enter the cafeteria. Scanning the room, I spotted a table by the window and led the way. As soon as Noah and I slumped into our chairs, I glanced down at my watch.

We had about five minutes before the warning bell rang and fifth period started—English Lit with Mrs. Saunders, which was usually just time spent scrolling through Instagram. Mrs. Saunders was retiring at the end of the year and had reached the point where she just didn't care, so every class was spent reading or watching a movie adaptation of a book. Today we were watching *A Midsummer Night's Dream*, and I had planned to pass the time by brainstorming my way through the article I needed to finish tonight.

Once the movie was playing and the lights were off, I pulled out the mess of papers that I'd shoved into my backpack. I immediately regretted my decision to push them in haphazardly and cringed as I tried to smooth the wrinkles out. Falling into a daze, I held the paper against my chest when suddenly inspiration struck. I quickly pulled out my favorite pen and my notebook and let the words flow out of me.

I JUMPED when the lights turned back on in the classroom. Finally, lifting my head to find everyone around me was yawning and stretching after being brought back to life after their fifty-minute nap. A huge smile pulled across my face and mentally I high-five myself for lifting the writer's block that had been plaguing me as I looked back down at the notebook in front of me. Not only had I drafted the article about our upcoming big game, but I had revised and completed a second draft that was now ready to be typed and completed.

Gathering all of my belongings, I placed them into my backpack more carefully this time, before standing up to leave. Looking around the room, I laughed when I found Noah still asleep in the next row over. I walked over to him and stood above him at his desk.

"Noah, get up. Time for you to go to Art," I whispered, gently pushing his shoulder to wake him. He shot up straight with a grumble, yawning before rubbing his eyes. I took that as my sign that he would be all right and hurried toward the door, the minute warning bell ringing loudly overhead. I hardly made it two steps before choking on a gasp of air as my eyes connected with my favorite shade of green again.

Ryder.

He was leaning against the lockers directly across from where I stood with his arms crossed over his body, looking relaxed while my heart plummeted into my stomach. My palms began to sweat as his eyes burned directly into mine, setting a fire that coursed through my veins while my whole body came alight under his stare. I bit down on my lower lip, refusing to let him see how he affected me. I had slid under his radar for this long, I didn't dare get on it now. But this was twice in one day. *Why was he here?*

He smirked, and I felt that smirk all the way to my core.

I couldn't do this.

I couldn't breathe.

I wasn't this confident.

I wasn't this girl.

The last bell rang, breaking me out of my trance and reminding me where I was. I narrowed my eyes at him and walked away, leaving him standing there, but leaving me wondering if he finally had noticed me.